A SILENT CRADLE

A SILENT CRADLE

SUE PACEY

First published in Great Britain in 2017 by

Bannister Publications Ltd
118 Saltergate
Chesterfield
Derbyshire S40 1NG

ISBN 978-1-909813-29-8

Sue Pacey asserts the moral right to be identified
as the author of this work

A catalogue record for this book is available from the British Library

Typeset in Palatino Linotype by Escritor Design, Bournemouth

Printed and bound in Great Britain

This book is dedicated to all the wonderful midwives at Chesterfield Royal and its community who have been treasured friends and colleagues for many years.

Chapter 1

They came to the edge of the small Limousin town with engines roaring, drawing to a halt with a screech of brakes. The hot tyres of the canvas-covered vehicles sent swirling clouds of dust skyward. It was quite deliberate. Announce the arrival. No mercy!

Jackboots thudded on the baked, summer earth as men jumped from the transports and took their places in line. The hot sun glinted from each button and cap badge with the insignia of the Waffen SS. They stood at ease … and waited.

From his hiding place in the grass, Pascal watched with growing curiosity.

What are they doing here? He asked himself. Papa said only last night the war was all but over and in a few days, France would be free once more. Had not the British and Americans landed on the northern beaches?

He shivered, wishing he'd gone to school instead of choosing to spend the day idling and searching for birds' eggs. Instinctively, he crouched lower in the grass.

The arrival of the officer triggered the men to brisk attention, rifle butts poised stiffly on the ground.

Pascal's heart beat faster, his mouth drying as he recognised the uniform of a high-ranking Sturmbannfuhrer in the SS. This was no patrol. He looked around for escape and seeing no other alternative, began to crawl on his belly toward the far edge of the field – and home.

*

They stood in two lines under the hot sun as the orders were given. Not one man dared to move under the relentless scrutiny of Sturmbannfuhrer Dickmann's ice-blue eyes as he scanned each face for weakness. Satisfied, he raised his arm in salute.

"Heil Hitler!"

Each man followed with faultless precision.

The village bell began to ring. Dickmann's mouth twitched into a smile, which didn't reach his eyes.

"So, the boy heralds our arrival. It is fitting, but there is to be *no* panic, so smile. Help the old ones if they need it. They will cooperate and go willingly … then it will be too late." He looked down the dirt road to the village beyond, the smile disappearing. He turned to the young, blond Lieutenant on his left, "And, Kessler, stop that bell." He drew a gloved finger across his throat. Clicking his heels, the young Lieutenant walked towards the village.

*

Each inhabitant of the tiny Limousin village stopped what they were doing, startled by the unaccustomed ringing. Madame Chourade continued to stir her soup, deaf for the past five years. Anouk Ferrier hurried across the kitchen and took her arm gently.

"Grand-mére, the church bell is ringing … we must go outside. I think perhaps the war is over!" The old lady raised her wrinkled hands in a salute to God, soup dripping from the spoon she still held.

Scooping up her sleeping, new-born son from his crib in the corner of the kitchen, Anouk helped her grandmother outside. A similar scenario was being played out in each dwelling, hope rising in every heart that, at last, this filthy conflict was over. Folk gathered in the main street outside their houses. Some shook hands and slapped each other on the back, rejoicing that their little corner of France had escaped the war largely untouched.

The hum of excited chatter abruptly ceased as a lone figure was seen approaching from the edge of the village. Even at such a distance the uniform was recognisable. Some of the women ran back to their houses, ushering the children inside. The men remained, curious at this lone officer. For he didn't goose-step or even march, but walked into the village at a steady pace, nodding courteously to each group of men as he passed. Without comment, they followed with their gazes as he walked on past the café, questioning each other with looks. The diminishing figure continued on towards the church.

Albert Benoit, long-time schoolmaster, was first to break the silence.

"Now, what do you suppose *he* wants?" The majority still stood in silence watching the uniformed man, now almost out of sight as he reached the door of the church. It was the huge figure of the village butcher, Jean Toulon, who answered with a sneer of irony in his voice. With a guttural hawk, he spat on the ground.

"Maybe he is going to pray for his soul, my friends. I don't think there is much hope of salvation, do you?" He laughed, fleshy jowls wobbling, and the tension was broken as the others joined in. "If he expects absolution from Papa Matthias… then…" He paused abruptly.

The church bell had stopped ringing.

There was no panic. The company of soldiers who followed into the village were courteous and unhurried. When the Sturmbannfuhrer requested that all the population should assemble in the town square for the purpose of an identity check, it was accomplished quickly. No one was anxious to stand outside for too long in the heat and humidity of midday where there was little shade. Only a few mothers of the very young had stopped to get their prams out and most carried their infants, including Anouk Ferrier who held her new-born son close to her chest. Most of the women chatted to their neighbours.

Nevertheless, machine-gun posts had been set up at all four corners, which alarmed some of the women. The officer addressed the crowd. He spoke through a megaphone in impeccable French, though heavily accented, his dark eyes steady.

"Do not be alarmed." He held up a hand for quiet. "We must be cautious, for despite the reported Allied landings, we *are* still at war! Listen carefully. To make this process easier and quicker we need to separate the men from the women." There was general consternation and gasps of anxiety. He raised his hand again for silence. "Don't be afraid. We do not want to keep you out in this heat for too long, and so the men will assemble on this side of the square with myself in command and the women and children on the other with the Lieutenant." He inclined his head toward the tall young man at his side. "Boys of less than ten years of age will go with their mothers. Now move, quickly!"

Presently, the two groups were established on opposite sides of the square.

The Sturmbannfuhrer raised his megaphone again. "Will the Mayor kindly identify himself?"

There was movement and Monsieur Roubier stepped forward. He wore no chain of office, but carried an air of authority that went with the position, his grey moustache tweezed and oiled as always.

"I am the Mayor." He stood straight in front of Dickmann, who addressed him curtly.

"Have you weapons concealed in this village?" The Mayor replied that he knew of several men who had sporting rifles.

Dickmann's mouth tightened. "It has come to our attention that there are Resistance weapons concealed here." Monsieur Roubier stood taller still, meeting Dickmann's piercing gaze.

"Non, Monsieur," he replied firmly. "We have taken no part in this wretched war. We hide nothing!"

"Then it will be necessary to search your homes and, while that happens, you will all be held elsewhere. When we have completed our search, the innocent will be set free."

The Mayor inclined his head. "As you wish, Herr Sturmbannfuhrer."

*

Jean-Claude began to cry. Even shielded from the worst of the midday sun beneath his mother's light cotton shawl, he was still overheating ... and becoming hungry.

"Shuuussssh, mon petit." Anouk rocked her child, fanning him with her free hand to little effect.

The young Lieutenant stepped forward to where she waited with Grand-mére at the edge of the square. "The child is ill?" The grasp of her language was impeccable. His eyes were soft, the colour of cornflowers; compassionate eyes.

"Non, Monsieur. It is very warm and he is but two weeks old."

The Lieutenant smiled, and, reaching forward, stroked the child's face with a gentle finger. Anouk did not snatch the child away, for this man looked kind and did not match up to her perception of the average German soldier.

He smiled again. "It will not be long now."

"Merci, Monsieur." For a split second their eyes met before he turned and moved further down the line.

On the far side of the square, the men were being marched away in the direction of the farm on the edge of the village by soldiers holding rifles.

Then, an order was given in German and the women were led back along the road that led to the church. Anouk patted the old lady's arm. "It is all right Grand-mére. We will be safe in God's house."

Tight lipped, the old lady crossed herself.

*

Hans Kessler stood by the church door, supervising, as the old and the young entered the cool sanctuary, grateful for respite from the hot sun. In an orderly fashion, the women began to find places to sit, children of all ages settling on laps or sitting at their mothers' feet on the cool flagstones.

Eventually, there were a couple of hundred people packed inside the church, their anxiety growing to see what would happen next. The heavy oak door had been locked. The stale smell of sweat from the sheer numbers mingled with unease and growing fear. Near to the sacristy door, Anouk busied herself with feeding her infant, who was hot and fretful.

Some of the younger children, taken from their lessons unaccustomedly, began to cry. Their school mistress, Madame Fournier, drew a few into a tight circle on the floor and clapped her hands for attention. Despite an unsteady voice, she began to sing a nursery rhyme and presently the children joined in.

"Allouette, gentile allouette…"

The German guards looked on. One licked his dry lips as he wiped his brow on his cuff, an automatic weapon slung against his shoulder.

"Look at them!" Grand-mére said out of the side of her mouth, gimlet eyes narrowing. "They are all no more than boys sent to guard old women and children. Is this what remains of the conquering heroes?" She threw back her head and laughed, displaying a few yellowed teeth.

Suddenly, the great oak door was flung open and, thinking they were about to be set free, some surged forward.

"Halt!" The young Lieutenant entered the church, his weapon cocked. There were shouts of alarm as the women at the front retreated, clutching at their neighbours. "Sit down!" The guards levelled their weapons at the women. Everyone sat.

From her seat by the sacristy door, Anouk could make out little through the sea of people, the baby suckling quietly. Two burly soldiers marched up the aisle carrying a large, wooden box; the throng parting to let them pass. From it hung tapes that trailed on the floor. They deposited it by the choir stalls before marching briskly back down the aisle.

Anouk reached for the old woman's hand and squeezed it. It was but a year ago that she had walked down that same aisle dressed in lace on her father's arm. There had been flowers and soft music. She took a deep breath. These men had defiled the place and, with it, her memory of the wonderful day she had married Guillame. She hoped this would all be over by the time he got home from work. As it was, the meal would be late! She held on tightly to Grand-mére's hand.

A terrific burst of gunfire came from outside, closely followed by two large explosions. Women shrieked and huddled together as more shots rang out. Having nowhere to run, they crouched, trying to protect their children from the unseen foe. Anouk threw herself on top of her infant in the shadow of the sacristy wall.

By her side, Marianne Le Roc was screaming her husband's name. Then, reality shot through Anouk's mind like a white-hot arrow.

"Sacré bleu ... they are shooting the men!" Her voice was unheard, lost in the cacophony of panic.

Then came running feet; the sound of boots on stone. Anouk lifted her head to see two soldiers crouching over the box, then, a moment later, fleeing back down the aisle toward the great door as if running for their lives. They turned to guard the opening, guns levelled at the crowd.

The trailing fuses had been lit and the box exploded with a huge bang, giving off thick, black, suffocating smoke. Screaming in terror, women and children ran to the far areas of the church where the smoke had not yet reached, choking and stumbling as they went.

The terrified crowd rushed for the sacristy, barging and flattening anyone and anything in their path. Anouk gasped as, flattened against the wall, she felt feet stand on her back as she crouched in an effort to protect her son.

Screams filled her head as, with a terrible crash, the sacristy wall gave way against the sheer weight of pushing bodies. Debris scattered inward or she would surely have been crushed beneath the ancient stones.

Then gunfire.

Hardly able to breathe, she watched in horror as automatic weapons opened fire on the crowd. Women and children were cut down where they stood. Neighbours and friends, shrieking and bleeding as they fell in heaps, clutching at their children and thin air. A group tried to rush the door and were felled like rag dolls; the automatic weapons spinning them around in a macabre dance of death. Two soldiers made their way up the aisle seeing that people had escaped into the sacristy, shooting to either side as they went. Anouk lay under the bodies that had pinned her to the cold floor and prayed, not daring to move or knowing whether the child beneath her was alive or dead.

Deafening automatic fire came from the sacristy. The fiends were shooting everyone who had survived the collapse of the wall. The screams of torment could not be lessened as Anouk's arms were pinned underneath her and she could not raise them to cover her ears. Silent tears of anguish and unbelievable horror coursed down her face onto the cold stone. Then, stillness, save for the soldiers moving around, no doubt checking if anyone was still alive amid the carnage.

Anouk retched as a wave of cloying odour hit the back of her throat. She had never smelled blood before … not human blood.

From her hiding place, she could just see as the soldiers passed down the aisle, their grisly job in the sacristy complete. The legs of their uniform trousers dripping with the blood of innocent French women and children.

Anouk shifted from beneath the weight of a body, trying not to cry out in agony as the blood returned to her limbs. Something moved under her stomach. Jean-Claude was alive and unharmed, still sleeping, protected by his mother's body. Her silent tears gave thanks to God.

She raised her head cautiously from behind a heap of bodies. There were just two soldiers left and she watched with growing horror as straw and chairs were piled on top of them, lying on the flagstones.

Smoke began to rise again as the horrific pyre was lit with a volley of machine-gun fire.

Suddenly, from alongside, a bony hand grasped at her arm almost making her cry out in terror. Afraid to allow her eyes to wander for what she might see, her body began to shake. The hand moved down her arm to her wrist, gently. Taking short gasps, Anouk looked down. The hand bore a familiar gold ring. She grasped it.

"Grand-mére?" she whispered softly. The old woman was alive and lying at her feet. Anouk rested her head on the older woman's shoulder to whisper. "Are you hurt, Grand-mére?"

The old lady fixed her with a steady gaze and mouthed the words. "Go to the sacristy ... the window behind the altar ... crawl slowly ... use the smoke as cover."

Anouk shook her head frantically, the butchered bodies shielding them from view. The old lady tightened her grip. "Go!" she whispered, "for the child!" Anouk peered down to where the fire was taking hold. Smoke was already sweeping up the aisle toward the sacristy. Just one uniform could be made out in the gathering gloom – the young Lieutenant – and he was occupied by the door, checking that no one was still alive, pistol in hand.

"Grand-mére, I ... I ..." Tears ran down her cheeks, her voice a mere crackle.

Grand-mére held up her hand. "Do one last thing for me, Anouk. Help me up ... then go!"

In the gloom, Anouk began to crawl over bodies in the sacristy, her precious cargo tied securely in the shawl across her chest. Stumbling on, tears fell from her eyes, mingling with the blood and tangled limbs under her feet in a final desperate attempt to live.

The old woman stood amongst the carnage of the charnel house, soaked in the blood of neighbours and friends. Painfully, she began to walk up the aisle toward the soldier. She watched as he stiffened, sensing movement behind him. He turned slowly and raised the pistol.

Marie Chourade's dark eyes fixed him with a hard, uncompromising stare that bore into his very soul and the pistol in his hand began to shake. Who was this woman who faced him with such pride and defiance?

Kessler could neither move nor speak, held by her malignant gaze.

She raised her arms and began to intone softly, a medieval curse, her eyes never leaving his. From deep in her sub-conscious it came – long forgotten, down from the past. The words spewed from her mouth; from generations long gone to their uneasy rest. From the furthest reaches of her soul they came, piercing and pricking him like the point of a bayonet.

And he could not move.

She lowered her arms and pointed a bony finger.

"J'accuse! For what you have done today, there will be no rest … no forgiveness … not for you or your blood folk. I curse your soul for the innocents."

And, for the first time in his life, Hans Kessler was consumed by fear.

She walked toward the burning pyre, flames licking upward as if to welcome her. Still holding him fast with her eyes, she walked into the fire, her gown catching alight at once.

A terrible scream came from within her, not of pain or anguish, but of sheer malevolence. From her gaping mouth came a great plume of black smoke, which shot toward him, spinning him off-balance and knocking him to the ground. There came a deafening roar of flame and when he dared look again, she was gone – consumed by the fire.

He lay on the floor, breathing hard. All was silent save for the crackling fire and, from the direction of the sacristy, the plaintive cry of an infant.

Slowly, deliberately, Kessler reached for his pistol.

Anouk had reached the altar, crawling and stepping on bodies, the gall rising in her throat, all the time trying not to vomit. She stepped into the space behind it that was providing a blessed shield from the rest of the church. The windows above had been shot out and she took long gasps of fresh air.

Carefully, anxious not to make a sound, she retrieved the stool used for lighting the altar candles and placed it beneath the middle window, the largest of the three. On it, she could just about reach the stone sill with her fingertips, terror giving her strength. A fragment of masonry loosened by the bullets gave way and she lost her foothold, falling heavily back to the ground. With the unexpected jolt, Jean-Claude began to scream.

In horror and panic Anouk rocked him vigorously. "Shuusssh, mon petit … please do not cry … not now … please." The baby quietened and she cocked her head to catch the sound of footsteps.

In blind panic, she scrambled up onto the stool once more, heaving herself up toward the windowsill. This time she found a firm foothold and began to climb, cuts from shards of window glass going unnoticed.

Breathing hard, she reached the stone sill and hauled herself up to stand on it, a sudden bout of dizziness almost causing her to fall back down again. She grasped the lintel tightly with bleeding hands and looked out. Five metres … five metres to the ground and escape. Anouk took a deep breath and prepared to jump.

"Halt!" The staccato command cracked the silence of the church.

She froze and grasped the now whimpering baby, her lower lip bitten in prayer.

"Turn around!"

She obeyed, forcing herself to look away from the gun barrel and once again into the Lieutenant's cornflower eyes now locked on her own.

"Sir, I beg you … spare us." She grimaced as a stream of hot urine ran down her legs. "For pity's sake!" her eyes pleaded.

He raised the gun levelling it at her head.

"No …" Anouk screamed and turned to jump, Jean-Claude clutched against her.

The bullet hit her between the shoulders, a clean shot which passed through her body and that of her son pitching them forward through clear air into blessed oblivion.

Chapter 2

Mike Duval was delighted with the result of his well-kept secret. All those whispered phone conversations and clandestine meetings with friends and family had been worthwhile. He'd wondered if he could *really* pull it off. After all, he'd never been *that* good at keeping secrets and, like most men, was not known for his organisational qualities at home. Any worries about the success of the thing evaporated the moment Denise rushed towards him like a speeding train, arms held out like a child to be picked up. He'd obliged; swinging her high off the ground, her doll-like frame almost lost in his arms, eyes sparkling like a five-year-old on Christmas morning.

"Thank you, darling. This has been one of the best days of my life."

He laughed, his face snuggling her neck, then setting her down at last.

"So *that's* what all the creeping about was for, *and* the secret phone calls. Honestly, Mike, I was beginning to wonder if you were having an affair."

"Shame on you," he remonstrated, wagging his finger. "I should have thought by now you'd have realised there'll only ever be one woman for me. God knows, I can't afford another one!" Denise threw back her head and laughed, pirouetting on the spot out of sheer delight.

It'd been a truly wonderful party; the kind of occasion that most families always intend to make happen, but rarely get around to. It'd been sold to her on the premise of 'having a few friends round' for her birthday and to celebrate their ten years together. He'd never doubted she'd look lovely, but was amazed at just *how* lovely. His wife never went anywhere looking less than perfect, but, as she walked down the stairs, she'd taken his breath away.

The black, washed-silk dress outlined Denise's slender figure, its colour giving her skin the appearance of porcelain. Her natural blonde hair framed a heart-shaped face, further emphasising her doll-like qualities; tiny feet in tall stilettos. She could have graced any Paris catwalk, though the 'killer' heels *had* been abandoned the second the last guest left. Her feet probably hurt like hell, but she'd rather have died than admit it or risk looking less than elegant. Mike allowed himself a self-satisfied smile as he poured a well-earned brandy.

My God … ten years! Michael James Duvall – the man they said would never settle down – just look at you. Cheers, my friend! He raised his glass to the reflection in the mirror and drank deeply. Ten years' married already! Who'd have thought it? A decade with the most stunning woman in the world. He still got an erection thinking about her! Mike grinned and took another long slug of brandy and sat in the armchair.

It'd been a good idea to pull all the family in from the four corners of the country for a party, and long overdue. A welcome change from meeting at funerals; he was really glad he'd made the effort. He thought back to how the family had loved his prospective wife from the outset. That was important as she'd none of her own.

Denise told Mike a few days after they'd met that she'd been orphaned at three, the result of a tragic skiing accident in the Austrian Alps. There'd been a period when she'd talked about it a lot, as if needing to make someone special understand how it was. She knew little of the details, except that there'd been an unexpected avalanche that killed both her parents. She'd been left with a nanny in the ski resort on that fateful day and had little memory of her family apart from a few precious photographs.

It was clear from those black-and-white snapshots that she looked like her mother, a tall, elegant blonde of Swiss origin.

She wished she could remember Papa, though from the photographs her eyes were certainly like his. The few folk who'd known them both said he was a quiet man, yet powerful and muscular. Mamma, it was said, was the strong, sensible one of the partnership who'd not shown emotion easily. Denise liked to think she'd inherited the best qualities of them both. In some small way it seemed to make up for their absence because they were unable to give her anything else.

Sometimes, on waking, she'd remember fleeting details, but didn't really know if they were imagined. As a child, she'd been so anxious to remember even a little, so perhaps it was wishful thinking. But one thing she did remember was her father singing her to sleep with a lullaby. She remembered the tune vividly, but only later learned the words of the old, German folk song. As an adult she still found it strangely comforting, catching herself humming it from time to time.

Roses whisper goodnight, 'neath silvery light

Asleep in the dew, they hide from our view.

When the dawn peepeth through, God will wake them and you.

When the dawn peepeth through, God will wake them and you.

Throughout all the lonely years of growing up deprived of her parents, she'd plenty of time to wonder if indeed she *had* been loved.

All that ended when she met Mike. Suddenly, it was as though all those lonely years without a real family didn't matter anymore. She was gathered up into *his* family, quickly becoming part of it. For Mike, who was five years older than her, it'd been wonderful to see her respond to them, and they to her.

So, Mike had been determined that *this* celebration would go some way to make up for all the birthday parties she'd missed as a child. Not that Denise went short of affection. The 'aunties' at the Belmont children's home were a wonderful bunch; kind, caring and always available for cuddles. Today, care workers often stay for six months and move on. The staff at Belmont worked there for years – sometimes for their entire careers. It was a real vocation. If there'd been anything good about being brought up in a children's home, it was that. Denise considered herself to have been lucky, though Mike knew it couldn't have been easy. A little girl suddenly alone, confused and probably frightened. Her parents gone, she was taken away and left in an unfamiliar place with strangers. He'd always found the thought unbearable. There'd only been one elderly aunt of her mother's in Surrey, far too old and infirm to bring up a child of three. There'd been no choice.

The 'house' mother and father at Belmont were a married couple and their lives revolved around its children. The 'Home' was just that – a home to all who came to stay. If there'd been a down side, it was often the continuity that was missing.

"When you cried in the night," Denise once told her husband, "it wasn't always the same 'auntie' who came to comfort you. No amount of 'aunties', as good as they were, could replace a *real* mother's love." At last, with Mike, she had a *real* family.

And he was particularly proud that he'd been able to bring together the past and present for the party. After much searching he'd managed to track down two of the favourite aunties from Denise's early years in Belmont.

What a pair of characters they proved to be!

Henrietta Lange was in her eighties and affectionately known as 'Hennie'. Lucy Harpur was a sprightly, plump and, now, almost blind, gem of a woman in her late seventies. She'd, not surprisingly, been nicknamed 'Goosey Lucy'. At least there would be someone from her childhood for Denise to greet.

She'd been so utterly surprised and delighted to see them, and had hugged them both in the same fashion they used to hug her.

'Aunt Hennie' was barely five feet tall – and as far around – dressed in sombre black. Her blue-rinsed hair had been specially coiffured for the occasion. On top of it sat a black, sequinned hat adorned with a large, blue feather that once belonged to a peacock. She'd the kindest eyes Mike had ever seen; twinkling with mischief despite her age. Her skin was as smooth as silk, never having seen a trace of make up in its 80 years.

'Aunt Lucy' was also dressed in black, save for a glimpse of intricate, white cutwork lace at the neck of her blouse. Tall and elegant with not a scrap of excess fat on her frame, she wore stiletto heels that made her look taller than ever. Her pencil-slim skirt and silk, seamed stockings bore not a single crease. She'd rather a cadaverous face until she smiled and *when* she smiled it lit up the entire room with the same candescence as a lighthouse in the ocean's mist.

They looked a formidable pair perched in the two armchairs either side of the fireplace, resembling a couple of temple guardians. Denise suppressed a smile as she watched them sip their respective cups of tea in near-perfect synchronisation. They sat chatting easily as if no years had passed; their faces transformed into the giddy young women they once were, animated by the reminiscing. This was what Denise remembered as a child, the fun and the laughter; happy memories brought back by two wonderful old ladies, now enjoying themselves thoroughly and giggling like schoolgirls.

"I wonder how many children the pair of them cradled over the years?" said Mike as he gazed at the pair.

"Too many to count." Denise sighed. "I can't believe you found them. Where on earth did you find them?" She served cake with ridiculous amounts of cream on pale-blue china plates.

"Actually, it wasn't too difficult. The charitable trust that ran Belmont is still listed with social services. They had the records, believe it or not, and contact numbers for previous long-term employees. The trust made provision of small pensions to those who'd worked there for over 30 years, and that included Hennie and Lucy. I had to formally ask permission to contact them, of course, but they were so helpful and as good as their word when I explained what it was for."

"So, they're provided for?" said Denise looking up. "I'm glad, because they deserve to be comfortable in their old age."

"The two of them certainly look it from the outfits they're wearing," said Mike. "That's quality stuff! Even *I* can see that. Do you know that Hennie worked at Belmont for nearly 50 years and Lucy for 48? They must have been mere girls. Imagine looking after someone else's children all that while, given that they're both spinsters and never had any of their own."

"I don't expect they had time," said Denise as Hennie let out another hoot of laughter. "They may well be 'Misses', but I doubt they've missed very much."

"I'll make sure they don't go short of cake and drinks," said Mike with a glance toward the pair through the open door of the sitting room. "You go back to your guests. Though I wouldn't be too surprised if those two are up doing the conga later." Denise passed him two large slices of pink-and-white cake before disappearing into the cacophony of the conservatory with a laden tray.

Mike stood out of sight for a moment, plates in hand, and listened to the laughter coming from the sitting room. Oblivious to the loud music coming from the rest of the house, the two elderly ladies were clearly enjoying themselves. He smiled, thinking how much he owed the pair. For it was they and perhaps a few others that were responsible for Denise being the person she was after such a terrible event. How were they able to give so much to someone else's child and to keep giving day after day? He was just about to walk into the room to ask just that when Hennie stopped laughing and leaned forward.

Mike stopped, masked by the partially-open door.

"Do you think she knows?" Hennie asked, pointedly.

"How could she?" Lucy's voice was steady and soft. "What good could it possibly do? She's turned into *such* a lovely young woman."

"Everyone has a right to know where they came from, my dear, even if …"

"No!" Lucy cut her off in mid-sentence. "She must *never* know. It would destroy her. Remember the promise. She must *never* be told!"

"Knock, knock." Mike pushed the door open and offered the tray. He sat in the silence that'd suddenly descended. "Now ladies, what must she *never* be told?" He looked from one to the other. Lucy sighed and ate her cake in silence.

*

In the early hours of the morning after all the friends and relatives left, they lay on the sofa, Denise in Mike's arms their bodies touching.

"I love you so much, Mike. It was a wonderful party, and do you know what made it perfect?

"Don't tell me – Hennie and Goosey Lucy?"

"Yes."

"And the best thing is you need never lose touch with them again. They only live in Wensley, a few streets away from each other."

"Good grief!" Denise snuggled down in Mike arms. "I still find it hard to believe they never married and had children of their own, though. But how could they, looking after us all day long? Still, you always assume ..." She shrugged. Mike quickly put the unanswered question to the back of his mind. This wasn't the time to address it and nothing was going to spoil today.

He silenced his wife abruptly by kissing her throat and moved to her mouth as her arms encircled his neck. She shuddered and responded to his rising passion and growing hardness. Their lovemaking brought a natural end to a perfect day *and* started a sequence of events that would change their lives forever.

Chapter 3

Denise woke with a violent start, her heart pounding. For a moment, unable to breathe properly, panic spread through her body before she realised that it was a nightmare – only a nightmare. With huge relief, she turned over and looked at the clock. It was almost 6.00am and the alarm would ring at any moment. Quickly, she pressed the cancel button and reached for the glass of lemon Perrier she kept by the bed. Leaning back against the pillows, she took a long drink, her breathing still erratic.

Whew! What was that about? She blew out through pursed lips.

It was years since she'd had a nightmare like that, which left her shaking and sweating. Denise knew all about nightmares. Around the time her periods started she'd had them in abundance. It was normal, or so the doctor said when her mother took her to see him.

"It's just your hormones beginning to work overtime." She'd once read that nightmare sufferers take a little time after they wake to convince their conscious mind that their body's not in mortal danger. Once the senses have been whipped up with the adrenaline surge that comes with the nightmare, it all takes a little while to settle down. Nevertheless, she still felt disturbed for hours.

Later that day, Denise was desperately trying to remember what it was upset her so much. The damnedest thing was she couldn't recall anything apart from the feeling of panic.

Mike had still been asleep when she left for work, being 'well-oiled' from the night before. He was never at his best in the mornings, anyway, until after two cups of coffee at the very least.

By the end of the day, she felt better and her sense of unease disappeared.

Work's often the best therapy when something's on your mind. It was probably the party with its reminders of childhood that set it off; a resurrection of forgotten memories. And hormones! She smiled. Denise was well acquainted with those. Puberty had come at an impossibly early age. At ten, it was such an inopportune time. She'd been barely capable of understanding the new and alien feelings that accompanied the monthly visitor. The nightmares that followed had come with sickening regularity. They were something else!

They always began in the same way. She was standing in the centre of a large room, with an overwhelming compulsion to get to all four corners at the same time. And she must because if she failed, then she knew something awful would happen. Her life depended on it and, as she looked down at her hands and feet, they became huge – completely out of proportion to the rest of her body. She'd likened it to *Alice in Wonderland*, but *far* more sinister. The worst part was it was a hopeless dilemma and, each time it happened, she feared she'd die if unable to complete the task.

When Denise woke, it was with the same pounding heart and feeling of suffocation, her body wreathed in perspiration. When she'd dared to open her eyes, it was often Aunt Hennie or Lucy who'd be sitting by her bed, alerted by the terrified, dream-state screams.

And then the nightmares became less frequent. It was a blessed release from her nightly torment and much to everyone's relief. By her 14th birthday they were a distant memory never to return – until the night of the party. So, it was with some trepidation that Denise settled down to sleep the following night. She needn't have worried for all stayed peaceful, and she soon fell into a deep and blessedly dreamless sleep. It seemed that life had returned to normal.

**

Six weeks later Mike and Denise were out celebrating. Not that there was anything *special*, but there'd never been the need for an excuse to visit Giovanni's restaurant. It was a particular favourite, and Joe and Eleanor Duffy, their best friends, had joined them.

It'd been a wonderful evening. The 'awesome foursome', as they liked to call themselves, hadn't been together since the night of Denise's party. All four drank a considerable amount of Giovanni's exceptional house wine and were merry, to say the least.

Dining at Giovanni's wasn't just 'going out for a meal', but the full Italian experience. He'd been quite a celebrity in his home town of San Gimignano in Tuscany. The family restaurant, Da Graziano, was renowned throughout all Italy for its speciality fish dishes. Giovanni brought the same flair to England in the 1960s; an expertise that would ensure the family business would flourish for generations to come, as it had in the old, medieval town of his birth.

Conversation was never stilted when the four of them were together. Tonight it'd been buzzing, tongues and imaginations loosened by the increasing consumption of alcohol. The jokes and innuendos became smuttier with each glass consumed.

The art of enjoying themselves was never difficult. Joe and Eleanor had been at secondary school with Mike, and when Denise appeared on the scene she'd slotted effortlessly into place. At first, she'd been regaled with the antics the trio got up to at school; the tales had been added to and 'embroidered' somewhat over the years. Secretly, Joe and Eleanor were relieved to see Mike settling down at last.

The evening ended with the four around the microphone singing *Volare*, while Cesare, the owner's son, played guitar. It'd been a passable effort despite them having to hang onto each other for support.

*

"Oh, somebody put me to bed!" slurred Mike as he practically fell from the taxi, trying not to be sick. Denise was relieved to get home. After all, it was a £25 fine if you were sick in a taxi, or so Joe said, and *he* obviously knew about such things.

"Don't worry," Mike said, with a drunken leer, "I can always do it in Eleanor's handbag."

Eleanor took a swipe at him, incensed that *anyone* would consider using her expensive Louis Vuitton handbag for such a purpose. Mike ducked instinctively. He knew Eleanor was more than capable of defending her property if she had to. Her black belt in karate was a testament to that. He'd been on the receiving end more than once when he'd teased her a little too much.

Having paid their half of the fare, Mike and Denise tottered up the path with a backward wave. They made it as far as the pot plants before Mike's squid in garlic with linguine put in a reappearance. The pair fell into bed and consciousness flew to some far off place where even the cat's insistent calls didn't reach. The animal climbed to the topmost branch of the cherry tree outside the bedroom window and yowled loudly to no avail.

However, deep within Denise's subconscious, something *was* happening. Had Mike been awake he'd have seen his wife's hands clench and unclench. He'd have seen her eyes open in a terrified stare and her lips, from which no sound came, move frantically. Then after several minutes, she gave an enormous sigh, turned over, and all was still again. Whatever caused her disturbance had gone away.

For now.

*

Mike woke with a *very* thick head in the late morning, gingerly raising his head to look at the bedside clock. A piercing pain shot between his temples reminding him further movement wasn't a good idea.

"Bloody hell!" A whole roll of drummers beat a tattoo inside his skull. Denise roused and fumbled for the painkillers in the bedside drawer; a well-practised ritual after a night out with their friends.

"Here, take a couple of these. God! Mike, *how* much did we drink?" He rolled over, wincing, careful not to move his head too quickly.

"A lot! Darling, could you possibly make coffee this morning? I'm completely wrecked." Denise threw back the quilt.

"Phew! I don't feel so good myself. Dehydration probably … I'm hot and sweaty."

"Nothing to do with several bottles of wine followed by rampant sex, I suppose." He considered laughing, but thought better of it.

"I only remember the wine," said Denise with a petulant purse of her lips.

"Only joking, so do I! Now go and make the coffee." He gave her a playful shove with his foot.

Denise sat on the side of the bed and ruffled her fingers through her hair. "Okay then, coffee. I'll make it black and *very* strong."

She'd almost reached the bedroom door when a wave of vertigo hit her. The room spun like a crazy merry-go-round. She clutched her head and gasped before falling to the floor in a dead faint. Mike scrambled out of bed in a vain attempt to catch her. The last thing she heard was the cat's insistent call after making another unsuccessful attempt to be let in.

*

Over the next few weeks, Denise fainted a few more times, usually on getting out of bed. Never a person to worry about her health, she quickly dismissed it as unimportant. At Mike's insistence, though, she started to take iron tablets just in case she was anaemic.

"I'm sure it's only women's problems," she told him. "We do this from time to time, you know." She did, however, feel very tired for the rest of the day whenever it happened. And, there was something else. She felt disturbed – and scared.

Chapter 4

The days became colder and winter arrived. It was time to decorate the house, and they always had great fun doing it. The end product was worth all the falling out that invariably happened. Denise was, in Mike's words, "too much of a foreman and less of a labourer". They entertained frequently during the dark nights, and planned a break with Joe and Eleanor, skiing in the French Alps near Val d'Isère.

It proved to be a rather *unusual* holiday.

*

Poor Joe fell awkwardly and broke both bones in his lower leg on the first day. He'd only been going for a trial run on the nursery slopes. Sporting a full-length plaster, the rest of the holiday had to be arranged around his needs. Unfortunately, the art of patience and sitting still were not amongst Joe's attributes. Eleanor deserved a medal for putting up with his ill-disguised grumpiness. One morning he came down to breakfast sporting a black eye and a bruised nose where he'd, allegedly, fallen off his crutches. Mike swore that Eleanor attacked him with the bath brush whilst he slept as the only way to get her own back.

Incapable of going to the slopes, he was more than content to be 'parked' each day outside one of the bars. He'd happily sit in the sun with his leg resting on a cushion. It was a prime location to elicit sympathy from all the female ski instructors, who'd fetch beer and take him wherever he wanted to go. He was in heaven! Crutches abandoned and with his arms around the shoulders of assorted Nordic beauties, he hopped happily from place to place. The 'little-boy-injured' look that he wore in those puppy-dog, brown eyes ensured his every need was catered for. He probably had a far better time than if he'd been out on the slopes.

All four returned home in a happy and relaxed mood. Joe was fussed over by the stewardesses and given priority seating on the flight; they flashed their smiles at the 'poor injured boy'.

"Enjoy it, Joe," said Eleanor with a smirk, "*this* is where the carrying about ends. And, you can take that look of indignation off your face. We *all* know what you've been up to."

"Thank goodness," sighed Mike as the taxi drew up outside the house. "It's great to go away, but it's even better to come home." Later, after climbing into their own bed, Mike held Denise briefly before they both drifted into sleep.

*

The moon came out from behind a cloud, bathing the room in soft ethereal light through a gap in the curtains. Denise awoke with a start, but it was only an imploring "meow" from the topmost branch of the cherry tree outside. Clambering out of bed, she reached through the window, grabbed a somewhat miffed Bunbury by the scruff of the neck and hauled him inside. Before long, a contented purr told her he was settled on the bottom of the duvet and had forgiven them for going away.

Bloody Bunbury! Why can't he come in at a decent hour? It was her last waking thought before she slipped into sleep.

Bunbury wasn't sleeping. Through half-closed eyes he was watching. For what, he didn't know, and he wasn't sufficiently interested to move. The moon cast shadows on the walls as the clouds moved across its face in the winter's air, and Bunbury continued to watch, thinking better of sleep.

*

Denise was choking as unseen hands tightened around her throat, forcing her down into chilling darkness. She fought for her life, trying to get a handhold on whoever or whatever it was who gripped her. An enormous weight was smothering her, draining her very soul, pushing her down towards the raptures of endless sleep. She was losing consciousness and the battle for life as she fell onto cold stone from which there was no escape.

Is this how it feels to die?

With a final tremendous effort, she lifted her head. There was a child crying and the cry became a long tortuous wail. The wail became a scream, louder and louder until it filled her head. Then, from out of the cold darkness, someone was grabbing her shoulders, snatching her from the cold floor, shaking her back to consciousness and calling her name.

With a jolt, she awoke to realise that the scream had been her own and the grasping hands the familiar ones of her husband.

"Denise, for God's sake, what is it? What the hell's happening? His wide eyes were filled with fear.

"Nightm … mmare," she managed to gasp, her throat as dry as dust. "Night … mmare … nightmare." With shaking hands, she fumbled for a glass of water and, with his help to steady it, drank deeply and greedily. "So hot … I'm so hot." Her skin was burning as if in the grip of some horrible fever. She sobbed, her head buried in Mike's chest for the remainder of the night until exhaustion overcame them both.

*

The next day, Denise didn't go to work for the first time ever, but, by the middle of the afternoon, she felt much calmer; though still very weary and a trifle foolish for missing work over what was *only* a stupid dream.

Mike came home and after supper they sat and talked. She hadn't told him about her recent nightmares, but now she could keep them to herself no longer.

"The whole thing is so foolish," she told him. "Look, I'm an averagely intelligent human being and I've tried to rationalise it. Honestly, Mike, this is starting to get me down. I'm so tired the next day. I'm sure I'm using so much energy dreaming by morning I'm worn out."

"How often is it happening, Denise?"

"It began a while ago. Then, I thought it'd gone away. It didn't happen at all whilst we were away."

"How often, Denise?" Mike persisted, his hand gentle on her arm.

"Three or four times a week, I suppose, but nothing like the ferocity of last night's episode." She caught his expression of horror and closed her eyes for a moment, unable to meet his gaze. She was embarrassed and knew she should've told him before. It seemed to portray such a lack of trust in this man who loved her.

He put his arms around her, as if to compound her shame, lightly kissing her on the forehead.

"Whatever's causing it, Denise, we'll get through it together." She looked up into his strong, trustworthy face.

"I know we will, Mike." Whatever Mike really thought, he didn't say – not then.

**

Three months on, things had gone from bad to worse.

Denise went to bed early, the frequent nightmares taking their toll. Mike poured a large whisky and sat in the dining room thinking over the events of the past few months. In that short time his lovely wife had changed from a fun-loving, immaculately dressed 30-year-old into someone he hardly recognised. Denise was depressed, and slow of thought and speech. Some days she'd not bothered to wash or comb her hair, staying away from the job she loved. She rarely cooked, opting for quick meals needing little preparation. At first, he'd been as guilty as anyone of only seeing what he wanted, blaming women's problems for her mood swings. He'd had to admit to himself that men do that when presented with quirks of the female psyche they don't understand. But he couldn't fail to notice she was pale and weary-looking. Her skin had lost its usual healthy glow and she'd lost weight. All the time he'd known her, Denise had been slim. Now she was skinny and that was *far* less attractive. The clothes seemed to hang on her frame and dark circles under her eyes betrayed a lack of rest. He knew she slept, but was that sleep restful? He thought not. It was as though she was afraid to go to sleep, preferring to read or iron into the early hours. As a consequence their relationship in bed and out of it had suffered terribly. Sex was a distant memory. Putting down the empty glass, he walked upstairs to the bedroom and sat beside her.

"What about a chat with the doctor?" He half expected a refusal.

"Oh, I don't know whether ..." She grimaced.

"Denise, it can't hurt. Perhaps it's something as simple as being run down. Let's make an appointment and I'll come with you. Please, darling."

She nodded her reluctant assent.

*

Dr George Green listened carefully and followed up with a full physical examination.

"Thank you, Denise. Take a seat for a moment, will you?" He'd known Denise Duval from a child – Denise Ashworth as she was then – and he liked her. He wished he could have said that about all his patients. She wasn't a regular visitor to his surgery, apart from for the annual hay fever medication and the odd ear infection. That was about it. He'd watched her grow from a small, shy orphan in a children's home into a confident and beautiful young woman, delighted she'd made a happy marriage to the man who sat beside her.

George leaned back in his brown leather chair, case notes in hand.

"Well now, let's go through it. Your blood pressure and urine test are both normal, and there's no sign of an ear infection. So that's not the cause of your dizziness. I think perhaps it's best if we do a few blood tests for anaemia, and urea and electrolytes to check your chemical balance, with all this sweating and fainting. Oh, and perhaps hormone levels and thyroid function whilst we're at it." He smiled at the pair of them. "Don't look so anxious. I can't find anything wrong; well nothing obvious, anyway. Let's see what the blood tests tell us, shall we? Make an appointment for a week's time and I'll see you then."

"Thank you doctor," said Mike as they left. "It's good of you to see us so quickly."

George sat back in his chair again and looked at the notes. He picked up his pen and pushed his spectacles back firmly onto the bridge of his nose. He wrote up his findings and recorded all the tests that were to be done. There *was* something unusual, something different about the young woman. She was pale, but it was the anxiety and her strained expression that struck him. And she wore the dark smudges under the eyes of one who's not sleeping well. He sighed, weary, too, after such a long and busy day, and then pressed the intercom button to call in his next patient.

✶ ✶

A week later, Denise returned to the surgery.

"Hello Denise, nice to see you again. On your own today, I see."

"Mike's working late."

"Oh well, that gives us plenty of time to talk as my next patient has cancelled." He was secretly grateful. Minnie Abbott was the biggest hypochondriac on his list and he'd have been lucky to get away before dark. He motioned to Denise to sit and did so himself, leaning forward, attentive. "Now, how are you doing?"

Denise relaxed as she always did in this man's company. He was easy to talk to, and she'd known him as long as she could remember.

"Well, I did all the things we talked about. I've cut down on alcohol, and stopped drinking coffee or anything else too exciting before bedtime." She gave a nervous laugh. "When it gets to 9.00pm my brain's too tired for anything but sleep."

"Still feeling weary, then?"

32

"Yes. A warm bath and a milky drink, and that's me away to bed, I'm afraid."

He noticed that she smiled much more readily than she'd done a week ago.

"Well, Denise, the news is good. All your tests were normal, so I expect that's a relief." She nodded and he sat back. "Let's talk some more about you."

George Green was not only a good family doctor but a shrewd and expert counsellor. During the conversation that followed, he was able to extract a great deal of information from what, to the untrained ear, was a normal, friendly conversation.

"Well," he concluded, "I think you could be suffering from something called seasonal affective disorder; SAD for short." Denise raised her eyebrows. "It's actually very common. It's due to the lowering of light levels in winter time. This causes the amount of a substance called serotonin in your brain to fall. We call it the 'feel good' chemical because that is exactly what it does. Now, there are two options. We can give you a box that emits a bright light, which you sit in front of for a couple of hours a day ..."

"I'd much prefer a walk at lunchtime," Denise interrupted.

"Yes, you could do that if you want, but, with these nightmares, I'd suggest a mild sedative, just for a short time." Her anxious look told him she wasn't keen and he held up his hands pre-empting her objections. "Now, before you say you don't take pills, it's only one at night for a few weeks, at the most. I think if, perhaps, we can get you *really* relaxed *before* you go to sleep, you'll stay that way. I think you'll find those nightmares go away, too, and then you'll start to feel better."

"This SAD is aptly named," said Denise, "because if that's what it is, that's exactly how I feel." She paused to consider. "Okay, let's give it a try."

"Good girl. Now come and see me again in another couple of months. I'm sure by then the tablets will have done the trick. If it's any consolation, it happens in nature, too. There are some other mammals that suffer in the same way. It's all to do with long nights and short days. Some animals are even able to control their breeding cycle if the weather isn't right. It happens with sheep and some deer, I think. Oh, and hamsters." Denise laughed, amused at how anyone could possibly know something that obscure.

"Well Dr Green, I'll see you in a couple of months, or before if I start running round in a little wheel." It was George's turn to laugh.

"The tablets *will* do the trick, Denise. Be patient and don't expect to feel better overnight." She got up, shook his hand and left.

✶ ✶

And, indeed the tablets *did* work, or, at least, something seemed to. It helped considerably that Bunbury had ceased his nocturnal wanderings, opting for the warmth of the kitchen, where he'd settle on top of the Aga and purr contentedly. The cat was definitely a fair-weather animal, hating the unpleasant feel of the cold ground beneath his paws.

After a few weeks of medication, Denise began to regain her zest for life and the energy she'd been so lacking, much to Mike's delight. Her memory began to improve. She joked that, at last, she could go shopping without forgetting where she'd left the car. When the nightmares started, sleep deprivation made her short-term memory terrible. Now, getting through the day was no longer an effort and she began to enjoy going to work again.

Denise was the secretary to the managing director of a local, and *very* exclusive, chocolate factory for eight years, and was very well thought of. However, spending all her working life in close proximity to the endless confectionary meant she never touched the stuff. Joe was a confirmed chocoholic and constantly begged for samples. He was provided with a constant supply, usually the misshapen ones that couldn't be sold. Joe didn't care; chocolate was chocolate. Before going shopping one Saturday morning, Denise called to drop off a bag at their house.

"My favourite other woman bearing gifts; the best kind of mistress," said Joe as he greeted her with a hug and grabbed the bag. "You're looking *so* much better."

"So are you," said Denise, extricating herself. His leg was healing well now and he was off crutches with only a mere trace of a limp.

"Ellie! Den's here." He leaned forward and whispered, "11.00am and *still* in her dressing gown." Denise gave a wry grin and raised an eyebrow.

"Hope I haven't disturbed you doing anything important." She winked.

"Absolutely not. I'm afraid Ellie had rather a lot to drink last night. She's feeling decidedly dodgy this morning." As if on cue, Eleanor shuffled into the room, obviously having just got out of bed, her hair tangled and spiky.

"Hi Den. Sorry ... had a lie in." She took in her friend's neat appearance. "Good God, where are *you* off to dressed up to the nines? No need to ask if you're feeling better. Good." She wandered off to the kitchen in search of coffee.

"I'm going shopping," called Denise, "and wondered if you wanted to come. It's the first time I've felt like it in ages." Ellie returned.

"Would you mind terribly if I didn't today? Coffee?"

"Not at all, and no thanks," said Denise. "Now take your coffee back to bed and sleep off the hangover. Get Joe to wait on you hand and foot for a change, now that his plaster's off." Ellie groaned.

"I think I will." She headed for the door. "Oh, Denise, it's good to see you looking better."

Joe and Eleanor, being the good friends they were, had been as alarmed as Mike at the speed their friend was losing weight, but decided to give them a bit of space and not badger them for information. If there was anything to tell, they knew they'd be told sooner or later.

Joe watched as Denise walked down the path and got in her car, waving as she pulled away. Whatever it was, apparently it had got better, but Den had always been a bit emotional. She *was* lovely though, the sort of woman he'd have asked out had it not been for Ellie … and Mike. He rubbed at the stubble on his chin. Then again, Eleanor was much more self-assured and he found strong women incredibly sexy.

With a huge grin, he followed her upstairs.

Chapter 5

Denise came out of Debenhams, laden with carrier bags, and bumped squarely into an old-fashioned, coach-built pram someone had left unattended by the doors. The worn-down tyre on one of its huge wheels scraped her shin painfully and she dropped a couple of her bags. Swearing under her breath, she bent to retrieve them, stopping for a moment to rub her leg. Gathering the bags, she was about to walk away when a whimper from inside the pram made her stop. Transferring her shopping to one hand, she peered inside. Lying there was a baby, its face wrinkling in preparation to howl. It was the sort of pram you saw on the council tip, piled with rubbish, often minus its wheels. Local kids usually took them to make a trolley.

It was so grubby. Who in their right mind would put a baby inside that? Denise was horrified. And, even worse, who would be so stupid as to leave a child alone in the middle of a busy shopping centre in this day and age? She looked around anxiously for signs of a mother. Maybe, she'd been distracted by an unexpected meeting with a friend and was watching nearby. But there was no one in sight who seemed to own the pram or the child.

Gosh, she thought. *Anyone could walk away with the pram and its precious contents in a flash. The child looks no more than a few weeks old.*

The baby began to wail; a long, insistent howl of hunger and indignation. With a hint of growing desperation, Denise looked around her. None of the busy shoppers seemed to be paying much attention to the pram, or the row that came from within. She rested her bags up against the shop window and, taking the large ivory handle, began to rock the pram.

"Please don't cry," she whispered, peering inside. "There, there." She rocked harder as the infant continued his repertoire of screams. "Oh, where's your mother, for heaven's sake? Fancy leaving you like this! Don't cry please. I don't know what to do to make you stop. Shuuusssh. Oh, please … I don't like it when you cry."

An overwhelming sense of panic rose in her tightening chest, her breath coming in short gasps as the infant cried louder still, its face puce. Instinctively, she bent to pick up the squalling infant, but checked herself almost immediately.

Someone may think I'm trying to steal it! Denise was sweating, but the urge to comfort the distressed infant was overwhelming. The cries filled her head, piercing her very soul. Fighting her instinct to reach inside the pram, she merely rocked harder. The rusty, old suspension protested with a series of squeaks.

"Please stop," she begged, peering inside again. Her hand reached out to stroke the infant's flushed, angry face.

A huge woman rushed from the shop. She grabbed the handle of the pram from Denise, sending her sprawling with carrier bags falling to the ground. The woman's face was inches from Denise's, her lips drawn back over nicotine-stained teeth bared in a snarl. It was the face of a wild animal and Denise cowered under the threat. The woman's grubby, blonde, loose mane of hair flew behind her. She grasped the lapel of Denise's jacket, pushing her until she fell heavily against the shop window. Mercifully, the toughened glass bowed, but held fast, as she sank to the ground in shock.

"But, I was only …" she began.

The woman spat out her words, setting loose facial flesh in motion and poked a dirty finger close to Denise's face, hissing between clenched teeth. "Curse you lady!" Denise gasped, her face as pale as that of the snotty-nosed toddler the woman dragged behind her.

"I know your sort, lady." A dirty finger nail jabbed at Denise's cheek and she recoiled cowering against the shop window. She tried to turn her head from the rank breath, which spewed from the mouth with its brown teeth. The fingernail held fast, threatening to pierce her skin. "You should keep your 'oity 'toity nose out of it, *if* you know what's good for you." Her black eyes held a threat; a warning delivered with pure venom and brooding malice.

Suddenly, Denise found her voice. She was angry now, but even though still on the ground, she was not ready to be bowed by this harridan.

"He was crying!" The voice which came from her was surprisingly strong.

The woman pushed her sallow face towards Denise's. "I *heard* him. I were in t' shop and I were watching him." She held up a clenched fist. "Now, get away from him, yer bloody cow!" Denise recoiled again, fearing she may be struck, hands instinctively going up to protect her face from a blow that never came.

The woman grabbed the pram with its still protesting occupant and, dragging the toddler behind her, disappeared into the distance.

Denise leaned heavily against the shop window, panting more from shock and humiliation than anything else, her shopping bags still scattered about her. Tears welled in her eyes and spilled over to run down her cheeks as she sat on the cold, tiled floor.

No one came to help her. A few shoppers regarded her curiously, but most gave her little more than a passing glance. No doubt busy and not wishing to become involved with someone they saw as no better than a baby snatcher.

Denise closed her eyes for a second to shut out the horror of what had just happened, then a voice close by made her start in renewed panic, expecting to be attacked again. This time, however, the voice was gentle.

"Come on, luvvie, up you get. I saw it all. Now let me help you. It's alright now. Up you come."

Denise opened her eyes to see an old lady bent at the waist retrieving her scattered parcels. The effort left her gasping noisily. Her breathing rasped like someone with severe bronchitis.

"Come on then, luvvie," she said, before straightening up with some difficulty and propping the carrier bags against the window. "'Ere, grab hold of me and let me help you up." Denise did so, hoping she wouldn't pull over the frail old lady who was smiling down at her.

"She's always down here; the silly bitch! One of these days, somebody's going to take off with one or t' other of those brats. Or my name ain't Alice Arbourthorne. Now, let's go and get us both a *nice* cuppa and calm down. All this excitement's doing my old ticker no good at all."

Still shaking, Denise allowed herself to be led to the little café opposite. The old lady ushered her to a corner table before going to the counter and returning with two mugs of steaming tea. Gratefully, Denise wrapped her hands around the mug for its warm comfort.

The old woman parked her capacious behind on the chair opposite and it creaked alarmingly, protesting at the weight. She, in turn, cradled her mug with its steaming contents, her old elbows resting on the table.

"There you are, luvvie. Now that's better, ain't it?" Denise nodded gratefully, unable to drag her eyes from the old woman's face. "Wants shooting she does, leaving little mites outside shops in this day and age, especially with t' kind o' people that's about nowadays. And she needn't fool anyone she were watching neither … shoplifting! Nicking! That's what she were doing, as flippin' usual. She goes home with that pram so full o' stuff, there's hardly room for t' nipper." Denise looked at the old woman, amazed at her keen perception.

"Oh yes! I know. I'm here every day. Now, lass, are you feeling a bit better?"

With the calming effects of the tea, Denise's pounding heart began to slow, her breathing steadier. She began to relax enough to produce a smile for her rescuer. "Yes, thank you. You've been very kind."

For a couple of minutes they drank in silence, watching each other easily.

The woman really was a funny, old stick with wrinkled, weather-beaten skin, and seemed of indeterminate age. She was one of those people who could either have been in her early sixties or late eighties, though Denise fancied it was probably somewhere in the middle. For someone so pleasantly plump, her hands were like claws with long dirty fingernails that hadn't seen a manicure in years. She wore a battered, old, grey felt hat, over which was a striped woollen scarf with the ends tied under her chin to keep out the cold.

More holy than righteous.

The thought struck her as something one of the 'Aunties' at the home would have said. The old lady's dark-green coat had once been good, and Denise reckoned that it'd probably come from a jumble sale, many years ago! It hadn't been what you'd call stylish for as long as she could remember. Denise tried not to stare whilst sneaking a look lower down, on the premise of fiddling in her handbag for a tissue. On her feet, old Alice wore wellington boots with red socks turned down over the tops. Denise smiled and shoved the tissue back into her bag.

But it was the old lady's face that held her fascination. From the wrinkled features shone the blackest gimlet eyes she'd ever seen. She watched as they darted to and fro; bright, alert and missing nothing. When she smiled, her few remaining yellowing teeth were displayed with obvious pride as, between sips of tea, she watched Denise's every move from beneath the brim of her hat.

"Ahh wasn't always like *this*, luvvie," she said suddenly. "Couldn't half turn a few heads once upon a time. Old age comes to us all one day!"

It was as though she'd read Denise's thoughts and she blushed, realising she must have been staring. Embarrassed, she looked at the empty mug.

God, thought Denise *I hope I never ...* The old lady held up her hand.

"Oh no, lass! You'll never end up like me! I can tell you that for nowt. You'll be beautiful until the day you die." Denise was once again shaken by her new friend's perception.

"I'm sure I won't," she whispered, aware of her flushed cheeks. The black eyes fixed Denise with a stare she found hard to break.

"Oh yes, my dear. You will. Believe one who knows." She tapped the side of her nose with a claw-like finger. "Beautiful until the end of your days you'll be. That I do know, so don't you go feeling sorry for owt you may be thinking. What your eyes tell you is not always t' full picture. I am what I am. I could see straight away you were only trying to help t' little nipper. You've got a way with you, so you have." She paused. "Got none of your own, or so I fancy?"

Denise smiled and shook her head, finally able to break the gaze. "No."

"Well lass, some things are just not meant to be. Then there's others best left alone." She leaned forward and spoke quietly. "Do you know what I mean?"

Denise looked puzzled. "No."

"You will one day. Now, lass, away to your place and don't give it any more worrying. No harm will come to that nipper; not with *me* watching."

"At least let me pay for the tea." Denise reached for her bag.

"Nay lass, nothing's owed, already paid in heaven." The old lady got to her feet, with some shuffling and wheezing. Denise bent to pick up her parcels and rose to thank her again for her kindness.

To her utter amazement, there was no sign of Alice and she stood alone, looking around in disbelief.

Chapter 6

With the evening meal over and the dishes consigned to the dishwasher, Mike and Denise settled on the sofa to chat, as was their long-established custom.

At first, Mike had been horrified at the near assault on his wife, but somewhat amused by the story of the old woman. He was a person who always gave people the benefit of the doubt, looking for easy explanations. Whilst Mike generally looked for the best in people, he was in no doubt that there were those who did others harm for the sake of it. Fortunately, such evil doings had never touched his life personally. Knowing how Denise had lost her beloved parents in such a tragic way, the minor irritations in *his* life had become rather insignificant.

"I can just imagine it," he began, pouring two glasses of white wine and handing one to Denise, "I bet the old girl hangs around that shopping centre all day long. Probably the only company she gets, poor thing. Can't you just see her? Like an elderly 'Lone Ranger'; coming out of nowhere and going back the same way? Only with a shopping trolley instead of a horse." He drank and smirked. "Hey, you don't suppose she was part of the gang do you?"

"Mike, what an awful thing to say!" exclaimed Denise. "She was the only person to help me. All those damned folk going about their business, too busy to even help me up. She was the least physically equipped to do so. Sometimes people disgust me!"

"Well," said Mike with a philosophical shake of his head, "people are not *always* what they seem. Did you check your bag to make sure your purse was still there?" Denise stared at him.

"Mike Duvall, you're horrible, but you're right about one thing. I haven't unpacked, what with all this. I was so glad to get back in the house that I left all the parcels in the boot." Denise put her feet up on the occasional table and held her glass out to be refilled.

"Yes, your Majesty!" retorted Mike. "Now don't exert yourself further after all that retail therapy. You sit there and drink your wine whilst I, your obedient servant, traipse out into the cold and empty the car for you." He bent and touching his forelock, backed out of the room. Denise gave him a royal wave, laughed and sipped her chilled wine.

*

"Good God, woman, how much have you spent?" Mike gasped, when he returned, bowed under the weight of many bags; there were more than it was possible to carry in one trip. "Bloody hell, you must have been in every designer shop in the precinct." He set down the last of the parcels on the sofa next to Denise.

"None of it'll go to waste. I thought I'd do some early Christmas shopping."

"What? In May?"

"I got some great bargains; honestly, Mike."

"Well, am I allowed to look?"

"Of course," said Denise "Oh, don't go thinking that I spent money on you." She laughed and her face shone. It was a long time since Mike heard her laugh like that and it felt good.

Maybe ... just maybe, he thought. "Come on then," he grinned, grabbing the first bag and tipping the contents onto the sofa. "Let's have a look at where all our money's gone this month and probably next as ..." He stopped abruptly, the red designer carrier still clutched in his hand as the contents tumbled out.

"Denise, who are all these things for?" The smile died on his lips, replaced by a quizzical look as he tipped out the remainder of the bags.

Denise stared at the piles of gifts, her own happy mood disappearing as the heap on the sofa grew. Mike sat crossed-legged on the floor and, without a word, examined the fragile items, placing each carefully on the floor beside him. Denise watched him, a look of abject confusion on her face.

There were small pink and blue teddy bears, and soft toys with rattles and squeakers. There were dresses, bootees and sleep suits; a white, heavily embroidered, soft woollen blanket; mittens; and a packet of nappies designed for boys.

"Didn't know you could get them *just* for boys," said Mike in a matter-of-fact way. He shook his head dismissing the one sensible, yet ridiculous, thought inside it. Then, there were bottles, teats and baby formula.

Denise stood up as though in a trance, mesmerised by the pile of soft, fluffy baby things on the floor.

"Denise?" Mike whispered. There was no response. "Denise!" His tone was unaccustomedly harsh and she jumped, the trance broken, but still with a strange, faraway look on her face.

"Mike," she began, "I bought a coat, gloves, make-up and some early gifts for Christmas." She looked at him desperately. "I did, Mike ... I did!" Mike took the last bag from her that she'd been holding. It was smaller than the rest, a little afraid of what it may hold.

There was another box of formula milk, some teething gel and a dummy – no, *two* dummies. He reached further into the bag and pulled out what was left. In all, there were 15 dummies, all blue, though different shapes and makes. Mike laid down the last bag and stared at his wife.

"What the hell's going on, Denise? Is this some sort of around-the-houses way of telling me it's time we started a family?" He took her by the shoulders and held her rigid body gently, his arms around her. With a sudden jerk, Denise thrust him away. "I bought ... a coat ... handbag ... and some make-up!" The words were spat out between gasps of a voice breaking with emotion and rising panic. Mike sat in the armchair, his eyes not straying from her face and his voice gentle, controlled.

"What's wrong, Denise? Tell me, because I have no idea what's happening here. Is this about me? Is it something I've done, or am I *so* insensitive that you can't talk to me anymore?"

With a look of despair, Denise shook her head, her eyes saucer wide.

"Help me out here, for God's sake," he pleaded, "because I *don't* know what's happening to you, to *us*." He rose and encircled her with his arms once more, her head sinking onto his shoulder, her body becoming limp in his grasp.

"I bought … I bought …" she began again.

"No, it's okay." Mike stroked her hair tenderly.

"Mike, I don't remember buying any of it. God help me, I don't. I can't remember choosing it, bagging it, paying for it or carrying it away. Not any of it!"

She began to sob, her head resting on his shoulder. After a few moments, he carried her to the sofa.

"Denise, are you certain they're *your* bags? I mean, you couldn't have just picked up someone else's shopping by mistake?"

"I just don't remember anything from parking the car to finding that kid outside Debenhams. Mike, for God's sake, tell me I'm not going crazy." There was fear in her eyes as she searched his face for some snippet of comfort. Lifting her again, gently, he carried her, sobbing, to the bedroom and laid her on the bed, covering her thin frame with a soft blanket. He sat by her side, tenderly stroking her hair.

Presently, her sobs ceased and she slipped into an exhausted sleep.

*

Pouring himself a generous measure of whisky, Mike went through all the bags again, meticulously checking the purchases against the credit card receipts in Denise's purse. There *was* no mistake. She *had* bought everything he saw spread out across the floor. Had she not used her Visa, the theory of someone else's bags may just have been credible. However, there was no refuting it. Denise had gone out shopping – his lovely, sensible

Denise, who'd then spent over £600 on baby equipment when they hadn't a baby or weren't even planning one. And she couldn't remember doing any of it!

He needed answers. This was beyond his understanding. Quickly, he downed the contents of the glass and poured another measure, equally large, and sat at the computer.

With a press of a button, the screen flickered into life. He connected to the Internet and typed in 'seasonal affective disorder'.

The myriad pages of information staggered him and, laying the whisky aside, he tiptoed to the bedroom. Mike stood watching for some minutes as Denise slept peacefully, breathing gently. He *must* understand this tonight before it went any further. He *had* to understand what was happening. If he didn't, then he feared for his marriage, but, above all, he feared for Denise's sanity. She was on the edge of the abyss and they both seemed to be on the point of taking a headlong plunge toward destruction. This must end here – *tonight*. Gently, he settled the quilt around her and returned to the computer to begin his search for an end to this nightmare that was fast-overtaking them both.

"No bloody way!" said Mike aloud, as he sat facing the screen. "Not if I can help it. I *will* understand this."

He set the whisky aside for what was expected to be a very long night and began to read. Above all, he needed a clear head.

*

The first rays of the rising sun crept across the horizon and, with the dawn, a single blackbird began to sing its plaintive tune. Mike rose and stretched. He yawned, the cursor still blinking on the screen in front of him. Killing the power with a sharp jab of his index finger, he stretched again, wincing as blood flowed back into muscles inactive for hours. He made black coffee and laced it with sugar, whilst looking out of the kitchen window to the open countryside beyond, watching thoughtfully as the dawn broke.

Many more birds had joined the dawn chorus. It was unbelievably loud. Mike couldn't understand why it hadn't wakened him more often. There was just a little high cloud and it looked like shaping up to be a warm day for early May. As the sky lightened, it was as though the whole world was new; the fields and hedgerows cloaked in green and fresh at this unearthly hour. He couldn't remember the last time he'd been up to greet the dawn. It was as if he were on the outside looking in and really shouldn't have been there; an outsider in a world that was the province of the birds and their wonderful song, and privileged to look out on a scene that few witnessed on a regular basis. Somewhere he didn't belong.

Mike drained his coffee cup, grimacing at its bitterness despite the sugar, and placed it carefully in the sink. He probably knew all there was to know about seasonal affective disorder after his night's research. The main facts had been memorised and, when he'd become too weary, he'd printed the rest for future reference.

The house was quiet, save for a faint noise from an air bubble in one of the lounge radiators that was only apparent when the central heating clicked on. He made a note to deal with it later. Despite his fatigue, facts continued to fly around his head from the night's research.

Seasonal affective disorder or SAD for short; that was ironic! Cause unknown. Thought to affect the body's clock and its circadian rhythms; the natural annual cycle that becomes disrupted. It's also called 'winter depression'. With the days being much shorter and, with a lack of sunlight, some individuals experience a severe lowering of mood. Thought processes are affected, as is concentration. Not to be ignored as it can lead to severe mental illness. May be tied to melatonin, the sleep related hormone that increases during the long nights of winter and disrupts sleep, leading to further depression.

"But," said Mike to the cat who'd wandered in to rub against his leg, "it's May and the days are longer." He struggled to accept the theory of everything he'd learned, as although Denise had a few of the symptoms there were others she definitely *didn't* have. She'd no craving for carbohydrates and was certainly not gaining weight – quite the reverse, in fact. And there were the nightmares. What about those? Far from sleeping *too* much, she found it was often the wakefulness that was hard to bear.

"Well, Bunbury," said Mike as he continued to stroke the cat, "I don't pretend to know what's happening to your mistress, but I'm *very* sure of one thing. It's not bloody seasonal affective disorder!"

Shooing the cat from his lap, Mike rose and carefully packed away all the shopping from the previous day, placing it on top of the wardrobe in the spare room. *Maybe, it'll come in handy one day*, he thought as he closed the door. The rational part of him, however, was thinking that it seemed less and less likely.

He needed to go and see the two old ladies. They could give him some answers, maybe. He was *sure* they knew something. He yawned and, stepping out of his clothes, slipped quietly into bed.

*

When Denise woke, it was like nothing had happened and she seemed completely back to her old self again. Later, they discussed the events of the previous day, calmly this time, much of the emotion removed with a good night's sleep. If anything, Denise was even able to be philosophical and accept that occasionally things happen for which there's no explanation.

A follow-up appointment at the surgery yielded little that was new, except to reassure them that Denise was *certainly* not mentally ill. Dr Green suggested that, maybe, the odd bit of bizarre behaviour was just one of those things that happened to everyone sometimes. Denise was adamant about one thing: she didn't want any more tablets.

"My memory's bad enough as it is," she told him, "without making it worse with sedatives. Maybe the tablets had something to do with it. Do you think that's possible?"

"Could be," said the doctor, "could well be." He could tell, however, from the look on Mike's face that *he* really didn't believe that.

Mike was certain of something else, too. If they were to survive as a couple, he'd have to take positive steps to put a stop to the almost imperceptible unravelling of their marriage. Maybe Denise was unable to see it, but he wasn't. For that reason, he'd been to the travel agent's and bought two tickets to Amsterdam. Maybe a trip away might do the trick.

Chapter 7

Cordelia Jayne Dujonois had just endured a *very* difficult day.

Once inside the front door, she shook the rain from her hair, threw her coat at the hat stand and kicked off her shoes. They were most probably ruined anyway from the muddy puddle she'd stepped in getting out of the car.

"Those workmen want shooting," she muttered. "I just *knew* they'd got the camber wrong when they laid the drive."

At the foot of the stairs, she dropped her capacious handbag, which was bulging alarmingly, distorting the fine leather.

"Handbag abuse!" she snorted and with a sigh began to ascend the stairs. There was a sudden scuffle from the lounge as a blue-point Siamese cat careered around the door towards her. Delicately taking the bag handles in his mouth, he followed her up to the bedroom. She grinned broadly; the performance never changed. He sat like a temple guardian, bag in mouth, as she divested herself of her uniform, dropping it contemptuously at arm's length in the corner of the room. Then, she fell backwards onto the bed as if struck by lightning, raising her legs in the air and wiggling her toes.

"Ahhaaaah. What heaven! My legs deserve an Oscar nomination for the performance they gave today. I've been on my feet for eight hours and 47 minutes to be precise. And that's 47 minutes too long." She raised her head, frowning. "Max! Drop that bag! Don't you know it's a Radley? Look at it – covered in slobber!" The cat obeyed instantly, though the well-known tag of a Scottie dog had been bitten through and was now stuck in his teeth. He spat furiously to dislodge the offending piece of leather.

"Oh, Max!" CJ, as she was known, huffed and sat up. "That's completely buggered it. There goes my street-cred again." She flopped down heavily onto the bed again, spreading out her arms.

With an effortless leap, the cat landed on her chest, purring loudly. They regarded each other, nose to nose.

"Did you cook my tea today, buddy? Perhaps you made me some coffee? Or maybe warmed my place in bed?" The cat stared back, enduring the daily ritual with unblinking patience. "Then where," she continued with a raised voice, "is the fella who took a vow to do all those menial things for me?"

"In the shower," came the reply in a rich, though greatly exaggerated, West-Indian accent. "Have a moment's patience will you, wo-man?"

"Oh, hurry up! I've just had a day you would *not* believe, honey." She sighed dramatically wiggling her toes in the air again. "There was …"

"Never mind," interrupted the voice, "I'll make you a cup of tea."

"And there was … *and* you are *not* going to believe this."

"Probably not, but I'll take you out to dinner anyway."

"Good! I didn't get any lunch. There were twins, a breech and then two C-sections in half an hour. We'd just got sorted when we had a prolapsed cord *and* all in the space of …"

"Don't tell me any more," cut in the voice again, "you know I can't stand suffering!"

CJ stretched, pushing the cat onto the floor. "Oh, none of them suffered. We don't allow them to."

"I was referring to you! The same goes for self-pity. You are home now wo-man. Forget the day. What's done is done."

"Yeeees." She punched the air triumphantly. "Home until Monday."

"Just keep telling yourself babies are wonderful. You *like* babies."

"Yes, darling," she quipped, "but I couldn't eat a whole one!"

"What a pile of manure you talk, wo-man."

The owner of the deep voice appeared in the doorway, wrapped from the waist down in a pink, fluffy towel. She raised both eyebrows and smiled broadly.

"Ahhh, the colour suits you, sir." Sam flopped down on the bed next to her displacing Max with a small flick of his hand. The cat grunted. After all, he saw the bed as *his* rightful place. Sam kissed her, drawing his wife close so their bodies touched.

"Hello darling, I love you. You smell like a dead horse. Now take your clothes off." He bit her ear lobe playfully.

"Ouch!" CJ pushed away his advance and sat up. "How can you *possibly* love me when I smell this bad, and will you just look here? I've got a spot on my nose." She pointed to it with horror.

"I love the way you smell *and* I love your spots." He growled playfully, nuzzling her neck.

"You're kinky!" she exclaimed, pulling a face and rolling away from him.

"Yes" He whispered, lapsing again into broad West-Indian dialect. "Cause *you* is my wo-man." Sam's eyes rolled in his head showing the whites only.

"God, stop it. You look like a witch-doctor!" CJ propped herself up on one elbow, stroking the dark skin of his chest and tracing her fingers through its black curled hair. "You're completely barmy."

"What the hell is 'barmy'?" Sam's eyes returned to their normal position. "I can't understand you half the time!" CJ allowed her fingers to tantalise the skin of his lower belly.

"That's because you're foreign, my darling, and not au fait with our customs here in Derbyshire. You need a bit more practise, that's all."

"What *are* you talking about? I've been here nearly as long as you." Her hand slipped beneath the towel and she felt his body tense.

"So, what's all this?" her fingers stroked his skin gently.

"Wrapping paper!" he gasped breathlessly and pulled her on top of him, discarding the towel and silencing her with a firm, urgent kiss.

They'd been together for ten years; blissfully happy with none of the problems of some. In the medical profession, mixed marriages were far from rare. Hospitals tended to be a melting pot of people from every corner of the world. Sam and CJ were like the two arms of the letter 'M' – both leaning on each other for support and needing each other's existence to live.

They'd their moments, of course, like most couples, but nothing serious. The one thing that hadn't lessened over the years was their passion for each other's bodies. And, today, when that passion was sated, they lay close together in the warm afterglow of lovemaking. The cat thought better of staying and found his basket in the kitchen a better and more peaceful prospect.

It'd been an unlikely kind of passion that brought them together in the first place: cricket.

*

"You remember that favour you owe me?" CJ's friend asked, one day.

"What's that? I don't remember owing you a favour." CJ looked a little worried, wondering what was coming.

Hazel had been a good friend for years, but not *so* good she didn't remember the time CJ enrolled her in a dating agency as a joke. It'd been disastrous. Poor Hazel got lumbered with a bespectacled trainspotter who'd taken six months to get rid of *and* she'd not forgotten!

Hazel Cummings was tall and willowy, not unlike the tree that bore her name. Her raven hair was woven into a French plait that hung down to below her slender waist. Her long, elegant legs were usually crossed when sitting, as they were today. She carried herself with a confidence that could have graced any Paris catwalk. She was a chemist working for a science laboratory researching genetics.

CJ was tiny by comparison and about as far as you could get from the old-style image of how midwives were portrayed in Victorian times. She was not big, buxom, nor permanently tipsy, and preferred orange juice to gin. Her rather boyish, elfin face was framed by short, dark hair cut geometrically over her ears. CJ didn't particularly like her body shape, feeling she was 'bottom heavy'. In fact, she wasn't out of proportion at all. Her tiny, size-two feet supported quite a slim frame.

Her most striking feature was 'the streak'. In her hair, from crown to fringe, was a stripe of purest white, a full half-inch across, making her stand out from the crowd. As a young girl, she'd hated it, but the thing defied all her efforts to disguise, dye or even cut it out as she'd once tried as a child. It was, of course, inherited and could be traced back in the family's female line for generations.

With it had come something else: *'the knowing'* as her grandmother called it. And CJ certainly had 'the knowing.'

She was one of those rare people blessed with second sight – clairvoyance or the ability to talk to the dead, whatever was in vogue to call the phenomenon. The streak of white seemed to point like an arrow down to her face as if to say *"Look! This person is different"*. CJ preferred to call it 'insight', as *'the knowing'* sounded like something London taxi drivers had to acquire before they were trusted to ferry people around the capital. In fact, it was the streak that had been responsible for her meeting Hazel and their subsequent friendship.

CJ had been to a study day on genetics at the local university in Sheffield; reluctantly, as it happened. Each year, midwives are required to attend several lectures as evidence of ongoing study in order to stay on the register of practitioners. She'd looked through the list of what was on offer, huffing as there seemed to be nothing remotely interesting. Choosing the talk on genetics was the lesser of two evils, the alternative being sexually transmitted diseases, and she'd done that one an interminable number of times. Nevertheless, it didn't stop the perennial moan about having to do it.

She nearly didn't go as heavy snow had fallen the previous night, making the journey to Sheffield hazardous. The lecture was due to start at midday, but by 9.00am the sky was blue and the snow seemed to be melting. If she hurried, she'd just make it.

Oh, what the hell? Let's go! Nevertheless, the back route over the hills into the city would still be tricky, even with only a small amount of snow. It was the prospect of the stunningly beautiful drive over the hills that swayed her.

Donning her waxed jacket, she set out across the waste ground to where her vehicle was parked; the 'old gal' as it was affectionately known. Whatever the weather, her old Land Rover coped. She'd *never* failed to get to patients for home births, even in dark winter months. There'd been only a few occasions when, having reached remote farms, it hadn't been possible to get home again and she'd bedded down in the warmth of the old farm's kitchen.

Community midwives are versatile if nothing else! CJ grinned at the triggered memories. Derbyshire hill-farmers were well-known for serving sumptuous breakfasts, especially after a night's labour. They were used to long sessions of lambing in the early hours. Sustenance before sleep was the done thing, and human birth was viewed no differently.

Oh, those wonderful breakfasts! CJ drooled at the memory as she climbed into the Land Rover and turned the key. The engine, reliable as always, kicked and roared into life.

Bacon, a quarter-inch thick. None of your watery supermarket rubbish! Eggs, their yolks golden, freshly-gathered from all the nooks and crannies, as free-range means just that. Then, on a huge platter came tomatoes, fried bread, mushrooms and more buttered toast than one person could comfortably manage – and home-made black pudding! Oh my God!

She knew it was pig's blood with lumps of pork and seasoned herbs fried in bacon fat, but, from the moment the smell reached her nostrils, she'd decided that this was not a time to be concerned with calories. CJ ate and enjoyed as if it were her last meal. Before leaving, she thanked her hosts for their wonderful hospitality before being towed to the main road by the proud father on his tractor.

"Oh, those breakfasts," she said aloud while adjusting the mirrors. Still salivating, she reached into the glove compartment to fumble for the Mars bar she kept there. It was a poor substitute and she sniffed disdainfully as she bit into it, knowing the sensation would not be comparable. Then, revving the engine unnecessarily in a fit of pique, she set off down the track to the main road. The wheels spun briefly before finding purchase, sending a shower of snow into the air.

CJ made a habit of packing and preparing the vehicle for the coming winter in October; a habit from the days of working regularly in the community. Nowadays, CJ was based in the hospital and only worked as relief in the community in times of sickness.

In the boot was a large shovel and assorted warm clothing, including sturdy wellington boots with thick socks. There was a cardboard box filled with high-calorie foods in case she was ever stuck in the snow and blankets to keep warm while she awaited rescue. It hadn't happened yet, but was a sensible precaution. As were the powerful flashlight, bag of grit to sprinkle under the wheels and a whistle for attracting attention. She fancied Shackleton had taken less on his expedition to the South Pole than she had in the back of her Land Rover, except for a few Huskies, perhaps.

The roads were surprisingly clear of snow. The ploughs had obviously been out during the night. It was only when she started to climb over the moors that the road surfaces became more slippery. But it presented little challenge to the Land Rover's powerful engine and four-wheel drive.

The sky was clear and blue; the snow banked up where the wind had caused it to drift against the sturdy walls bordering the fields. Flocks of sheep huddled beneath the dry-stone walls for whatever shelter they afforded. The farmers had been out to tend their stock, judging by the fresh bales of hay. Thick, hardy coats protected the pregnant ewes from the worst of the weather. CJ liked to think of them as 'ladies in waiting' – soon to lamb and so begin the cycle of life once more. She liked the thought of new life. After all, it went with the job.

Her mood was broken by a wild rabbit in the middle of the road ahead. She braked gently. The creature sat on hind legs, sniffing the air, totally unconcerned by the approaching vehicle. CJ blew her horn.

"Come on bunny, hop off!" she shouted as the rabbit regarded the Land Rover with disdain. CJ wound down her window. "Rabbit stew," she called again, blowing her horn sharply. The animal reared and fled, as if understanding the threat. CJ laughed and burst into song. "If I could talk to the animals, walk with the animals, run, squeak, dah-de-dah and stalk with the animals ..." Still singing, she pulled into the university car park with only five minutes to spare before the start of the lecture.

The lecture theatre was nearly full by the time she found it amongst the unfamiliar surroundings, and the lecture had started. Quietly, she lowered herself into the only spare seat on the end of the back row, trying to cause as little disturbance as possible. Nevertheless, a few students started to shuffle their papers. The speaker paused, allowing them to settle and CJ nodded her thanks.

She learned a lot in the next hour and a half, and was glad she'd made the trip. The time had flown and CJ couldn't remember the last occasion she'd attended such a riveting and absorbing lecture. Afterwards, there was coffee laid on, of which not many people seemed to avail themselves, but CJ was reluctant to make the journey home without one. Most of the audience were students at the university and probably much preferred to head for the Students' Union bar.

*

"May I join you?" CJ paused, the cup halfway to her lips as the young, female speaker sat opposite without waiting for a reply.

"Sorry," said CJ, "I tried to creep in as unobtrusively as possible."

"Oh, it doesn't matter," said the woman pushing a long plait of raven-black hair behind her back. "It was good to have someone so interested in what I have to say for a change. You know what students are like – probably still bladdered from last night." She held out a slender hand. "Hazel Cummings."

"Cordelia Jayne Dujonois" she replied with a grin, taking the proffered hand and shaking it gently. "Known as CJ, and you can see why with a name like that. But *not* CJD please!" Their eyes met and they both laughed at the reference to being called after such an awful disease. It hadn't been lost on Hazel, though she was much too polite to have mentioned it if CJ hadn't done so first.

"It wasn't that infamous when I married," said CJ. "It's a bit like being called Anna Isabel Dobbington-Smythe or something. You just wouldn't sign your initials on anything. So, I'm CJ to everyone."

"You're very interesting, nevertheless." Hazel quickly held up her hands at CJ's worried expression. "No, please don't get the wrong idea. I'm not hitting on you or anything!"

"Thank God for that," said CJ, leaning back. "I like men far too much."

"Let me explain," said Hazel sitting back in the chair. "It's your 'Mallen' streak, you see."

"My what?"

"The white streak in your hair." She gestured towards it. "I suppose it *is* genetic and not dyed in?"

59

"Oh, it's genetic all right," said CJ running her fingers through it. "I spent half my life trying to get rid of it. I never knew it had a name. What was it again?"

"It's become known as a 'Mallen' streak because Catherine Cookson wrote a book about a family called the Mallens. All the men had it and so it was obvious who all the illegitimate children in the area belonged to, and there *were* rather a lot of them!"

"Tell me more," said CJ. "Now, this is interesting! Let's have another coffee."

CJ listened as Hazel explained there was a trilogy of books written about the Mallen family and how the streak, a shock of pure white hair at the front, was passed genetically down the male line.

"Now, CJ," Hazel continued reassuringly, "please remember that all this is fiction. The Mallens were a cruel, vengeful lot and most of them came to a sticky end, I'm afraid. Few of them died in their own beds. They were an odd bunch with strange characteristics but, like I said, it's fiction. The books were so popular that any white streak in hair became known as a Mallen streak. I don't want you to go thinking that anyone who has it is doomed or anything. It's just one of those genetic idiosyncrasies that make you a bit different. I spotted it as soon as you walked into the room."

"Oh, I think you can say I'm different," said CJ with a wry smile.

"And that brings me to what I *really* want to ask you," Hazel ventured. "It's quite rare this phenomenon and at present I'm doing a study on things like it and I was wondering if you'd be interested …?"

A friendship was forged that day that lasted long after the research had been completed and written up to great acclaim in the *New Scientist*. Much to her delight and gratification, Hazel found that fame opened doors. It lead to the position she now held at a life sciences laboratory and the department she now headed up at the comparatively young age of 32.

*

"So what's this favour I'm supposed to owe you, neighbour?" Hazel lived in the next village. Their friendship had flourished and they met weekly at The Feathers in Moorside for a pub lunch.

"I've not yet quite forgiven you for fixing me up with that awful trainspotter who took me weeks to get rid of." Hazel frowned. "And I think it's going to take a *few* more favours before I'm able to erase the unpleasant memory." She placed the back of her hand to her brow in mock tragedy.

CJ sighed. "Okay, okay. What do you want then? God, Hazel, you missed your vocation, babe! You should be on stage at the Old Vic." Hazel drank the remains of her gin and tonic. "I was wondering if you could help me next Sunday afternoon."

"Doing what?"

"Making tea."

"Tea? Is that a two-man job?"

"It's a cricket tea for the local team. It's my turn and I'm not much good at it. We only have to get it ready for the interval. All the food will have been bought. It'll only involve cutting up cake, making a few ham sandwiches and brewing tea in a giant teapot."

CJ scowled. "Hazel, my dear friend … as you *well* know, I don't make teas. I'm a woman of the 21st century. People make teas for me and then invite me round. It's the only way they can ever expect anything decent to eat!"

Hazel set her mouth in a thin, determined line. "That favour. Remember the trainspotter, and even worse – the bell-ringer!"

CJ sighed, holding up her hands in submission. "Okay! What time and where?"

Chapter 8

Although CJ would never have dreamed of admitting it to anyone, she'd a distinct liking for the game of cricket. Aware that it was hardly an approved pastime for a thirty-something, trendy woman like herself, she didn't speak openly about it.

In her mid-twenties, she'd broken her ankle playing hockey and that meant a lot of sitting about that CJ was unused to. With her leg in plaster, she'd been bored to tears by the end of the first week and it was heavy to drag around. She was sure that the orthopaedic surgeon who'd inserted the pins had purposely not put on a walking plaster.

"Go home and enjoy the peace and quiet, and allow the maternity unit to have a few weeks respite, too," he'd guffawed. Mr Cripps – Crippen behind his back – knew CJ well from her general training on his ward. She was sure he saw an opportunity to get his own back after all her practical jokes. She'd been sent home with crutches and had fallen headlong within the first ten minutes.

CJ sat ... and sat ... and sat ... until, one day, flicking through the Sky channels in near-suicidal boredom, she began to watch the West Indies playing Australia. From that moment she was hooked. Understanding the rules of the game happened much later: its googlies, silly mid-on and the lbw rule. For years she remained a closet cricket lover until Hazel intervened and, as a result, her life was destined to change forever.

*

So, on a hot June afternoon, she'd repaid her debt to Hazel. The two stood side by side frantically buttering bread for sandwiches.

He'd seen her before she saw him. In fact, he noticed her the moment she walked into the old, wooden hut that served as the cricket pavilion. A few moments later when she did see him, she found it hard to tear her eyes away. She positioned herself so that she could get a better look out of the window whilst seemingly occupied with food preparation. Hazel wasn't fooled for a second and allowed herself a little smile.

Every time he ran in to bowl, CJ was overtaken by the need to stop what she was doing and stare, mesmerised by his jet-black skin against pristine cricket whites. For a tall man, he moved like a gazelle. So great was the compulsion to watch that the kettle boiled over and Jonny O'Reilly's mongrel ran off with the ham.

"Hazel, who is that? Doesn't he bowl well?" In vain she tried to sound matter-of-fact.

"I wouldn't know good bowling from a bucket of frogs," Hazel replied, wiping her hands on her apron, "but I *do* know, if you stand there staring much longer the game's going to be over before this tea's ready." CJ picked up the bread knife and began cutting slices of Madeira cake. "I know something else though," Hazel continued, "he's been watching *you* like a hawk all afternoon."

"Don't be so silly," retorted CJ, unable to drag her eyes away as he ran in to bowl again. The bales flew and she screamed with excitement almost upending the cake and causing Hazel to nick her finger. "Owzat? Wicket! Oh, Hazel, I'm sorry. I'll get you a plaster. Lovely tight bum though!" She clicked her tongue twice in appreciation.

Hazel raised her eyes to heaven.

"That's the tea interval. Brew up for God's sake, will you?"

*

"Tea, please, and a couple of ham sandwiches." The dark eyes with their impossibly long lashes looked deeply into hers.

Don't you dare blush! "Sorry, no ham I'm afraid."

"No ham?" He folded his arms and looked at her reproachfully.

Oh shit … I'm blushing! "No ham, but I'm afraid it *was* your fault."

"How's that?"

Oh, very good! CJ wondered if the pun was intentional. "I was watching you bowl and O'Reilly's mangy mutt ran off with it. He held her gaze and raised an eyebrow.

"Well, it'll have to be empty sandwiches and scones then, I suppose." He winked at her and grinned. "I'll expect extra cake and a big mug of tea to make up for it." CJ's legs turned to jelly.

"Come on, Sam, mate! There's a bloody queue forming here," a voice came from further down the line.

*

Tea led to dinner several days later and, after a few more days, dinner led to breakfast, and little had changed since. They moved in together after two months and married a year later; the guest of honour being O'Reilly's old mongrel. The dog had been specially washed and de-flead for the occasion, and wore a garland of flowers around his neck, which he promptly ate.

*

By her own admission, CJ was a lousy cook and after a hard day's work, Sam knew the best chance of getting a decent meal was to eat out or cook it himself. He'd developed a technique to spare his wife's guilt by pretending it was to spoil her. That particular evening, they dined late at their favourite Indian restaurant in nearby Darley.

"Was it *really* such a bad day?" Sam asked, spooning lime pickle onto a poppadum. "Or did you just need a good moan?"

"Not really bad, just on the run every minute. Satisfying though, but it would be even more so if we'd more staff. The health service will never be any different so we might as well get used to it." The main course arrived and was set on warming trays. Sam sniffed appreciatively, closing his eyes.

"How can I ever hope to diet," CJ said with little conviction, "when you will insist on taking me out to dinner all the time?" Sam opened his eyes.

"You don't need to diet, I keep telling you."

"But I'm fat. My bum's enormous. When I bend over it blots out the sun."

"What rubbish you talk, woman." Sam helped himself to pilau rice, lamb curry and sweet potato dahl.

"Well, darling," began CJ piling up her plate, "I'm a stone heavier than when we met. Nine stone. God forbid! I've never been nine stone in my entire life."

"Back 'ome," said Sam lapsing into Barbadian twang, "a big bottom is extremely desirable. Big ass means big dowry, baby."

"Man," she mimicked him and pulled a face "that's what I says to meself when I looks in de mirror every mornin'. Will you look at the size of me dowry?"

They laughed throughout the meal, relaxed not only in conversation but in the silences, too; wrapped up in one another, each like the other's comfort blanket, totally in love with life and each other.

Chapter 9

Mike's idea of a trip to Amsterdam proved to be just the thing needed to ease the tension of the past few months. The moment they boarded the ferry in Hull, Denise's mood lifted and she became the person he married: happy, talkative and great company. It was a far cry from the melancholy little waif of the past year.

Up on deck, he watched her as they leaned on the ship's rail, her hair blowing in the wind. He thought how great life was, just looking out to sea and sharing a joke. Mike was aware they couldn't always be away travelling, but he was happy to accept what was here and now. Maybe, just maybe, this was the start of her recovery from whatever affliction pushed her to near-breaking point – and their marriage towards abysmal failure. As he looked down at the water, Aunt Hennie's hushed tones still echoed somewhere in the back of his mind, whether he gave them credence or not.

"The past is only important, Mike, if you make it so. Remember that." He wished he'd never overheard Hennie and Lucy's conversation, or asked the question.

*

May in Amsterdam was warm and the sun shone, making the river sparkle as it snaked its way through the city. Denise sparkled, too. They'd never actually fallen out of love, though feelings *had* been sorely tested. On a canal boat, seeing the sights of such a wonderful city, the problems all seemed to be from a very long time ago.

Mike clicked the camera shutter again, wanting to preserve the memory of this wonderful trip. But it was more than that. He needed to have a record of Denise looking well and happy in case it all went wrong again on their return. The thought was constantly in the back of his mind no matter how much he tried to make it go away.

"Smile and say 'cheese'. Go on! Pretend you're on the bow of the Titanic." He pointed the camera in her direction yet again.

"I doubt I'd be smiling," Denise replied with a grimace, then posed provocatively, lifted the hem of her skirt and pouted. Mike clicked the shutter.

"Good grief, Mike! You're really getting your money's worth out of that new camera. Boys and their toys, eh?" He joined her at the rail. Ever since he'd bought it she'd heard little else from her techno-obsessed husband than how wonderful it was.

"Latest model ... so many pixels per screen size ..." He was off again. "And the beauty of a digital camera, of course," he said, leaning towards her, "is you don't need to take the film to the chemist and risk being arrested." Denise turned, her eyes wide with amusement as he framed her face on the LCD screen yet again. "So you'd better watch out when we get back to the hotel, my girl! This little gem has a video facility."

"You filthy beast! You wouldn't dare." She kissed him before he'd the chance to reply. "Now let's go to the Rijksmuseum. At least you won't be able to take photos in there."

✶ ✶

Mike yawned, already on his third cup of coffee when Denise appeared at breakfast next morning. He also was recovering from too many units of alcohol at the beer tasting. Normal reasoning had been suspended at around 11pm the previous night, and the black coffee was just beginning to awaken the cognitive parts of his brain.

Denise sat, scraping her chair across the marble floor. Mike winced.

"Sorry, darling." He watched as she demolished a full English breakfast, three slices of toast with jam, and two croissants. Finally, setting down her empty tea cup she leaned back. "Whew, that was lovely."

"No kidding." Denise had certainly got her appetite back. He'd rarely seen her even *eat* breakfast lately and it gave him a warm feeling he hadn't experienced for months. It was hope and contentment; anxiety was receding with each day.

"Oh, Den, hasn't it gone quickly? Now, what shall we do for our last day?" Mike held up his hand. "But, before you answer, I don't think I could stand another museum of any description. I'm all 'museumed-out'. The Anne Frank house nearly finished me off yesterday, being directly after the zoo. I couldn't believe it. There was even a ruddy museum in the zoo!"

They'd spent two hours queuing to get into the Anne Frank Huis on Prinsengracht, and Mike had left Denise in the snaking line of tourists to go and get coffee – twice. However, the wait had been worth it. Denise laughed heartily.

"Don't tell me you're getting too old for it all. Maybe I should take you to a café near the canal and cover you with a blanket so you can watch the world go by and perhaps have a doze." She pursed her lips thoughtfully and patted his hand. "You can sleep on the ferry tomorrow, old chap." Mike bared his teeth in a mock growl.

"Okay, but no museums, please; I'm begging." Denise reached for the teapot, refilled her cup and leaned back in the chair.

"Mike, do you know what I'd *really* like to see?"

"I think it's a month too late for the bulb fields, Den."

"No," she said with a grin. "Nothing as prissy as a few flowers. I can get a bunch of tulips at Tesco."

"What then?"

Her eyes lit up, the old mischievous grin returning.

"What I really want to see is the Rosse Buurt!" Mike shot her an incredulous look. "Let me get this right, Den. You want to see the red light district?"

"Yes, I do. We can't come to Amsterdam without seeing the seedy side." Mike raised his eyebrows, genuinely surprised.

"Okay, then. You're on! We'll go at dusk. That's the time to see it at its worst. So they tell me, that is." Denise's eyes widened.

"Oh yes, and how would you know that, pray?" Mike spluttered.

"I must have read it somewhere. Or maybe Joe told me. Yes, that must be it – Joe told me!" His mind was clearly working overtime.

"And how would Joe have known?" Mike opened and shut his mouth like a stranded fish as Denise threw back her head and howled with laughter. "It's okay Mike. Stop struggling. I'm not going to grill you further, or Joe for that matter. There are some things it's probably best for a wife not to know." Mike coughed. Out of his wife's view he exhaled deeply, unable to believe he was off the hook. It'd been Pat Grady's stag weekend in Amsterdam some years ago. The event had become a distant memory, *if* a rather sordid one. Denise wore a smug expression that lasted for the rest of the day.

✱

"Let's eat dinner early," said Mike, after they'd packed. Denise always liked to pack the morning before they left anywhere to take full advantage of their final day; be it on the beach or wherever. "I want to take some shots of the floating flower market on the Singel. Did you know that it's the oldest canal in Amsterdam?" Denise gave him an amused look and raised her eyebrows. "And, before you start asking me how I know that," he tapped the book he held, "it's in the guide book. So, I'm going to tell you about it whilst you get ready, whether you want to know or not!"

"Go on then. Shoot!" Mike grinned. The easy, light-hearted banter as they verbally played with one another brought echoes of how it used to be. He never wanted to let it go again. Maybe the whole episode was over at last. He began to read aloud.

"All plants used to be transported by barge from the inland regions around Amsterdam. Now they all come by lorry, more's the pity. It's one of the sweeter-smelling spectacles of Amsterdam and ..." he looked up," it'll make some gorgeous pictures for the hallway. I may even allow *you* to be in a few if you're good."

"How good do you want me to be?"

"What?" he said, looking at the guidebook again.

Sidling over, she slid her arms around his neck raising a bent knee to rub the inside of his thigh. "Is this good enough?" Her lips moved to his ear lobe, caressing before delivering a playful nip. "Good enough for you yet?" Denise felt him catch his breath.

"Not yet," he whispered, hoarsely. "Perhaps I should tell you a bit more history of ..." She seized the book and tossed it over her shoulder.

"Screw history."

With one movement she pushed him backwards onto the bed moving quickly to straddle him, her hands inside his shirt stripping it away. Gazing into his eyes, she felt him harden beneath her, straining against the thin fabric of his chinos. Not yet! She'd make him wait. Penance for the stag weekend she knew all about from Ellie, as one night Joe had drunkenly confessed. With a wry smile, Mike put his hands behind his head in a gesture of surrender.

"Do your worst!"

Sitting upright to pull off her shirt and bra in one movement, the pressure of her body was unbearably erotic. Her breasts freed, she leaned forward allowing each erect nipple to brush his lips. Every nerve in his body screamed and he could barely control himself from throwing her over on her back, ripping off her remaining clothes and taking her there and then.

Denise moved backwards to kneel between his spread legs busy with the zip on his bulging chinos and, as he arched his back, she slid her hands inside to lower them. He gasped, his hands firmly on her shoulders, eyes rolling, begging for release.

Her head moved down not quite touching him, tantalising, delaying the moment. Then, she brushed her lips briefly over his bulging manhood, kissing gently, her tongue flicking in a circular motion until he felt he'd burst.

Deftly, she moved to sit astride him ready now, as slowly she took him into her. Breathing hard, she reached to pull him upright and as he thrust deeply into her, she allowed him finally to take over; to have her completely and she him.

*

Thoroughly spent, Mike gazed at his wife. Her skin glowed with the aftermath of lovemaking. He couldn't remember the last time they'd made love with such passion and intensity. Whatever horrors she'd been through in the last year, whatever nightmares were inflicted on her, it was well and truly over and she was back with him. It was how it used to be and would always be so. He was sure of it!

Chapter 10

It's hard to describe the spectacle of the floating flower market on the Singel to anyone who hasn't seen it, apart from using the words 'colourful' and 'fragrant'. The all-year-round Bloemenmarkt is set on moored houseboats along the canal's edge. Its picturesque nature lured Mike and his new camera in pursuit of any shots he could frame.

"Good God, Den!" he exclaimed, stopping at one of the stalls. "How about taking some of *this* home, then?" Even for a country with such liberal drug laws, it was unexpected to see 'grow-your-own-cannabis kits' on sale.

"Huh," groaned Denise. "That's all we need. You getting arrested and strip-searched going back through customs. The dogs will smell it before the plane lands. You can take my photograph in front of the stall. That'll make a good talking point to put on the lounge wall."

They walked the length of the gently swaying stalls, Mike stopping from time to time to snap, occasionally insisting Denise pose in the shot. She sneezed violently.

"Ahhhhtisshoo." Okay Mike, that's enough. My hay fever's starting." She pointed. "I'm off to that café over there for pancakes and coffee whist you do the 'Lord Litchfield' bit." She sneezed again. "That's unless you want me to spray the camera."

"Yeah," murmured Mike, distracted and framing yet another shot on the screen of his new toy. Denise shook her head in amusement, turned on her heels and headed for the café.

*

It wasn't immediately apparent they were in the Rosse Buurt, the 'red light' district, until darkness fell and the street lights came on. Denise was mesmerised. It was unlike anything she'd seen before – if only for its blatancy. Suddenly, they were surrounded by crowds of people who'd also come to look and some, no doubt to experience what was on offer. There were couples, young and old, holding hands, giggling groups of girls dressed up for hen-parties and busloads of Japanese tourists with the obligatory expensive cameras slung round their necks.

The old city oozed charm, with many of the old buildings leaning at odd angles, though Denise doubted few were there to admire the architecture. In the daytime, the dingy streets would have been seedy to say the least. But, after dark, bathed in light, with music coming from a few newly-built, classy eateries, you could linger safely and for much longer.

"Close your mouth, Denise," chuckled Mike. "It's been open since we walked in here. Now keep close to me. We don't want to get separated in these crowds."

"Why? You afraid I might be off to earn some extra money?"

"Come on." He pulled her toward the red-fringed windows where women of all nationalities were parading their wares. In one sat a young woman of middle-European descent, legs apart on a stool. Her hands cupped each full breast, accentuating her form against the skimpy, black basque she wore. Pouting her lips provocatively at the assembled crowd, her sultry eyes invited them in. No words were necessary.

A group of young men leered in at the window, egging each other on. The woman leaned forward, her breasts straining against the fine silk fabric of the garment. She fixed her gaze on one of the gangly youths and beckoned. In a show of bravado he made for the door and was ushered inside by two huge minders. His mates cheered as did the crowd. The girl rose from the chaise and drew the window curtains. The deal was done. Not five minutes later he was escorted back out on to the street grinning broadly and 50 euros poorer.

"That's some work rate," commented Mike. "I've just worked out what she earns in a night."

"I don't think I'd want to earn *my* living like that," said Denise scowling, "no matter how much it came to." Mike paused to whisper in her ear.

"Well, if this morning is anything to go by, I'd pay double."

"Only double? Get on your bike, mate!" They laughed and held hands, Mike with a warm feeling in his stomach again.

"Come on, let's walk a bit further."

The red-curtained window was larger than all the rest. The lighting was more subdued. Low voltage lamps dimly lit the background and the fittings were cheap. A single spotlight was trained on a black chaise trimmed with fake fur. On it reclined a beautiful woman, her skin the colour of butter muslin. She'd the finest bone structure and her forget-me-not-blue eyes surveyed the potential clientele from the safety of her prison. For a prison it certainly was. She wore a red, satin teddy, boned to push up her small breasts to their best advantage. But it was her long legs that caught the eye, tapering down to small delicate feet clad in black high-heeled boots. Her long, jet- black hair, woven into an elaborate switch, snaked down to her knees and emphasised the translucent paleness of her skin. This woman had a look of class about her and seemed totally out of place amongst the others; the common tarts plying their trade openly from the pretty windows.

The crowd sensed it, too, for there was a hush as people stood before her. A sad caged bird out of reach of the yobs on their alcohol-fuelled sex trips from England. Beyond the reach of the men who'd come from all over Europe in search of a cheap thrill. Here was something different and Mike was fascinated. He pulled Denise through the crowd towards the window.

"Mike, what …? Where are you going? Steady on! You're hurting my hand." He paid no heed, dragging her behind him until they were directly in front of the window. He stood watching her intently, a strange look on his face.

As if expecting the attention, the woman turned her head and looked directly at Mike, her blue eyes locking onto his in a deep, penetrating gaze. The red painted mouth smiled in an unmistakable invitation, more subtle than the others as though she *knew* he'd be there. Denise could only stand and watch as a sudden chill cut through her. Slowly, haughtily, the woman lifted her chin and her long white neck stretched upwards like a swan, her eyes never leaving Mike's face. Denise shot her husband a curious glance as he continued to stare mesmerised at the spectacle.

"Mike!" She gripped his arm forcefully as a shudder seemed to go through his body. With horror, she saw him raise the camera framing the woman on the LCD. The flash seemed to light up the whole square and dozens of pairs of eyes sought its origin. The woman rose from the couch and pointed at Mike, her mouth opened in a silent scream; the red lipstick now an open slash across her face as though someone had drawn a knife across it.

There was a crash as two mountainous bodyguards burst from an adjoining doorway, pushing through the crowd in search of the offender. Denise had seen enough, grabbed the camera and Mike's arm, galvanised into action.

"Run, Mike. For God's sake, run!" They took off, trying to push and elbow their way through, the burly minders yelling in pursuit, but restricted by their sheer bulk and the closeness of the crowd. Breathless, Mike and Denise reached the edge of the square and turned the corner. The crowd had thinned and it was clear that they were no longer being followed. Denise crouched to catch her breath.

"It's okay, Den. We lost them!" She glared at him.

"Why the hell did you do that, Mike?" she demanded. You very nearly got us both beaten up. You and that damn camera. For God's sake, man! What the hell were you thinking?" Mike shrugged his shoulders, nonplussed and looked a little embarrassed.

"Honestly Den, I don't know what came over me. It wasn't real somehow. It was just like she was a dummy staring out of a picture at me. Whew!" He shook his head. "Now, let's put some space between us and this damn square."

Chapter 11

The trip to Amsterdam had been as good as a second honeymoon. The phone was ringing even as Mike put the key in the lock.

"Hey Mike, you two had a great time?" Joe never *had* a concept of the lateness of the hour. Mike glanced at his watch. It was almost 1.00am. He raised his eyes.

"Hi, Joe. We've just this second walked in."

"Listen mate, I'm not going to keep you. Come round for dinner tomorrow, will you? We're cooking and drinking, and I knew you'd have nothing in. Just come and eat. Got some news to tell you and I've got a rather pleasant proposition to put to you. Will about 8.00pm be okay? Fine … see you then." He rattled off the words with the speed of a machine gun, hardly waiting for a reply.

"Looks like we're going to eat out tomorrow," said Mike as they climbed the stairs.

** **

"So," said Ellie as she cleared the remnants of the pasta, "we want to hear *all* about your trip. Just a minute … Joe, get another couple of bottles of Chablis, will you?"

They'd never yet managed to match the countries with the food and wine whenever they got together, but, as Joe said, "after a couple of glasses … who cares anyway? You save all *that* effort for people you really *need* to impress."

Interrupting each other constantly, Mike and Denise regaled their friends with the details of how it was possible to make love in a bunk during a force nine gale on the return journey. And, whilst singing the rude version of *Tulips from Amsterdam* at the tops of their voices, with the ship pitching and rolling. True friends didn't require sophisticated conversation, just a few bottles of wine and a good story, revelling in the joy of all being together again.

Mike was more relaxed than he'd been for ages. Joe refilled their glasses again and sat. "Now then, Mike ..."

*

"Shooting ... you must be joking?" Mike's eyebrows disappeared under his hairline as he laughed. "Shooting? What, with guns? Furry animals and things with feathers?" Joe nodded, his forearms resting on the table as Mike went on. "No bloody fear! I haven't held a gun since I was five, and then the kid next door always made me be 'Tonto'." He drank deeply.

"No," said Joe patiently, "not animals, you foolish peasant! Targets. There are rabbits, of course, but they're so used to the bangs that they run around underneath totally unconcerned and nobody's ever hit one yet."

"So, Kemosabe," said Mike "How did you get into this?"

"Someone I met at work, actually. He took me along to one of those corporate things, just for the day as a guest. That was it. I was hooked! Seems I've got quite an aptitude for it. It's wonderful on a Saturday afternoon and the chaps are a real good bunch. I'm a full member now; just completed my six months' probation *and* been checked out by the police. So, now I can invite someone along."

He looked at Mike. "So, mate ... how about it? We shoot in an old stone quarry over at Westingbury, not too far from the estuary bridge."

Mike ran his fingers through his hair and sat back, hands linked behind his head, and thought for a moment, then nodded. "Yeah ... yeah! Why not? It sounds great. Mind you, let me warn you I can't hit a barn door at 30 paces. So be prepared to take cover and don't expect too much. Remember, I've only been allowed a bow and arrow before."

"So you'll come?" Joe's unruly blond curls danced to and fro like those of an over-excited child.

"Yes. I think I'm going to enjoy it."

For the first time in perhaps 20 minutes, Mike looked at Denise. The girls had been engaged in one of those deep, conspiratorial conversations only women have. Now, she was looking at him steadily, unease written all over her face.

"What's wrong, love?" he said. "All this is okay with you, isn't it?"

"I don't like guns," said Denise quietly, looking down at the tablecloth. "In fact, they scare me to death." She turned to her friend. "What about you, Ellie?"

Ellie sipped her glass of orange juice and sighed. "Well, I have to be honest, I was fairly uneasy myself at first, especially when you remember things like Hungerford. But, I've been to the club loads of times and I'm satisfied it's as safe as it can be." Joe took over the explanation.

The cops regulate the members carefully, and the guns and ammunition are kept in an underground safe at the club. Nothing's kept here – I couldn't live with that and Ellie wouldn't have it either. You have to have serious security if you want to keep any of *that* stuff at home. There have to be window locks, alarms, safes within safes – and the rest."

Mike was watching Denise carefully, hoping this wouldn't trigger another crisis, but she seemed reassured that Ellie was happy with it. Good old Ellie, thought Mike. She's always so level-headed.

"And," Ellie continued, "it really wouldn't be the thing to keep a gun in the house especially with …" She looked at Joe who nodded.

"Tell them."

"Especially with children running around the place."

For a few seconds no one spoke. Mike and Denise both stopped and stared at one another, glasses halfway to their mouths, then at Joe and finally Ellie.

"Yes!" she started to laugh. "I'm pregnant. We're going to have a baby – well, two babies, actually. It's twins!"

Mike stood up and clasped her hands in his. "Oh my God! That's wonderful. It's great news. Congratulations! He moved around the table and slapped Joe on the back before turning to kiss Ellie again. "How far?"

"Only 14 weeks. I've got ages yet." Ellie beamed and patted her stomach.

"So *that's* why you're drinking orange juice. I wondered. Now we know don't we Den ...? Denise?" He shot his wife a questioning glance. She'd said nothing and looked stunned as if struggling with how to react.

Mike couldn't help himself. He was suddenly overcome with anger. What was wrong with her? Couldn't she even make the effort to share their happiness? Joe and Ellie were their best friends. No! This was out of order. He turned to Ellie again and with an arm around her shoulders, pulled her close. There was an unmistakable note of irony in his voice as he said, "Eleanor, darling ... this is your lucky day. We can really help you out. Do you want to buy some cheap baby gear, perhaps?"

The moment the words were out of his mouth he regretted it. With a scream, Denise leapt from the table, knocking over her drink and chair, which fell with a clatter. She fled to the bathroom where she was violently sick. Stunned silence followed as Mike put his head in his hands making no effort to go after her.

"Mike, whatever's happening?" asked Joe gently. "I know life hasn't been easy of late, but we thought that was all over. She seemed so happy until ..."

Mike held up his hands. "I need to talk, before one of us goes crazy."

"Then, let's go and sit comfortably," said Joe standing up and gesturing towards the sitting room.

"Well, I'm going in there to Denise," said Ellie. "I'm not leaving her alone in *that* state."

What followed was the first admission by Mike – to anyone – that he feared for his wife's sanity and, ultimately, their marriage. Only there in the sitting room with his oldest and most trusted friend was he able to spill out all the events of the past year and how he *really* felt about it. Joe sat quietly listening to Mike's account of a woman spiralling downwards in a pattern of bizarre behaviour. No longer the person they both knew and loved in their different ways, she alternated between acting normally one minute and some profoundly disturbed person the next. It was becoming impossible to identify a trigger with her changing over next to nothing.

"It's the dreams she finds the most disturbing, Joe. She says it's like a malevolent force pushing her in a direction she doesn't want to go. 'Something evil that calls to her in the night', that's what she says." Joe gave a doubtful scowl.

"I know, I know!" said Mike. "But that's what she believes. God, Joe! She's always been so focused and in control. Now she thinks she's going mad and there've been times this past year that I've wondered about that myself. What the hell's happening to her Joe – to us?" Joe remained silent. "There's one thing I *do* know though, it's not bloody seasonal affective disorder!" He knocked back his whisky in one gulp and winced as the smoky liquid stung his throat. "The nightmares happen every week now. The only time they don't is when we're away, like this last weekend, but we can't keep travelling *forever*." He paused. "I know what I said was crass, unkind and cruel, but I've got to the stage where I can't help myself. He put his face in his hands and wept.

Joe listened to it all, thoughtfully sipping his whisky, biding his time.

"Look Mike," he began, "I'm not just saying this because we decided it was the right time, only, have you considered this possibility: is it some weird subconscious desire of Den's to start a family of your own?"

Mike shook his head. "I've thought of that and even the doctor picked up on it. We talked about it. You see, Denise has been adamant since the day we met that our relationship

83

wouldn't include children. She decided years ago that she didn't want any and she's as strong in that conviction today."

"But things change, Mike. What about you?"

"It didn't matter."

"Does it matter now?" Mike paused, looking at his friend.

"One of the things I loved about her *was* her conviction. Nothing else mattered. I loved her *because* of the person she was. Just the way she was."

"And now?" said Joe. Mike put his head in his hands again.

"I just don't know. I'm trying to understand. God knows, I'm trying."

"You said 'loved', Mike. Past tense."

"Did I?" He didn't look up, merely pressing his lips together tightly in frustration.

"Yes, you did. You said it twice. *Do* you love her, Mike?" Mike looked at his friend with an air of desperation. It was a few moments before he spoke and, when he did, it was with a voice cracking with emotion.

"To be truthful, Joe, at this moment, I really don't know!"

*

In the spare bedroom, something similar was happening. Denise was sobbing, her head on a pillow, clutching a handkerchief tightly in her hand. Ellie listened for nearly an hour's about the past year's events.

"Tell me, Ellie," she'd pleaded, her eyes red, "am I going crazy or not?"

Her friend looked at her intently. "I don't know, honey, but what I *do* know is whatever this thing is, it's destroying you both. Look at yourself! Now, for heaven's sake let's *do* something about it."

"The doctor must be sick of me and I don't think more tranquillisers are the answer. They make me feel terrible. I'm so spaced out all the time."

"Maybe," said Ellie, "more pills are the last thing you need right now. They're probably what's made you feel crazy, not the nightmares. Drugs have a place, but they alter your powers of reason, Den. They suspend your ability to think so you can't rationalise your dreams and, as a consequence, you stay disturbed. You never really deal with it and, when eventually you come off them, the problem's still there. It stays unresolved and the more you dread it happening, the more likely it is to do so. Do you follow?"

Denise thought it was the most sensible thing she'd heard in ages. Here was someone, at last, who wasn't patting her hand and telling her that it'd all be fine or that she'd get over it. And it was comforting. Ellie went to the bathroom, fetched a glass of water and handed it to her.

"Denise, look, you can tell me to mind my own bloody business if you want, but I know someone. She used to be a colleague when I worked at Broome surgery; you remember, that reception job." Denise nodded. "Actually, she's a midwife, but take no notice of that! She's a *very* good counsellor and sees people privately." A look of horror crossed Denise's face again.

"So, *you* think I'm crazy too!"

"No! Far from it. Counsellors aren't for *crazy* people, love. Mad folk don't *know* they need help. You do!" She put a hand on Denise's shoulder. "I know she'd be willing to see you if I asked her. You *really* need to talk and get to the bottom of this. This isn't just a bit of anxiety; there's more to it than that, but you *know* that already. Ask yourself, do you really want to spend all your life swallowing tablets and feeling like a zombie?"

Denise wiped her eyes and thought about it for a minute, running her fingers through her hair.

"No, I don't. That's the last thing I want. It's just that ... I'm not sure about talking to someone like that. Part of this seems to be about babies. Surely, the last person I should see is a bloody midwife!"

"But you're not going to be seeing her in that capacity, Den. Think of her as just another person who may well be able to help you. I tell you, she's good, damn good, and quite extraordinary."

"Okay," said Denise getting up and looking in the dressing mirror. "What have I got to lose?"

"I'll say one thing," said Ellie. When you see her, keep an open mind. She's a bit unorthodox; one on her own, you could say." Denise didn't dare ask what she meant by that, but her mood had lightened considerably.

"Thanks Ellie. You know I trust you. I'll make an appointment tomorrow. Though from what I've seen of midwives, she's probably 18 stone, with hips like a rhino, fierce as hell and will scare the living daylights out of me." Ellie laughed.

"I think you may be in for a bit of a surprise then. She's interesting and unconventional, and they certainly broke the mould after they'd made CJ. Come on, I think it's about time we opened another bottle of wine. I may have half a glass myself."

"No, you won't!" said Denise quickly. "Someone's got to look after your welfare." She turned, "I think you'll make wonderful parents."

Chapter 12

The conservatory, or the 'garden room' as she preferred to call it, had always been CJ's favourite room. And, on this warm spring afternoon, it was all hers. Sam was playing in an away match at cricket and would certainly not be back until at least 10.00pm. That was if he hadn't been persuaded to stay for a couple of pints!

As if he needs any persuading, thought CJ as she ran a duster over the cane-work chairs and coffee table.

"Cleaning is a very overrated pastime," she said aloud, throwing the duster back into the under-sink cupboard.

It was only mid-morning, but the sun was already hot through the glass, even with the windows open. It'd been a good idea of Sam's to leave the brickwork exposed on the side that wasn't glazed and it'd mellowed over the years to a rustic red.

CJ liked the idea of keeping things as natural as possible. The quarry-tiled floor sported a couple of ethnic rugs for comfort and contrast. All the niceties, such as decorating and dressing the place, were left to CJ. Sam really had no idea which colours went together. She stood by the window for a while looking out over the pretty garden. The border perennials were just beginning to come into bloom. The tall delphiniums were showing a hint of colour as they clambered up to peep over the fence. A clematis with its large, showy flowers was already sprinting along the top of the fence towards the greenhouse to greet the fledgling tomato plants clambering up their canes. The ridge vine was in full leaf and showing tiny, white clusters of flowers, promising grapes and eventually wine.

CJ jumped as a large frog hopped onto the sill. Sam had put the pond too near the house, despite what she'd said. The week before, she'd come downstairs to find a huge toad sitting in the cat's water bowl. It must have come in through the open door late at night, unnoticed. Max had been posturing and meowing, unsure what to make of the intruder. She'd have another nag at Sam about that pond. If she kept at him long enough, perhaps he'd give in and move it. She could imagine his voice chiding her.

"God wo-man, does a man *never* get a rest? All this talkin'. Those poor babies! I bet they get themselves born quickly just to get away from the sound of your voice!"

But CJ could also listen. In fact, she was an *excellent* listener and that's why Saturday afternoons were set aside for her counselling sessions. And there was plenty of demand.

She used the garden room as it was cheerful and light, yet relaxing. There were pale, vertical blinds that shaded the sun if necessary and wall-mounted heaters to keep the room cosy in winter. It provided a pleasant place to relax and forget troubles, so was ideal for her purpose. Swags of pale silk flowers adorned the space over the French doors leading to the rest of the house. An oil burner on the sill gave off a fragrance. Today, she'd chosen a combination of geranium and rose for peace and tranquillity. It was perfect – except for one thing. In the corner, on a stand, was a large, gilt cage in which resided a noisy occupant.

WG, the African grey parrot, Gracie for short, sat on his perch with his head cocked to one side, ducking and diving in anticipation of being fed.

"Hi, Gracie, how's tricks?" The bird excitedly ran the length of the perch and back again, squawking loudly. "Graceee, Graceee, gimmee, gimmee, gimmee," he chattered furiously. CJ shook her head. This must be the only parrot in England with a West Indian accent. Sam spent hours teaching the bird to talk and that wasn't all – he'd also taught him to swear like a sailor!

CJ fetched the boxes of food she kept in the fridge. "Okay, greedy, have a little patience."

"Gimmee, Gracie, Gracie," he screeched, the pitch getting higher. Opening the cage door, she filled his bowl with nuts and slices of fresh apple.

"Waarrkkk!" With one final cry the bird set about demolishing the food.

"Now, please be quiet, Gracie. I'm working this afternoon and I can do without your contribution. Thank you."

CJ looked out of the window again at the garden she loved. It'd soon be time to plant up the boxes that sat beneath the windows. The effect was always spectacular as scarlet geraniums cascaded, softening the stark white of the sills. It reminded her of France and the wonderful holidays she'd spent there with Sam and his family; just wandering, stopping wherever and whenever they felt like it. Freedom was wonderful and in complete contrast to the regimentation her working life demanded.

She glanced at her hands with their untidy, short nails, overdue for a manicure, and spread out her fingers. *Working hands those! Gardener's hands.* Unlike those of her friends with their beautifully painted nails and soft skin, and not horny around the knuckles like her own. CJ's looked like they belonged to a builder's labourer, though she hadn't time for such fripperies, preferring more practical pursuits.

Her daydreaming was interrupted by another loud squawk from Gracie. Max had strolled in purring loudly. He rubbed his cheek against her legs, and proceeded to weave in and out of them, as he often did. At the parrot's report, his body flattened low to the ground and with ears pricked, began stalking the cage. CJ watched this daily ritual with amusement. The cat never learned! He sat looking up at the cage and its occupant, emitting a low growl of warning, tail fluffed, ears back and ready to pounce. The parrot remained motionless and the two creatures held each other's gaze. Max began to salivate, licking his lips. He growled again. The parrot put his head on one side and eyed the feline from his perch on high with a gaze bordering on contempt.

"Gracee, Graceeeeeee," he chattered, then retorted, "Piss off, pussy."

As if deeply offended, Max turned away, his proud Siamese head held high. Then, with a flick of his tail he walked out of the room in search of less uncouth company.

"Sam, I could kill you!" CJ said, picking up a large, psychedelically-patterned cloth. "All right Gracie, time for silence." Standing on tiptoe, she draped it over the cage, never quite understanding why it worked. Perhaps, the bird thought it was night, but she suspected he was far too intelligent to be duped so easily. Maybe, he was hypnotised by the colours, but, whatever the reason, it silenced him instantly. The parrot wouldn't utter another word until the cloth was removed. All that was heard was the occasional crunch as he extracted nuts from their shells or spat out an apple pip.

She made fresh coffee in the kitchen before returning to sit on the sofa, feet up on the low table. Five sinister-looking faces watched her from the opposite wall. Their hollow, sightless eyes seemed to follow her every move. CJ put out her tongue at the one in the middle. Sam's collection of ebony tribal masks from Africa always made a good talking point and her clients never seemed to find them disturbing in the least.

Finishing her coffee, CJ looked at her watch. There would be just enough time to check all the work equipment she kept in the boot of the car. When her client had been and gone, there would be no further need to interrupt the remainder of the weekend.

"Yes!" said a gruff voice close by. "Gerr on wi' it and don't be so flaming lazy, woman! Never mind sitting there suppin' all day." CJ laughed, smelling something familiar: Brylcreem.

"Okay, Georgie, I hear you. I thought you'd deserted me these past few days. My life's been so *very* peaceful without your constant nagging, you old rascal."

The voice spoke again, louder this time. "Just go and get all t' stuff out of that new-fangled contraption of yours that goes at 90 miles an hour, will yer?"

The Jeep! CJ nodded. She didn't *need* to say anything out loud. He could hear her thoughts anyway; it just seemed more sociable to actually speak to him, but only when no one else was there.

"Aye, that thing wi' t' push-up lid on top; tha allus forgets to shut it when it rains. Well, go on, woman. Quick march!"

"Okay." She held up her hands in a gesture of submission knowing he wouldn't be quiet until he got his way. She gave a wry smile.

"The parrot and you are *very* alike, Georgie!"

∗

Three trips to the garage later saw all her work equipment deposited on the rug. Seated on the floor, she methodically began to check it. It was a weekly chore that all midwives working in the community had to do. No good getting to an imminent birth and finding an empty gas and air cylinder. Women in labour were vocal enough without chastising the midwife for her incompetence for neglecting to bring the pain relief. Carefully, she checked the contents of each bag and set it aside for return to the boot later.

"Okay, oxygen full; all sterile packs present and correct, and in date; dressings; Entonox ..."

"Nowt like that when my missus had our nippers," interrupted Georgie again. "Three days, my Agnes was, 'aving t' first. Midwife used to knot a towel round t' brass bedstead for 'er to hang on to." CJ carefully began to check the expiry dates on her allocation of drugs, placing each back in its own lockable case.

"Aye, and we dint 'ave any of them either!"

"Times have changed, Georgie, though not always for the better."

"Aye." There was a sigh, the voice saddened. "Four we lost, tha knows! Didn't see inside of t' church – none of 'em."

"I know, Georgie." CJ picked up the last bag, an old, black, saddle-bag style case designed years ago to fit over the crossbar of a bicycle and obsolete with the advent of cars. Outdated maybe, but *very* useful, "And with plenty of space for all the odds and ends which don't fit anywhere else," CJ told herself every week. She'd great affection for this old relic from the past. "A bit like you, Georgie." She glanced over her shoulder to the place from where she knew he'd be watching. "There ought to be a pouch for *you* in here; one I could buckle up tight."

"I 'eard that!" The voice rang with indignation. "Right, I'm off. I can't stay 'ere all day canting with a daft cat like you. I've got better things to do, you cheeky wench!" And, he was gone as quickly as he'd come leaving only the lingering smell of his old-fashioned hair cream.

CJ took her teaching doll from the bag and held it at arms' length, frowning. It was grubby, probably left lying around the garage after her last holiday. It really was an ugly creature! The soft-bodied doll stared back at her with sightless eyes. It was used to teach students the manoeuvres of labour and delivery, the head being marked with the individual skull bones and fontanelles. These are the soft spots at the front and back that close as the child grows. She re-attached the umbilical cord to the fabric placenta with its press stud and, licking her finger, rubbed a black mark from the doll's nose.

"You poor, old thing!" she said, shaking her head. "I'll give you a good scrub later." And she sat the doll on the low bookcase under the window before returning everything to the Jeep.

"Thank you, Georgie," she said. "You've a way of making me do those things I don't care for." There was no reply, though she suspected he wasn't very far away. She could still detect a very faint trace of his hair cream. The women in the music halls, where he'd been a performer had raved over it – or so he'd said. Yes, he wasn't far away. She knew that without a shadow of doubt.

For, as well as being Sam's wife, part-time counsellor, cat carer, parrot silencer and midwife, Cordelia Jayne Dujonois was an extraordinary medium. And what she'd managed to do was never let one influence the others.

So far.

Chapter 13

"Hi, you must be Denise. Call me CJ. Everyone does." The expected visitor was shown in. CJ noticed immediately how painfully thin and profoundly uneasy she looked, her mouth set in a thin line as if fearful of what was to come. She stood in the kitchen hesitantly, not seeming to know what to do next. Should she turn and run – or stay?

"Oh my goodness," began CJ, gesturing to the room, "you'll have to forgive the place! No one ever accused *me* of being house proud, I'm afraid. So, if you don't mind being mugged by the odd cobweb …?" She raised her eyebrows and waited. The woman's thin lips softened into the ghost of a smile. "Failing that, I could give you a duster and if you see one, just give it a flick, will you?" They both laughed; CJ watching her client, thinking she'd the most hypnotic blue eyes she'd seen. Their sheer size made her stand out and CJ secretly confessed to a little envy. "Just let me move these cups. Oh, would you mind passing me that cake plate and I'll get rid of the lot, and then we can begin."

Denise felt herself relaxing in the company of this jovial, ordinary-looking woman who was collecting assorted pieces of used crockery. With a clatter, she shoved the lot into the dishwasher and slammed the door.

"I don't know about you, Denise, but, no matter how much time I think I have, I always seem to be caught napping when people come. I must have been born disorganised."

Whatever Denise expected, and Ellie had told her very little, this woman fussing around in her kitchen wasn't it. So, what *was* she expecting? Was it a tall, elegant academic in a pinstriped suit with a clipboard? Or someone middle-aged and grey, with

95

a comfortable figure in an ethnic, elasticated-waist skirt? Certainly not this young woman who suggested coffee and a 'natter' as though it was the most normal thing in the world. The strangest thing was Denise felt that it was *just* that.

CJ spooned coffee into mugs, sensing Denise's eyes on her, watching every move. And what *Denise* saw in her appraisal was a tiny woman dressed in baggy jeans and a checked shirt with an elfin, cropped haircut. She'd obviously been decorating because she'd white paint all over the front of her hair. But one thing stood out. This was someone she could trust to talk to about her life and the mess it'd become.

"So, where shall I start?" asked Denise with a slight shrug of her shoulders.

"Why don't you begin by telling me a little bit about yourself? That seems a good place." CJ knew this was a good strategy to get clients to relax. It's easier to chat about happy times before the events that led them here.

"What about starting with your childhood?"

"Oh, I remember very little about my parents. I was orphaned at quite a young age. There was a skiing accident in the Austrian Alps and they were both killed instantly. I was told it was an unexpected avalanche." CJ shook her head sadly. "I was sent to England to an aunt of my father's to be brought up. There was no other family and certainly no one suitable to take on a three-year-old." She paused. "You see, I know nothing of where I came from and I don't suppose I ever will."

CJ reached over and touched Denise's hand softly, in a gesture of comfort.

"My aunt was called Janina and she was a lovely person, warm and giving." Denise smiled at the memory. "For two years, life was good and I was starting to settle, apparently. Aunt Nina, as I called her, became my mother, or as good as, and I was starting to think of her as such. Then, one day, she died – she just died with no warning, heart failure they said, and I was heartbroken." CJ shook her head again. "Then, of course, there *was* no one else and I had to go to the children's home."

So much pain and change for a small child to endure. It was little wonder she wasn't more damaged by the experiences, thought CJ.

Denise recounted her years at Belmont House. It was clear she'd been happy from the way she spoke with genuine affection about the two 'aunties', who'd not only cared for her but had given her so much more. Her eyes shone whenever she mentioned Henrietta Lange and Lucy Harpur, who lived in nearby Wensley. She paused in the telling and CJ took the opportunity to pour fresh coffee and offer cake. When they'd finished eating, Denise leaned forward.

"Do you know, CJ, when I was about 13 or 14, I went through a patch when I was *desperate* to know where I belonged. Does that sound stupid? I wanted to know where I came from."

"No," said CJ. "We all need to know that. It's our roots after all, isn't it? It's what makes us what we are."

"But you see," she went on with a frown, "no one could ever tell me, but I always felt there was something."

"Why?"

"I don't know. It was the *way* the subject was changed whenever I tried to ask. There was always something pressing to do. I'm sure that Hennie and Lucy knew more than they said. It was the way they looked at me. Not with pity. I don't mean that at all, but … Oh, I don't know. It was something about the way they looked at one another, whenever I asked."

"Well," said CJ, now you have made contact with them, why don't you ask again. You're a woman now and grown-ups can accept things children can't. It surely won't be all that terrible. Knowing might bring closure and settle your mind."

Denise nodded. "You know what?" She sat back. "I'm going to do that."

*

CJ deliberately allowed the session to overrun, just as she'd pretended to be hopeless and disorganised. It was a useful tool to gain confidence, to level the playing field, and it worked. It always did.

Denise went on to talk about recent events, stopping only briefly to stroke the cat who'd wandered in. CJ didn't interrupt the narrative, but merely sat in the armchair with her hands in her lap. Sometimes nodding in agreement, she made eye contact when necessary, her posture open and encouraging. This was the role of the well-trained and practised counsellor; never leading, but merely facilitating.

Denise talked about her dreams and how they began, the nightmares, panic attacks and her dread of sleep. She told of her fear of what this was doing to her and those she loved. And, when at last she'd stopped speaking, CJ saw the reality of how weary this woman was, every day of it etched on her face. Even with the telling, she looked completely exhausted; the very life force around her was dim.

There'd been no recognised trigger to these extraordinary events – no catalyst. But, as CJ knew, there would be, somewhere hidden in the past or the present. It was just a matter of identifying it and that was often the complicated bit! Later, when she came to write up her notes, it'd serve to remind her that rules must be followed and, to that end, she'd tell herself quietly what she always did.

You're a go-between, a buffer, a catalyst. You don't direct or solve. You're neither magician nor guardian angel. You only allow the client to reach the point at which they're comfortable enough to make their own resolution possible. Help them face their demons, and then empower them to move on and make their own changes.

Every time CJ did this, she'd hear the voice of her old tutor speaking in clear tones as though he were in the room.

"Remember, my child, if you get all these things right, the client will reach a special place. That is where they either solve the problem, learn to live with it or embrace things the way they are. *That* is compromise. Then you'll have done a good job." CJ allowed her thoughts to drift for a moment, absent-mindedly fingering the gold bracelet that adorned her wrist. Her fingers lingered over the trio of fine diamonds set at its centre.

Ah, Pieter! The wonderful Pieter Van Reger; the only man she knew who could both praise and destroy her within the space of one short sentence.

"So," said Denise, "do I see you again?" Though weary, she looked a different person from the frightened waif who'd walked into CJ's life less than two hours ago.

They agreed to meet again in two weeks' time and Denise left. CJ already had a plan in her head how the next session would go and what was required to allow the young woman to move on. She'd already asked the relevant questions and come to some conclusions. The woman wasn't in any immediate danger or in a crisis so deep that self-harm was a possibility. CJ had warmed to Denise. She liked her, but, as she watched her leave, there *was* just something ... a feeling of unease she couldn't *quite* put her finger on. But, it *was* there, a little disturbance in the psyche; the merest ripple on the calm surface of her otherwise clear mind. She'd talk to Pieter; not right away, as she'd see Denise in a fortnight. Then, if the feeling was still there, she'd *definitely* talk to Pieter.

As if to compound her unease, Georgie arrived in an unaccustomed rush, intruding at a moment when she'd rather have been alone with her thoughts. It was like a rough prod between her shoulders.

"Georgie! Stop that. It hurts." He rarely touched her. After all, she was so sensitive to his presence, there was no need.

"Careful, lass," he warned. "This one's complicated. Tha could easily get out of thy depth. That woman's trouble. Stay well out of it if tha' wants my advice. She's trouble."

"Is there *any* woman who hasn't given you trouble, Georgie?" said CJ aloud, trying to shake away the disturbance.

"Nay lass. Many haven't, but I've known thee since tha were a nipper. I know thee better than tha knows thyself and I'm just saying, be careful, that's all."

"Okay, Georgie. I hear you." There was a loud crunch.

"Now, for Gawd's sake, uncover that bleedin' overgrown budgerigar before it chews through t' bars!"

CJ drew her eyes away from the path along which Denise walked to her car and laughed. "There are times when I wish I *didn't* hear you, Georgie. You're always two steps ahead of me." There was a loud cackle that moved across the room towards the kitchen door.

"Yes, and there 'ave been times when I've learned things from thee that'd make me mates down t' pit blush."

"That's why we have rules, Georgie. That's why you stay *this* side of the bedroom door! Now, go away. I've got a husband to attend to."

"The poor bugger!" With a final throaty chuckle he was gone – out of her house and out of her head.

CJ wandered around the garden, picking roses for the table, unable to get the young woman's problems out of her mind. The early evening scent from the lavender calmed her. Maybe, Denise wouldn't return in two weeks' time. It'd happened before. She knew sometimes a good 'get it off the chest' session was all that was needed. It was often much easier to talk to someone you'd never see again. Didn't you meet people on holiday and talk like old friends, promising to write as you left to catch the plane home? You never did. You'd often told them your most trusted secrets and it'd been so easy, there in the sun, because you knew you'd never see them again. It was a low-risk situation and life – and trust – is all about risk.

Perhaps it'd be like that with Denise. Whatever was responsible for all this 'mind chaos' would merely melt away now she'd talked about it to someone who wouldn't think her crazy.

**

But Denise *did* return as arranged and, to CJ's delight, seemed so much better. She was more confident and self-assured, and a far cry from the frightened waif who'd suspiciously watched her make coffee two weeks before.

They sat in the conservatory.

"You've gained weight." CJ immediately clasped a hand to her mouth. "Sorry, I should *never* say that to a woman, should I? I meant that you look so well."

"It's okay. I needed to. My clothes were practically falling off!" Denise crossed her long legs.

"And you're feeling better?" The whole demeanour of her client had taken on a much more positive approach. CJ noted the care she'd taken with her appearance, and felt scruffy by comparison in her comfortable cropped jeans and T-shirt, her Saturday uniform.

Denise went on, "I'm sleeping like a baby, and no nightmares."

Good, thought CJ. *She's volunteering information without being asked. This is so much better.* There'd been no more strange encounters on shopping trips and she felt her memory had improved. CJ finished her coffee, and set the cup and saucer down on the low table, pondering the best way to bring up the next subject, when Denise stole her thunder.

"I didn't get as far as asking Hennie and Lucy, though." She looked almost apologetic as though a promise hadn't been honoured.

CJ had to check herself to avoid asking "Why?" That would have caused pressure, but Denise explained anyway. "I just have the feeling I'm better off not knowing some things," she said. "Maybe, it's better left alone."

Max wandered in, no doubt in search of a comfy lap. He was definitely an opportunist, knowing instinctively when anyone was sitting for longer than two minutes. With an effortless spring he hopped onto Denise's lap, padding and tippy-toeing until she stroked his head. He settled, purring loudly.

"Max, you're a terror! He'll cover you in fur," said CJ noting Denise's black skirt, and began to 'shoo' him away.

"No, he's fine. I adore cats." She turned her attention to the animal for a moment, gently moving her fingers over his silken fur. "You're just an old softie, aren't you? Just like my Bunbury." And for the next few minutes the conversation turned to the antics of their respective felines.

"He loves me," declared CJ without fear of ridicule. A cat lover can spot another a mile away. "He hates the parrot with a vengeance, or so he claims." She inclined her head towards the covered cage. "War was declared long ago and hostilities are continuing daily." They laughed.

"Oh, Bunbury's my big baby," said Denise, smiling. She paused. "It's the only baby I'll ever have." A sudden look of sadness crept into her dark eyes. It didn't go unnoticed and CJ wondered if she'd hit a nerve.

"Is that by choice?" said CJ, her voice casual.

"I always knew I'd never have a child, that's all. I neither wanted nor needed any."

"And Mike?"

"He accepts it's never been part of the plan." She rubbed the cat under his chin with the tip of her finger.

"Plans can be changed, Denise," said CJ. "They're not set in stone, you know". She paused, watching the other women steadily. "Would it be a disaster if it happened?" Denise didn't look at her, but continued to absent-mindedly caress the cat.

"It won't happen. I know it won't."

"How do you *know*? You seem very sure."

The woman gave a wry smile of the acceptance of the way things were. "I just am. You see, if I'm honest, babies scare me, especially when they cry."

Denise looked up and for a split second, their eyes met, revealing the panic that came with the revelation. It'd been made in an unguarded moment between the safe talk of cats and coffee. She'd probe the subject no further, but to her surprise, Denise began to explain.

"You see, I do *like* children – other people's. I'm the best 'auntie' in the world! My best friend's having twins in the next couple of months and there's no one more excited than me. I'm going to spoil them rotten, roll around the floor with them and have a great time. And, that's okay for a night or an afternoon," she paused, choosing her words carefully, "but as for all the rest? It's not for me. I couldn't deal with the responsibility, you see."

The cat suddenly leapt from her lap and she started as his claws gained purchase on her leg. The melancholy mood was broken and they both laughed.

"Coffee refill?" said CJ, getting up, "and a plaster?"

*

"Well," said CJ as they resumed, "we don't have any little ones either. It just never happened, but there's no hurry. Some things just aren't meant to be – yet."

"That's what the funny old woman said." She drained her cup. "You know what? I think I've got rid of my demons. I don't understand what happened here, CJ but I fancy it's done the trick. Thank you so much." She was unsure whether to kiss her or shake her hand. She did neither.

"No thanks needed," said CJ with a dismissive wave of her hand. "I'm just the go-between. You did it all by yourself, with a little help from Max, perhaps. Look, I'm here if you need me. Just pick up the phone."

"I will and thanks anyway." She took both of CJ's hands for a moment and squeezed them tightly.

"Remember," CJ said, as they walked to the door, "that nightmares are only the things we haven't faced during the day that come back to haunt us. They creep in when we're relaxed and our defences are down. Maybe, that's why we're here on this earth. We failed to do it properly the first time around and have been sent back, like a sort of school report that says 'must do better'. I wonder how many incarnations it takes to get it right?"

"God forbid!" exclaimed Denise, sharing the joke. As she left, CJ watched from the window as she walked up the path and got into her car, knowing they'd never meet again.

If, as she'd quipped, many return visits were required in order to get everything right, CJ suspected she might be here forever.

Chapter 14

Denise was ecstatic and hadn't stopped talking since Joe's phone call just after breakfast.

The twins were been born by caesarean section at 4.00am that morning. When labour threatened, Joe took his wife into hospital at once. It was a good job, as the first twin was lying in the breech position, presenting its bottom first. A quick decision was made that the safest way to deliver both babies was in theatre by caesarean.

Joe was weary when he rang, though completely elated.

"Ellie was wonderful, Mike. She was so calm, which is more than I can say for me! She'd been having some contractions when we went to bed at around midnight, and thought they might settle, but they didn't. We went in about 1.00am and by 3.30am we were in theatre."

"We?" Mike was shocked, knowing how squeamish Joe was. "Ellie opted for a spinal anaesthetic, so I was allowed in. Strictly at the top end," he said with a laugh. "I was gowned and masked like something out of an episode of *Casualty*. Then, in what seemed like minutes, out they came yelling their heads off, *and* two weeks early." Despite the long night, Joe was having difficulty stopping talking.

Eventually, when Mike put the phone down he was faced with an excited wife demanding to know *every* detail.

Shaun had been born first, weighing six pounds eight ounces. His sister followed two minutes later. Marianne weighed six pounds two ounces and, though slightly smaller, had a much louder voice from the moment she took her first breath. It was obvious that she was going to be the boss; the spokesperson in this symbiotic relationship, separated suddenly by the obstetrician's knife. To that end, she voiced her protestations loud and long.

When all the family had visited to fawn over Ellie and the new arrivals, it was Denise's turn. At last, she could indulge her long-buried maternal instincts. And, when she next went shopping, it was a very different Denise to the one who'd bought all those unwanted baby things before. This time, she returned with her arms full of bags again, but remembered buying and paying for everything.

Denise didn't share the view that twins should be dressed alike and neither did Ellie. It would've been difficult with one of each sex, anyway. She could see why the temptation arose in our mix-and-match, buy-one-get-one-free society. She believed children should develop their own tastes and diversities – even at this early age. When Denise was at junior school, there'd been a near-epidemic of twins. Not only did they look alike and dress alike, they stuck together like glue, hand in hand and not always making other friends. Although it looked quaint, Denise thought that surely this was not conducive to good development. Separation would have to happen one day. So she'd been very careful on her shopping expedition not even to buy the same colour for the little outfits, with their matching hats and booties. Happily, she headed for the car, realising she'd spent a fortune, then instantly trying to justify it.

Well, it is twins and twins are special – and Ellie and Joe are very good friends. I'll probably not get the chance to do this again, and, besides, I bought the second size, so they'll fit for a long time.

"That's a fine example of women's logic!" Mike commented when she told him in preparation for the arrival of the credit card statement.

Men can't possibly understand! So she wouldn't try and justify spending all that money any further. Quality always costs more. Oh yes, it does!

Seated by Ellie's bed later that evening, she gazed happily at the little bundles, lying side by side in their crib, angelic and sleeping. The midwife explained twins settled better if they were allowed to sleep together in the early days. After all, they'd been in close contact for the past nine months.

"How sensible," Ellie said. "Why don't the books tell you useful things like that? I'd never have thought of that. I suppose it only comes with experience." She sighed. "All those relaxation and birthing classes were a complete waste of time. It happened so fast, I didn't get chance to put *any* of it into practice. It never occurred to me they wouldn't be born naturally."

Denise found it hard to drag her eyes away from the little heads with their downy coverings of hair, the colour of ripe corn. Ellie laughed.

"Yes, I know. Where did that colour come from? Apparently, Joe's was the same when he was born, according to his mother." Denise stroked one perfectly shaped little head with the tip of her finger as Ellie continued. "The one thing I never expected was to have children with ginger hair."

"I expect it'll change with time," said Denise. "It's like their eyes. I read somewhere they're all blue at birth and change later on. It was most likely the problem page of *Woman's Own*." She looked at Ellie properly for the first time. "You look wonderful. Are they good?"

The little girl stirred as if to stake her claim to her mother's attention first. Ellie rocked the crib gently. "Well, at the moment, I wish they fed together. She's like a gannet with a suck like a vacuum cleaner and he likes a little and often. He's much gentler, feeds every four hours then goes to sleep for ages. What a child! I *do* hope it lasts. I suppose that's something else that'll change." She sighed happily. "There's so much to learn for all of us."

Ellie reached over and lifted the now squirming bundle of blankets. "Here you are, Auntie Den." She lowered the baby gently into Denise's arms. For a split second, Denise froze, stiffly holding the infant away from her body as if temporarily paralysed. She gasped, then some long-buried instinct took over and she held the infant close. Marianne nuzzled, her soft head beneath Denise's chin, tiny mouth searching.

"She's so warm, Ellie, so soft." She gasped again, this time in wonder at the sheer beauty; the sight and smell of the baby who instantly settled on the soft pillow of her bosom. "Oh Ellie, she's wonderful; they both are. I never imagined that anything could feel so … so … shnuggly." They both laughed at the invention of a new, but very apt word, cooing like women with hormones racing at full tilt can.

*

Later that night, over supper, Denise was still grinning with sheer pleasure as she regaled Mike with all the details. She was sure that she'd bored him out of his skin, as she'd never stopped talking about the babies since setting foot in the door. Even when his gaze wandered to the TV or out of the window, she barely noticed. After all, she knew that men get bored very easily, especially with baby talk. In fact, Mike was thinking how excited and fresh she looked tonight. Perhaps this was just what she needed; something good after all the problems of the past couple of years.

Later, he watched her as she undressed, bending to smooth body lotion on her long legs. She could still arouse him with the smallest gesture. He reached for her, drawing her close. As she sank into his arms, he breathed in the scent of her: the smell of rose petals at dusk. He kissed her neck and her arms went around him, their mouths meeting in an urgent kiss.

*

It was a humid night; oppressive and sticky. Denise got out of bed and opened the windows wide, though there was little movement in the night air. Then, drawing the curtain closed again, she got into bed and fell immediately into a deep and contented sleep.

Unobserved, the curtains moved from the gathering breeze outside. From his vantage point on top of the dresser, Bunbury was keeping his nightly vigil. He'd not gone out tonight. He'd stay at home to watch and, even though his eyelids appeared to be half-closed, Bunbury *was* watching. He saw a little moth as it fluttered through the chink in the curtains, following its erratic flight until it settled amongst the folds of the duvet, and he didn't stir.

He heard a train far away in the distance and the da-duh-da-duh-da-duh of its wheels going along some distant railway line, the sound carrying in the quiet of the night, and he didn't stir. He watched the forms in the bed shuffle, turning over before settling again, and still he didn't stir.

And he watched the shadows as they came – as they'd done so many times before. The dark shapes settled around those in the bed, growing until they filled the room with blackness. The one with the soft voice pulled up the covers around her neck, disturbing the little moth. He continued to watch until the shadows disappeared, leaving the fur on his back standing.

And, even then, he didn't stir, content to watch and wait.

✶✶

The babies were growing. The first six weeks of their little lives had flown. Ellie couldn't imagine what she'd actually *done* all day before they arrived. Between changing, feeding and the laundry, there didn't seem to be enough hours in the day. Joe helped – in his own way – by fetching and carrying, but looking after twins was exhausting to say the least. One or the other seemed to be attached to her at any given time of day and night. Joe was amazed; amazed how well she coped *and* still managed to look fabulous when he came home every evening. Her hair was always neat and she'd changed her clothes; still not completely fit after her surgery, but beginning to get out and about again. Although, after the umpteenth time she'd heard it, the comment "Oh, twins! Double trouble," had begun to wear a bit thin.

At times, she got emotional, usually as a result of tiredness and the explosion of hormones that can make new mothers cry at the drop of a hat. Just like their infants really; young Marianne could *really* howl. Her tiny face would screw up and become puce and Ellie would, once more, go through her mental check list.

Nappy – clean. Fed? Half a gallon, surely. Wind? The child could burp like a sailor. *Lonely, perhaps? No.* She was lying next to her truly contented brother who was shell-pink and sleeping like an angel. Ellie knew he wouldn't stir until his next feed in four hours' time.

"What *is* your problem, Marianne?" She lifted the squalling infant to rest against her shoulder. Instantly, she quietened. "You horror! You just like being picked up." The baby gurgled. "I can't walk around with you on my shoulder all day." Ellie sat in the nursing chair by the window and hummed a lullaby until the infant's breathing pattern suggested sleep. Slowly, she rose and lowered her into the crib beside her twin. Marianne shuffled against his back, briefly, and Ellie dropped the soft coverlet in place. With a sigh of relief, she drew the curtains and lay on the sofa.

What was it the midwife said? Become an opportunist sleeper whenever …

It was her last conscious thought before falling into the deep, satisfying, dreamless sleep of a new mother.

*

Consciousness returned with the same suddenness the moment Joe's car pulled into the drive. Ellie sat up quickly, a twinge from her healing scar making her grimace. She looked at the clock and realised she'd slept for three hours. Joe was home from work and it was nearly 6.00pm.

"Sorry, Joe … I fell asleep, and so did they." The bundle of blankets shifted in response to some unseen cue. "I hope this is the start of things to come. If it were, this job would be a doddle." An apologetic look crossed her face. "Sorry, darling. There's no food ready." Joe kissed his wife and the babies.

"Oh, don't worry. I'll go and get a takeaway. I expect you all needed the sleep. Don't get too hopeful, though. I bet they'll be up every hour of the damn night, just so we don't get complacent. I'll nip out and then we'll eat, shall we?"

* *

Incredibly, from that day forward, the babies established a pattern – with the odd hiccup for growth spurts. Life became much easier and more predictable; each developing their own little personality. Shaun was still gentle and quieter than his sister. One day he'd undoubtedly grow tall enough to protect her from the ills of the world, even if it *did* seem to be the other way around at present. Marianne was still the more demanding of the pair.

Ellie had always been organised and, apart from developing the secret weapon of napping in the afternoons, she had another – the magnificent Auntie Den.

Denise had taken her role of prospective godmother very seriously since Ellie and Joe had asked, and she'd been delighted to accept. When she wasn't at work, she spent nearly every moment helping Ellie out with either the ironing, the cleaning or simply keeping the cake tin full – much to Joe's delight. She was revelling in the role, so when the two of them were asked to baby-sit, Mike thought she'd *really* found her vocation.

Ellie and Joe were ready for a night out, if only for a quick meal and to see a film; a little 'how it used to be' time. The planning required needed to be done with military precision. Breast milk had been frozen and saved in bottles; nappies, creams and spare clothing were placed somewhere handy, *as was* a long list of emergency phone numbers that had to be seen to be believed.

When Denise and Mike arrived, Ellie was upstairs trying to find something that fitted and was 'having a strop', according to Joe. Denise nodded sagely and headed upstairs. By the time Ellie found something that didn't make her look, in her own words, "like a beached whale", Joe was nearly ready to call the whole thing off.

"I never thought she'd be this clucky," he said over his shoulder as he all but pushed her out of the door. "Bye guys. See you later." He stopped and turned. "Have you got the phone numbers?"

Mike threw up his arms in exasperation. "Just go! You're worse than Ellie."

Shutting the door quickly behind the retreating Joe, he leaned against it, laughing. He looked at Denise. "Tell me we'll never be like that. Will we?" Denise shook her head.

"No, this is fine for now. Three or four hours playing 'house' then hand over to the night shift." She bent over the lace-fringed crib. "They *are* perfect little angels, aren't they, Mike." He smiled and stood behind her, his arms around her waist.

"Oh, yes, they are."

*

The twins were on their best behaviour; only waking once for a feed, despite all Mike's surreptitious efforts to nudge the crib. Eventually, he was successful in waking them up and they sat side by side on the sofa, he with the boy and she with the girl. Their little heads pointed outwards as they fed, like a pair of bookends. Ellie had left precise instructions on how to warm the milk, and the little ones drained their respective bottles quickly. Mike was secretly dreading finding anything in the nappy, but his charge was only damp. Not so the girl. He looked in horror as Denise removed Marianne's nappy.

"Oh hell!" he exclaimed curling his lip, "how can so much muck come from such a small ... that's disgusting! It's everywhere. You'll need a bucket and shovel." "Come on, Marianne, let's get you cleaned up seeing that Uncle Mike's squeamish." She laughed Mike was just thankful he'd got Shaun.

Later, with the babies tucked up in their cots upstairs, they relaxed on the sofa, enjoying the bottle of wine Joe had thoughtfully left. Mike drank most of it. He lay stretched out on the sofa, his head on Denise's lap. She stroked his hair, the smell of baby powder still on her hands.

"Happy, Denise?"

"I'm very happy. This is the best therapy of all. Those little angels ... so dependent. Neither spoke for several minutes, wrapped in the glow of this new and pleasant experience.

"I love you, Mike," she said suddenly, "even if I haven't told you lately."

Mike took her hand and kissed it. "I love you too, babe, and nothing else really matters, does it?" He closed his eyes, her fingers caressing his brow. Winter would be here soon, and with it … He hoped beyond hope that her affliction wouldn't return. He'd been amazed how she was with the babies, so natural and happy. Maybe the spring would be a good time to broach the subject of starting a family of their own, perhaps? He knew what she'd always said, what they'd agreed, but that was before the twins came along. So maybe … That was something for the future. For now, Mike was satisfied. Tomorrow was another day.

Chapter 15

Pieter Van Reger was dozing. Strains of Solveig's song from his beloved Peer Gynt suite drifted over the old veranda where he reclined on a day bed. His hands rested across his rib cage, long fingers linked, rising and falling with his chest as he breathed. An old, straw hat shielded his eyes from the late afternoon sun. Beside him, on the ground, lay a pair of discarded espadrilles that had definitely seen better days. A low, tiled garden table to his left held a neatly folded copy of *The Times* and an empty wine glass.

Pieter wasn't asleep. Years before, he'd taught himself the art of self-hypnosis as a quick way of relaxing. These 'power naps', as he called them, allowed his energy levels to remain at maximum throughout the long working day. Though semi-retired now, he considered it a good habit to continue; every afternoon in summer when the weather was warm. His mind was far away in his native South Africa.

Pieter was a boy again, growing up in the Western Cape, on the edge of the savannah: the vast grasslands that stretch across the country and down to the ocean in the south. He was a child of Afrikaner descent; a child with the freedom to roam. The veldt was his playground and the savannah, with its dangerous wild creatures, held no fear for the young Pieter. His father, long gone now, had been an anthropologist; his mother, the daughter of the wealthy co-owner of a small, but very profitable, diamond mine.

From his hide in the tall grass, Pieter watched as the lifecycle of the African plains was played out before him. This was where he spent the long summer, as well as times when he *should* have been at his studies. Lions and cheetahs, with their different ways of hunting, would pass, often within yards of his den.

The folly of youth! He'd never contemplate such an act now, but all children are foolish.

He'd watch concealed, as the pride worked together to trap a herd of grazing animals. The lionesses would hide in the long grass, waiting to ambush any animal that became separated. Then, they would all eat, growling and tearing at the flesh in their turn, their fur stained with blood.

In a more placid pursuit, he'd lie motionless to watch the weaver birds build their great, hanging nests amongst the stems of the tall grass. Or simply lie on his back to gaze upward as harrier eagles circled above in the clear, azure sky, their sharp eyes scanning the hot plains for prey.

Kill or be killed. He'd seen plenty of that in the daily fight for survival on the plains and in the savannah. From the safety in numbers of the vast herds of gazelle and wildebeest to a solitary, thirsty elephant as it effortlessly tore apart a baobab tree to find the spongy, moist inner wood. Young Pieter watched it all from the safety of his hide.

And, now, from the comfort of his day bed, in the warm afternoon, relaxed and content, he was revisiting his childhood once more.

The incessant ringing of the telephone interrupted his rest and he sat up. It took a few seconds before he fully remembered where he was and, at nearly 56, was unable to move quite so fast these days. The phone continued to ring and, with a sigh, he went inside to answer it. The flagstone floor of the den was cool to his bare feet.

"Hello?" He suppressed a yawn. "Cordelia, my dear … how nice." Pieter smiled, happy to hear her voice. He was always pleased to hear from his protégé, even if he *did* refuse to call her anything but her given name; just as he'd resisted all her attempts to persuade him to buy a mobile phone.

"Sorry, I haven't interrupted Grieg's piano concerto in Z major or anything, have I?"

"You're a complete musical Philistine, Cordelia," he said, grinning despite himself. "Have I taught you nothing?" He paused whilst she chided him. "Now, what can I do for you? I don't suppose that husband of yours has left you?"

"No, of course not, Pieter."

"Shame, but I want you to know I haven't yet abandoned hope."

"Don't be silly, Pieter!" She giggled.

"So, this must be about your latest client, I presume. What's wrong? Migraine?"

"Not exactly."

"What do you mean? Related to what, then? Stress ... her marriage?" His voice took on a note or irritation.

"Who knows?"

"Then, don't be so ridiculous, child. You're not explaining this well," Pieter retorted. He called her 'child' whenever he felt she was being foolish. It gave him the upper hand. "Just one moment, Cordelia, then you can run the whole thing past me."

Slowly, he poured himself a fresh glass of his favourite Châteauneuf-du-Pape and settled down in the armchair before picking up the phone again.

"Now, my child, I suggest we begin at the beginning."

*

He loved her, of course. He'd loved her from the moment he met her.

She'd come for an interview for a degree course in psychology at the university where he was head of the department. She'd been accepted. At lectures, she stood out from the crowd and not *just* because of the shock of white in her dark hair. He'd recognised her for what she was: a small island in a sea of rather scruffy, less interested students. Her bright eyes seemed to hang upon his every utterance; possessed of an understanding and perception far beyond her years. He saw immediately that here was someone special. Her intuition was, at times, staggering. But, there was something about her that disturbed him. She knew things she wasn't supposed to. Nevertheless, her very voice was honey to his soul.

True love never came to Pieter as a young man. There'd been the usual awkward fumblings of youth, but the deep, meaningful kind had always been denied him. It was only in middle age that he felt it now – for his Cordelia; like a fine wine that leaves behind a warm feeling, mellow with age.

For Pieter Van Reger was mesmerised by her.

It came as no surprise when she graduated with a first class honours degree in clinical psychology. After the ceremony, she'd kissed him on the cheek and bought dinner to say 'thanks'. She never had any idea how much he wanted to …

He'd never tell her, of course. In that he was old-fashioned, but he often wondered if she knew. She seemed to know everything else – insufferable child!

"So, Pieter, do you think there's anything strange going on here? Have I missed anything?" She'd recounted Denise's case history as he listened without comment.

"No, I don't." The irritation in his voice returned. It was all part of the game he played with her. "As I've told you countless times, look for the obvious. Nine times out of ten, that's where the problem lies and you'll be correct, child."

"Pieter, you're bullying me again *and* you're shouting. I'm surprised to see semi-retirement's doing little to improve your temper."

He replaced the receiver with satisfaction. She'd come for lunch on Sunday while Sam was playing his damn silly game. By God! She was still feisty. If he'd been younger, he'd have asked her to marry him. He tapped his fingers on the soft leather of the armchair. All fanciful thoughts in that particular direction were set aside the day she married Sam. Her own father had died some years previously and it was he, Pieter, who she'd asked to give her away. And, with barely disguised tears in his grey eyes, he handed her to Sam as though she'd been his to give.

And that's another thing. Pieter shook his head. *Married in a field beneath the trees, like something out of a Robin Hood film and with a mongrel dog as the best man!* 'Hand-fasting' they called it. It was all done properly, of course, with a registrar there to make it legal. Their hands had been bound together with golden cord as they made promises to one another. *Ridiculous – and not a hymn book in sight!*

But Pieter Van Reger cried like a child when he saw her dressed in a scarlet gown with flowers in her hair. With closed eyes, he drank in silence, indulging in the memory of the feeling of fleeting pride – and not a little envy.

If Pieter had been lucky enough to have fathered daughters, he would've wished for one like his Cordelia, insufferable though she was at times. And now she belonged to another man, a good man – *a black man.* Coming from a country blighted by apartheid, he should perhaps be biased against mixed marriage.

He wasn't.

*

Pieter hated what apartheid had done to his beloved country. For him, the whole sorry business was summed up by the treatment of a little black boy. The child was employed – *if* that was the word, for he was given little more than food – by a local white farmer. Throughout the day, he sat in the searing heat by the gate waiting for his master to come home. Then, he'd get up quickly and open it for the Mercedes to drive through. He'd shut the gate quickly and run to the garage to open that door. His little legs rarely made it before the vehicle and he got a swift kick up the backside for his trouble.

He never cried, though it must have hurt; the blank expression on his face never changed. He *expected* this daily treatment, for when it'd been metered out he knew he'd eat. Only in those sad eyes did Pieter ever see the *real* truth. He was just a child, like Pieter, and only eight years old.

Twelve years later, as the hatred that was South Africa smouldered, a young, black man was taken out and hung from a tree. His crime? He'd shot dead a white farmer. Until that moment Pieter never knew the young man's name was Moetketsi and not 'Boy!' as was always shouted at him.

The abused child had grown up.

*

With the union of Sam and Cordelia, Pieter saw hope for South Africa. It'd been a long time coming. The two were joined by an invisible thread that would last forever and there was no place for the fanciful dreams of an older man. Yet he could still dream when he was alone, couldn't he?

*

"Hello Pieter." CJ kissed him on both cheeks and walked by his side to the bottom of the garden where the stream ran crystal clear. This was a special place, hidden from the house in summer by the foliage of the trees; a secluded glade for entertaining. "The garden looks beautiful."

"My dear, I wish I could claim the credit. But, as you well know, I *kill* things with a mere glance." Pieter shrugged his shoulders, spreading out his hands in gesture of acceptance. "So, I leave it to the gardener. He's worth his weight in gold."

Fragrant honeysuckle climbed the uprights of the arbour, its fragrance drifting around them where they sat. CJ put her head back and drank it in as Pieter poured Pimm's into tall glasses, handing her one.

"Thank you, darling," she said. "Now, how's the consultancy job going?

Pieter wafted a wasp away from his face and ran a hand over his short, greying hair. "The hospital is paying me quite an obscene amount of money for very little work," he said with a lift of an eyebrow. "But I'm not complaining *and* I'm not *quite* ready to give it all up yet. Consultant hospital psychologist. Sounds very ordinary, don't you think, Cordelia?"

"You'll never be that, Professor, and you know it." She laughed and sipped her Pimm's.

For Pieter liked the finer things in life, like the expensive, linen suit he'd donned for this very occasion. His cologne was made in Provence near Grasse and was sent to him from source, along with a regular delivery of champagne from Rheims every fortnight.

"Pieter, *why* do you want to work in an NHS hospital? Surely you don't *need* to work?"

"Just keeping my pension topped up." He tapped the side of his nose with a finger and chuckled. "And, for the sole purpose of spoiling you, of course. That reminds me, I've two tickets for the Albert Hall. Michael Manares is playing the concertos and I think it's time to further your musical education, my child."

"Grieg?" she ventured.

"Of course it's Grieg!" he snapped. "You don't imagine I'd be spending good money on a Simply Red concert, do you?" Pieter fumbled in the pocket of his jacket, which he'd slung carelessly over the bench. "Oh, and just a *little* something to match that." He pointed to her gold and diamond bracelet. "I want a well-appointed woman on my arm, after all."

CJ took the box and flipped open the lid. She gasped at the sight of the necklace inside: a gold collaret with three fine diamonds. A perfect match for the band on her wrist.

"Oh Pieter! It's exquisite. You spoil me terribly." Carefully, she removed it from its fitted box and, excited, turned for him to fasten it.

"I spoil you *wonderfully* and I love it. Please continue to indulge an old man in his dotage."

"Sam will be livid!"

"No, he won't. Tell him you've another man if he should ask."

CJ flung her arms around his neck, "Oh, Pieter …"

"Now, stop fawning child," he said gruffly, extricating himself, "and let's have lunch."

*

Pieter knew he'd enough money to travel anywhere in the world whenever the mood took him. He'd invested wisely, as well as having saved enough during his career at the university to ensure a comfortable retirement – whenever that came. Working in an NHS hospital amused him and Pieter liked to be amused. He'd continue to indulge his beloved Cordelia because he knew Sam didn't *really* mind. He never tired of spoiling her, and constantly invented new strategies for doing so. The trip to the Albert Hall was solely to further her education, wasn't it? Or perhaps it was the unbridled pleasure of a beautiful and intelligent young woman's company? Or a substitute for the family he never had?

"Pieter, you are *far* too generous," she constantly protested.

"Silence, child," he'd reply. "Who else would I spend my money on?"

What CJ wouldn't know, not for a long time, was that Pieter had *indeed* prepared well. For besides a generous university pension, his healthy investments *and* an NHS salary, there was the small matter of an inherited half-share in a South African diamond mine.

Chapter 16

Summer began to work her perennial magic once more. CJ found she was far from busy at work on her annual, three-month stint in the community. One evening she explained her theory on this matter to Sam.

"People don't plan babies during the summer months. It interferes with their holidays. So it's a great time to work in the community, in my opinion." He raised his eyebrows, never knowing whether or not to believe her. Hopefully, he held out his glass for a refill. CJ obliged and sat beside him, putting her feet up on the coffee table, which, for some reason, he always found rather endearing.

Macho man, he thought, *a primitive urge to protect the little woman.* She *was* small and quite unable to reach the floor if she sat back in the deep chairs. It was either that or allow her legs to swing freely in mid-air like a child.

"So, what do you plan to do with all the free evenings bountiful Mother Nature is about to bestow? Cookery lessons, perhaps?" He could dream. The enquiry was rewarded with a quickly hurled cushion that hit him square in the face. "Ouch … wo-man!" he complained with a scowl and brushing spilled wine from his shorts.

"I know exactly what *we* are going to do tomorrow, my darling" said CJ.

"'*We*'? Who said anything about '*we*'?" The conversation was rudely punctuated by a squawk from the corner.

"Sam … You is the man … the man. Sam loves CJ. SamSamSam."

"Shut up, you feckless bird," called Sam over his shoulder. "Or else ..." CJ ignored the interruption. "I believe you told me you've got a week free from cricket?"

"Yeeees?"

"Wasn't it something to do with the other side not being able to raise a team?" She'd no intentions of allowing him to change the subject.

"Yeeees?"

"So, I thought, I might clean out the garage and you ..." She leaned forward and took the wine glass from him, "my precious, darling husband are going to help me." Between each word she planted a kiss on his forehead. Sam visibly deflated as she refilled his glass to dull the pain. CJ found that plying a man with alcohol usually worked.

He took the proffered glass with poor grace. "Why do you *insist* on tidying everything?" CJ shrugged.

"It's a natural Virgo trait, my love. You lion, me virgin!"

*

It was a very tetchy Sam who appeared the following morning wearing old painting shorts and work boots. He hadn't any wish to spend his free Saturday clearing and cleaning. Old habits die hard – particularly when you come from the Caribbean! A man of the new age maybe, but those cultural habits weren't buried *that* far below the surface. The pretence of modern man was quickly stripped away as he heard the echo of his grandfather's voice muttering.

"Dis am wo-man's work, man!"

Sam complained silently as he got to work. Didn't he do his share around the house? He got out the vacuum cleaner – occasionally. He didn't move anything. What was the point cleaning what you couldn't see? And he always collected dirty mugs and put them in the kitchen. True, they didn't always make it as far as the dishwasher, but that was 'splittin' hairs'. He'd probably been distracted by the phone ringing, or the cat meowin', or something. Yes, that was it!

But, oh God! How he loved her. He still got an erection just thinking about her.

CJ was grumbling away to herself, too.

Sam *never* washed up. In his opinion that was what the dishwasher was for, even though he'd little idea how the clean crockery found its way back into the cupboard. She supposed he thought there was a small battalion of fairies – the 'ironing fairy' and the 'pick-the-grotty-underpants-up-from-the-floor fairy'. She'd no serious complaints really. Sam *was* a good husband and provider. That wasn't in question *and* he was easy-going and calm, which was annoying sometimes. He managed the local gym and kept himself in shape to the extent that every woman that went in drooled. Despite his physique, he wasn't vain and she never worried that he'd stray.

Sam only had eyes for one woman, and that was her. Since that first day they'd met at the cricket match, the passion had been electric. She'd assumed it'd dull and decrease with time, but there was no sign of it yet.

"Do you *really* mind that I'm a hopeless cook? I mean *really* mind?" asked CJ as she struggled with a huge bag of assorted rubbish.

"Nah!" he grinned displaying perfect teeth. "Anyway, I make passable attempts." Unlike most Barbadian women, Sam's mother had also been a hopeless cook. But for Aunt Clothilde, the family would've starved and it was she who'd passed the skill to Sam.

In 'his' kitchen, all the minor irritations of the day melted away the moment the rice and peas started bubbling on the stove. He chopped, baked and blended all the wonderful West Indian fruit and vegetables that seemed so out of place in England. The smells wafted around him as he worked, reminding him of the hot summers he'd spent as a child. His Caribbean kitchen was a place of sheer bliss, where he was lost in creativity.

Add to that a wife who was funny, crazy, sexy and beautiful all at the same time – even though she was hard-pressed to successfully boil an egg! It was the beginning of a memorable recipe. Add a contemptuous cat and a foul-mouthed parrot to complete the dish, and serve. Sam was a very happy man. But, clean out the garage? Oh man! That definitely was wo-man's work!

"Darling," he began, making one last futile attempt to get out of it. "No one has a garage to keep a car in. It's for all the other stuff." CJ's withering glance halted any further pleas to avoid the task. His wife had obviously got a 'burr under her saddle'.

In fact, they sorted and bagged so much detritus that came under the heading of 'just might need it someday', it was possible to get the Land Rover inside. *That* hadn't happened for a while. Sam beamed with satisfaction for the first time that morning.

"Thank goodness," said CJ noting the smile. "You looked like you'd just been given out leg before wicket for a duck by a blind umpire who was looking the other way. Now, darling, I think you've earned a coffee." Sam shook his head. At least she had the terminology correct, even if the rules *did* elude her.

*

They built a huge bonfire at the end of the garden with all the stuff not required for their immediate survival. CJ's diminutive frame matched Sam's efforts, bag after bag, and she raised her hands in triumph as the last one was stacked.

"Now, I can get to the freezer and tumble drier without breaking my neck or being mugged by the lawnmower."

The pair was so busy with the task that neither heard the knock on the open kitchen door or anyone calling. When CJ went to make coffee, she discovered a huge bunch of flowers lying on the conservatory table. A simple card attached said, "Thank you. Love, Denise".

"Good grief, Sam," she said handing him the mug, "I left the front door unlocked. Someone might have nicked WG! Probably wouldn't still have all their fingers, but still … I must be more careful in future."

*

At dusk, CJ lit the bonfire as Sam looked on. The paper that'd been stuffed in around the base caught quickly. He knew better than to interfere. CJ prided herself on being able to light a bonfire that wouldn't go out in anything less than a downpour. She insisted there was a definite knack to it and no advice was required, thank you, Sam! She had loved bonfires with almost pyromaniac fervour since she was a small child. He watched as her face exuded sheer pleasure, cheeks rosy from the heat as flames licked upwards. She clapped her hands with almost childish glee and Sam shook his head, bemused.

"Okay, I'm off to watch the match."

He knew she'd be out there at least an hour or two, stoking, prodding and poking at the embers. She'd rake up every last twig until all was consumed and only a grey ring of cooling ash was still visible on the earth. During this time, he knew she'd do a couple of turns around the house just in case anything had been missed. He'd not recognise the garden by morning as, when running out of tinder, she took to a little pruning by torchlight.

Once in the house, he showered and donned his dressing gown before pouring a beer and settling on the sofa. A new spurt of flame was reflected in the TV screen each time she fed the fire.

CJ sat on a stool looking into the flames – a child again. There'd been bonfire nights when the excitement of this once-a-year event had taken over the street. Dad used to take all the neighbourhood kids to collect wood from the hedgerows and nearby fields. It started around the middle of October with foraging, then the wood was spread out on waste ground to dry. On November 4th, the dads and older brothers would build the bonfire. No children were allowed and certainly no girls. Women were thought incapable of building a decent fire. Lofts and sheds were given their annual clearings out and garages prepared to receive cars for winter.

The women did what women do best. A rota was drawn up for the making of home-made toffee, sticky gingerbread, baked potatoes and all manner of sweets, to ensure the children had a good time. CJ licked her lips, warmly wrapped in the memory.

But it was CJ's father who was charged with letting off the fireworks, as he was a reserve fireman. The kids watched from a safe distance, well away from the odd stray rocket, whilst drawing circles in the dark sky with their sparklers clutched in gloved hands.

CJ inhaled deeply, legs drawn up and hands encircling her knees, staring into the fire. It was as if no years had elapsed at all. There were pictures in the fire: a lady gowned in silk and lace, grazing cattle and an old man's face. She remembered the Catherine wheel that flew from its post, sending cries of alarm from the mothers as they grabbed the children. There was the night when a jumping jack leapt into the box of fireworks setting the whole lot alight. It'd been a spectacular display – for about two minutes – and her dad had to dive for cover as a rocket whistled past his ear.

The magic moment was when the fire was lit as, with a crackle, dry wood ignited, sending billows of smoke heavenward. CJ imagined it was to cast out evil spirits, banishing them to the darkness forever. There was the smell of vine clippings, hot twigs snapping and the hiss of evergreens. It wasn't hard to imagine the delicious aroma of potatoes and chestnuts buried in the shallow earth around the fire's edge. When it was over and the dying embers raked, the mums put the children to bed, their faces glowing. With tummies full of toffee, they slept soundly, smelling deliciously of wood smoke, which lingered on the sheets and pillows until they were changed the following week. Next morning, her father took the ashes to sprinkle on the vegetable patch ready for the next season's early potatoes and the whole wondrous cycle of life would begin again. CJ sighed.

Ashes to earth – seed to earth – trees to earth – trees to ashes – ashes to ashes – dust to dust. She shivered, suddenly despite the fire's glowing heat.

"Georgie, is that you?" But there was only the crackle of the fire to disturb the still evening air. "Hey, you old rascal," she said louder, "talk to me." But there was nothing.

The fire was dying and CJ considered going inside to take a shower when a forgotten bag of rubbish caught her eye. She grabbed it and tossing it into the embers, gave it a prod. The clippings began to catch fire. One more turn with the rake would settle its fate.

There was a loud crack as a stream of molten plastic shot from the fire. Instinctively, CJ dropped the rake and raised her hands to protect her face. Boiling plastic clung to her right hand and she cried out, more from surprise than anything else. She fell to the ground trying to brush splatters away from her face as a wave of pain hit her and she screamed.

Searing, it enveloped her, as the intense heat penetrated deeper into the skin's layers. Unable to catch her breath, she rolled back and forth on the grass in agony as though her whole body was alight.

She was sobbing, her breath coming out in gasps. "Stupid bitch, stupid …!" she cried as anger became words, realising there must have been a plastic bottle with the lid on in there. The pain reached a crescendo and she screamed again; this time for Sam. Stumbling and half-crawling towards the house, CJ knew he couldn't hear her above the sound of the TV.

She reached the French windows, knees scuffed and bleeding from the roughness of the patio. With her uninjured hand, she hammered on the glass using her last ounce of strength, screaming her husband's name.

After what seemed an age, though in reality only seconds, the door opened. Sam's benevolent expression turned to horror.

"Oh my God! What …?"

"Water," CJ gasped through the agony. "I've burned my hand! Get me into cold water!" The world began to spin as Sam half-lifted, half-dragged her inside. With a cry, she passed out and he quickly carried her limp body up the stairs.

Chapter 17

When consciousness returned, CJ was lying on the bed, her hand wrapped in a plastic freezer bag taped at the wrist so no air could get in. The pain was only marginally less than before but Sam had done the right thing. She looked down fearfully at the ghastly mess of black, molten plastic that'd welded to the flesh and surrounding it were huge red blisters.

CJ winced, suppressing a cry; the slightest movement was agonising. Her clothes were filthy. The mirror opposite the bed told the rest of the story. A blob had caught her right ear lobe and dripped down the side of her face, luckily losing some of its fierce heat in the process. Nevertheless, an angry trail of red beads extended as far as her jaw-line, like the painted tears of a sad clown.

"Oh, help me, *please*, Sam," she pleaded, her face a mask of pain.

"I think we'd better go to casualty now," said Sam sitting beside her on the bed. He placed his hand on her arm. That was it. She burst into floods of tears. Sam held her close, the injured limb flaccid over his shoulder.

"I know it's hard to believe at this moment, but it could have been a lot worse. What if you'd tripped and ..."

"I couldn't make you hear, Sam," she sobbed into his shoulder.

"I know. I'm sorry. You and your bloody bonfires, CJ! Now, come on, let's get you to hospital."

"It'll be ages before we get seen. It's Saturday night and the place will be full of drunks."

*

That wasn't the case. By the time they'd driven the three miles to hospital, CJ had lost every ounce of colour from her face and she could hardly stand. Sam swept her up into his arms and carried her in, her head lolling.

The nurse in triage recognised her immediately and they were ushered to a cubicle and she was given a shot of morphine. Never so glad to see a hypodermic needle coming, her tears flowed like rain. Any embarrassment disappeared with the effects of the opiate as it ran through her veins bringing blessed relief from pain. Sam cradled her other hand in his, as between puffs of gas and air, the limb was cleaned. It lay, sticking out on a pillow as the doctor worked, like a signpost to disaster.

Ben Wright, the registrar on duty, was business-like but betrayed by the softest, hazel eyes. He looked at her from time to time, observing for signs of discomfort purposefully avoiding eye contact.

"When that morphine starts to wear off, CJ, just let me know and you can have some more," he said. "What *were* you doing?" She told him through a drug-induced haze, fascinated by the black ribbon that held back his rather outdated ponytail.

"I'm not going to even try to remove all this plastic," he said when she'd finished her slurred account. "That comes later." He layered paraffin gauze impregnated with an antibiotic over the area. "It'll probably need grafting though, I'm afraid."

"Oh, no," said CJ with a long look at Sam, thinking just how impressed her boss was going to be by *that* piece of news. The community was short-staffed enough as it was.

"As for work ..." said Ben reading her thoughts, "you can forget it for a good while. This dressing's going to need changing daily as it'll quickly soak through. You know how it is with burns."

"It's been a while, Ben," He finished taping the thick bandage in place.

"Okay then. I'll start at the beginning, like for anyone else."

He sat patiently and explained the 'dos and don'ts' whilst CJ tried to stay awake and attentive. When he'd finished, he leaned back on the stool, hands linked behind his head.

"CJ, you have a full-thickness burn to the back of your right hand, which extends to the webbing between your thumb and index finger." He pointed. "This streak over your wrist is superficial. The hand's going to need a hell of a lot of attention. It's going to take weeks to heal, if not months." CJ closed her eyes briefly and sighed. "In short, you've made a right mess of it, girl. I'm going to give you a shedload of strong painkillers and some antibiotics. The last thing we want is an infection. Now, do you need another shot of morphine?"

CJ declined, still drowsy from the last one.

"Okay then." He stood, pushing the stool back into the corner. "If it all becomes too much, come back at once and we'll admit you."

"Thanks Ben." He smiled before leaving. "Sam, take me home. I feel like a twit!"

"Well, if it's any consolation you look ten times worse than that."

"Thanks," she said, with a wry smile, as he helped her off the trolley. Sam picked up her bagful of pills, instruction leaflets and appointment card for the burns clinic. "Come on, babe. Let's get you home."

*

Sam deposited her on the bed once again. The mirror told her, in its uncompromising fashion, what she already suspected. She looked a sight with her hair sticking out at all angles. Even the usually distinctive streak was camouflaged by dirt and grime. There were grass stains all over her clothes from dragging over the patio, as well as the more obvious injuries of grazes and scratches. Her hand was protected by an oversized bandage. Though giddy and nauseous on the car journey home, she now felt better.

"Stay there for at least an hour before even *thinking* of having a bath," ordered Sam with unaccustomed firmness, "and I'll get you a cup of tea." He indicated the mess that had been transferred to the white quilt cover. "Stop worrying, wo-man! I'll just have to awaken my feminine side and change the sheets."

"Good grief," muttered CJ as he went downstairs. "I must injure myself more often."

She lay back against the pillows, suddenly weary from the evening's events and reproached herself. *How stupid I am! I can't believe I did that.* She gazed at her reflection. *Look at yourself. You're going to be off work for ages!* Her right hand throbbed mercilessly. *Just one inattentive moment of rank stupidity!* She looked disdainfully at the bandage and yawned.

✳

Two hours later, she awoke; the tea Sam had placed on the bedside table was cold. But, he'd also left a carafe of water and a glass beside it. CJ drank greedily as he came into the room. "Oh, you're awake at last."

"Sam … I really need a bath. Just look at me."

"Are you sure you feel up to it?" he asked with a doubtful frown.

"Yes, thanks, I'm much better. I can't really get into bed like this, can I?" She saw the look on his face. "Really, I'll manage."

"Okay, I'll be in here reading. Best leave the door open, just in case you want a hand." CJ glared. "No pun intended. I'll run the bath for you."

CJ undressed, allowing her clothes fall to the floor in a grubby heap and with Sam's help managed to climb into the tub. She sank gratefully into the warm water, dangling her injured hand over the side of the bath. It was throbbing dreadfully and the pain shot up to her shoulder. Perspiration dripped from her chin in the steamy atmosphere, despite Sam having left the door open. The warm water was comforting as she deliberately slowed her breathing and tried to relax.

There'd be no more bonfires for a while. She suspected the neighbours would be secretly pleased. They'd always been tolerant – outwardly at any rate – of her penchant for smoky fires. They didn't bang the windows shut *too* hard whenever smoke curled and ash settled on their pristine white window frames.

In the warm water, CJ began to relax and the pain lessened for the moment as a familiar smell drifted under her nose.

"Hello, Georgie," she whispered. "Look what *I* did."

"Aye, lass. I know. Dint I tell thee to be mindful? Kids shouldn't play about wi' fire."

"Oh, Georgie, don't say 'I told you so', please. I know it was my own fault."

"Yes, it was. If I told thee once, I've told thee a thousand …"

"Yes, I know. They used to burn women like me. Well, if that was a taste … Bloody hell!" The voice returned, loud and sharp close to her ear.

"Don't mock, lass. Don't ever joke about that." He was angry. She could imagine the raised finger wagging close to her nose.

"I wasn't, Georgie."

What must it be like to die by fire? Poor wretches! Women like me. They were no different. If I'd had been born 200 years earlier, who knows? It's unthinkable. CJ yawned again.

"Kids shouldn't mess wi' matches," he repeated firmly.

"Georgie, I'm not a child." She was irritated now, his self-righteous meanderings too much to bear.

"In some ways tha *are* still a child." Then, mercifully, he was gone.

CJ sank lower into the bath, allowing the water to wash over her shoulders; the warmth soothing mind as well as body. Her breathing deepened as she became sleepy and only vaguely aware of the cat who'd padded into the room. Max sniffed the bandage carefully and decided it was nothing of interest. It smelled *far* too clean and, as no attention was forthcoming, he turned and, with a flick of his tail, wandered out of the room. His sleek body brushed the door as he went and slowly it closed with a soft click, CJ unaware of it as she drifted into a dreamy state, her chin lolling in the warm water.

*

It came slowly in the air; an almost imperceptible whisper close to her ear. She barely roused. *Go away, Georgie,* the words not reaching her lips. It was not Georgie, but quite a different

135

voice, harsh and vengeful, and it repeated one word over and over.

"Witchwitchwitchwitchwitchwitchwitchwitchwitch."

The venom of its hissed repetition roused her violently and with her one good hand she tried to get up from the bath. She turned her head and there, written on the steamed-up mirror in ancient gothic script were the words 'Die, witch!'.

With a gasp of terror she fell back into the water as a jolt of pain hit her – pain that was nothing to do with her injured hand.

A sharp, searing wave began at her feet and moved upward over her legs and torso in a pulse of pure agony. She took a breath looking down at her body in horror, expecting to see flames. The stench of her own burning flesh made her retch, and she could neither move nor breathe. Then, she was being pulled down, the water now level with her nostrils. CJ tried to cry out, to scream, but there was no breath, only the blind panic of helplessness. Her brain cried out for air, but gasps were all she could manage as she fought to keep her head above the water, her mind racing.

I've got to get out. I'm burning. Oh God, I'm burning! How can I be burning in a bath of water? It wasn't rational; yet, she was still being pulled beneath the surface, desperately trying to grasp at the bath sides. The all-consuming pain crept up to her chest, like nothing she'd ever experienced – save for a small area on one hand.

Her head was now beneath the water, lungs bursting as she held her breath. Giant, unseen hands held her firmly and in the silence beneath the surface the only audible thing was the beating of her heart. She opened her eyes in defiance to face whatever held her, but there was nothing there. Her subconscious mind screamed.

I will survive, damn you! I will not die. And, with one superhuman effort, she managed to hook her foot around the chain that held the plug and pulled hard, her lungs on fire. On the third pull, it yielded and the water level to started fall. Then, CJ screamed and screamed and screamed.

Chapter 18

Sam dragged her from the bath and she lay naked on the bathroom floor, eyes staring, her breath coming out in little gasps. Coughing violently, she heaved and vomited soapy water. Sam grabbed a towel, swaddling his wife like a child against his chest as she shook with terror.

"CJ! Oh my God, what happened? Her eyes were fixed on his as though afraid to break away from the safety they held. Frantically, she pointed to the mirror.

"What …?" His head turned to look, brows knitted. "The mirror?"

She nodded, urgently, trying to get her breath.

"CJ, there's nothing there. What is it? Tell me." She fought free of the towel.

The mirror was no longer steamy. No words remained. When Sam had burst into the room on hearing her screams, the cool air had rushed in. The words and the unseen hand that had written them were gone.

Neither Sam nor CJ slept that night. He was afraid to take his eyes from his troubled wife as they lay holding each other in the darkness until morning. With the dawn, CJ fell asleep to dream of Georgie.

"Careful lass," he was saying, "all thy life I've protected thee, but now there are things here, and beyond, that I can't protect thee from."

*

CJ awoke at lunchtime; the bright, midday light bringing its own safe reassurance, and the horrors in her head gone with the darkness. Over a prolonged breakfast she told Sam what happened. Although he'd put it down to the combination of codeine and morphine, she knew he'd take her seriously. Behind his proffered explanation of 'drug-fuelled imagination and bad dreams', Sam Dujonois didn't dispute his wife's account. For he knew CJ better than anyone; not just every inch of her body, but her way of thinking, her sensibilities and her emotions, which were *always* in control. He also accepted that his wife was the custodian of certain abilities he sometimes struggled to understand. Nevertheless, he'd never doubted she had them or that she remained in control of whatever it was. This was different; he was afraid and didn't understand why. He'd grown accustomed to sharing his home with the unseen Georgie, regarding him as a sort of benevolent uncle. Last night, he knew from the look of horror on his wife's face that something evil had been at work, right here in his house.

Later that day, CJ was calm and reflective. "If you're stupid enough to go shoving your hand into a bonfire," she said over coffee and cake, "then, I suppose you must expect some sort of shock reaction, no matter how bizarre." By evening, she'd all but convinced herself that it was *definitely* the morphine.

A hallucination – yes, that was it. Sam left to get milk and bread. *Shock – and morphine. Imagination's a funny thing!* "No, dammit!" CJ banged down her coffee mug on the table. "No, it was *not* my imagination and I'm *not* going crazy." At that moment she needed to prove it, if only to herself. CJ knew the words would still be there, pressed onto the mirror's surface by the hand that'd written them.

All I've got to do is allow the mirror to steam up again. She shivered before determination took over and she climbed the stairs.

"Come on, then," she said, defiantly looking into the mirror. "Let's see what you can do. No one writes on my property but me. So let's have you." It was a challenge firmly laid down to whoever or whatever scrawled those words, and this time she was ready. A sudden blast of cold, evening air flicked at the blinds. CJ took a deep breath and, undaunted, closed the window.

Putting the plug firmly in the bath, she closed the door and ran the hot tap. Steam began to fill the room and she felt her heart quicken. A knot in her stomach tightened as the mirror began to mist, slowly at first, the edges obscured as steam crept towards the middle.

Panic rose in her chest. *No! This isn't right.* Grabbing a cloth she rubbed at the mirror frantically, threw open the door and stilled the flow of hot water. For a few moments she stared, steely-eyed, at her reflection.

"Yes, I know, Georgie. Some things are better left alone."

*

Two painful weeks passed with dreadful slowness, punctuated by daily visits to the burns unit at the hospital. The dressings were soaked off and the wound inspected carefully. The first time CJ saw her hand after that fateful night she was horrified.

"It'll surely need grafting," she told Sam, knowing full well what the process involved. It meant taking a thin slice of living skin from her thigh or buttock to place over the burned area. She'd explained it to him as a bit like putting a patch on a worn pair of trousers. She failed to mention the contraption used resembled a bacon slicer and the very thought made her shudder. Each day seemed to bring that process closer and she came to dread the daily ordeal. Quite apart from the pain involved, which often required an injection, the sickly smell of burned flesh made her physically sick, but the relief when a new soft dressing was applied was immeasurable, if short-lived. The next day would come around all too quickly.

It was hard to think rationally or concentrate for longer than a couple of minutes. To keep her pain under any sort of control, the medication had to be maintained. Codeine in the dosage she required to achieve this had equally unpleasant side effects. Nausea came in waves and all she could do was sit still and try to doze until she felt she'd go crazy with such unaccustomed inactivity.

*

Then, on the Tuesday of the fourth week, something wonderful happened.

When the bandages were removed, there, beneath the slough of dead tissue, was red skin; tender in the extreme, but living tissue regenerating.

"Well," said Ben Wright, flicking his ponytail back. "I think we may be winning here, at long last." He grinned broadly. "I think we're going to get away without a graft."

CJ breathed a huge sigh of relief and wiped the tears from her eyes – not from pain or sadness but elation that recovery was finally in sight. At that precise moment she decided to dispense with the pain killers and try to get back to some kind of normality. The boredom had almost been as bad as the pain.

A few days later, she found she could think again. It was like waking up after a long hibernation. The hand still needed to be rested and used minimally, but a couple of fingers were now free of the bandage and that helped. With only one hand, CJ quickly discovered how difficult it was to do things. She'd become completely dependent upon Sam for almost everything from peeling potatoes to fastening her buttons. She couldn't even write a letter or operate the computer effectively without extreme frustration. Now the bandages were much reduced, it represented a huge milestone. In the next couple of weeks she'd be able to start physiotherapy. Ben had warned her that the scarring would be quite extensive, though it seemed a small price to pay for stupidity. It was going to take another two months before she could even *think* of going back to work, and only if he was completely satisfied she was following orders. CJ felt like a naughty schoolgirl under his steady gaze, but she had to endure it weekly now.

"Focus on September for going back to work," he told her, "and not a moment before."

The novelty of being at home quickly wore off. It was surprising, therefore, that with spending so much time around the house, she hadn't realised the doll was missing.

*

"Where are you, you ugly little sod?" CJ scoured every cupboard and drawer, and under the sofa. With growing frustration she'd even looked in the freezer, lest, under the influence, she'd put it there. All searches turned up nothing. The doll was missing. Frustration turned to irritation and irritation to grim acceptance that it was one of those mysteries for the 'unsolved' file. It was probably in the same 'elephant's graveyard' where all the odd socks, pens, etc. go, only to turn up when least expected. The same place you *know* has been searched several times already.

"So, if I'm such a good medium," she studiously asked the parrot during a particularly boredom-filled afternoon, "why can't I find the damn thing? Look, I can tell what's going to happen to people – sometimes. I'm daft enough, sorry, *talented* enough ..." she spread her hands in a gesture of frustration, "talented enough to talk to dead folk and so far have avoided being put away. Why the hell can't I see where the blasted thing's gone?" She paced the room, stopping in front of the cage as if expecting a reply.

The parrot listened attentively, head on one side, maintaining a steady gaze. He had no answers, knowing when to be silent. At the end of any rant, he usually got a few nuts. He was motivated by food alone and what his bird brain could comprehend was that, when she spoke at that pitch, he must *not* squawk.

It was CJ's way of working things out; redefining her beliefs, her life. It'd always been so, this introspective questioning. It was her survival tool; her *other* face and far removed from the one she presented so confidently to the world.

This is what I am. Why me? Why now? The laughing extrovert often conceals a soft centre capable of being hurt deeply.

The bird remained silent, watching her steadily until the moment she pushed nuts through the bars. With a loud squawk, he grabbed one and, dancing on the perch, happily muttered to himself. CJ sat on the sofa, her feet on the coffee table, and yawned. She rested her head against the soft cushions and slipped into daydreams.

✱

"Would you like me to read a story, Cordelia?"

"No, Mama. The lady will read to me."

"No, I'll read. What is it to be tonight? Shall we read *Snow White* or *Cinderella*, perhaps?"

"No, the lady will read."

"Don't be so silly, Cordelia Jayne!" The reproachful look on her mother's face said "Liar!" Even though the word was never spoken, her expression said it clearly. She'd listen to the story whatever it was, cuddled against Mama's ample bosom as she told tales of witches and fairies in faraway lands; of elves, goblins and pretty gardens. After she'd fallen asleep, thumb in her mouth, the covers were tucked in around her. Mama kissed her gently on the brow and removed the thumb.

And the child dreamed of a beautiful lady with long golden hair and a pale green dress. The one who held her late into the night and told of witches, fairies and enchanted woodlands; CJ's hand rested on the soft satin of her gown as the lady told her it wasn't wrong to see things, for *all* children could.

There were neither reproachful looks nor harsh words as the quilt was settled gently around the sleeping child with her thumb in her mouth. At four years of age, all is well. All *should* be well.

✱

CJ opened her eyes. The parrot was crunching noisily, extracting kernels with a "tch tch" as he discarded them. Sleepily, she watched him for a few moments.

"But, I *am* different, aren't I, Gracie?" The parrot paused briefly on hearing his name before resuming his crunching. CJ smiled. She'd never gone down the route of experimentation with Ouija boards like some teenagers and hadn't even seen the inside of a Spiritualist church. She'd never needed to, assuming everyone was like herself. Children experiment when something is missing from their lives and, in CJ's life, nothing *was* missing.

144

"Was anything missing, Georgie?" she asked. He didn't answer, of course.

He'd once told her, in his inimitable style, that he didn't come to command.

"I'm not a bloody Alsatian tha knows! If tha *really* needs me, I'll be there. Just don't bloody yell."

"Where *do* you go, Georgie and what do you do there?" It was a question she'd asked many times. "And why did you attach yourself to me? I suppose you'd say we're only given what we need and not what we want, eh? Never refuse a gift or it'll be taken away."

What 'it' was exactly, she'd asked herself a thousand times over the years until acceptance finally came. It hadn't always been welcome – like with Jenny Dodd.

Jenny and CJ had grown up together, all through infant, junior and high school. She'd been the sort of friend you told your special secrets to; the sort of friendship that lasts forever. Except it didn't.

All the late-night giggling under the bedclothes with the 'sister' you always hoped you'd have, ended abruptly the day Jenny died without warning, without time to say 'goodbye' or even share a last hug. The car accident that'd taken Jenny from her family and friends was still raw, even after all those years. And, in her grief, the young CJ raved at Georgie.

"What's the use of a gift if it can't be used to stop things like this happening? Why have it if you can't use it?" She'd shrieked. "If I'd been better at it, I could have told her not to go that day. She was only 16, for pity's sake!" CJ had thrown herself on the bed and sobbed until she was hoarse.

Her guardian wouldn't speak. She knew he was there; she could smell that awful hair cream he used.

He watched as she wept, beating the pillow with her fists, demanding he comfort her and give her answers. He chose to stay silent allowing her work it out. She *had* to learn. Rules must be followed. It was for her own good.

Later, when she thought of Jenny, she realised there *had* been signs. On their last evening together there'd been the unmistakable scent of roses where none could possibly be. Later she'd come to recognise the smell as her own peculiar way of predicting death; the flowers on the way to heaven's gate.

"How can death smell so sweet, Georgie," she'd asked when finally he'd spoken to her again. She'd remember his answer forever.

"Accept it, CJ. For when we're all gone, only the flowers will remain."

*

The day CJ met Sam it was obvious to them both that the relationship was far more than a mere fling. As the weeks went by she knew there were things she must tell him because love – true love – is based on trust and there can *be* no secrets. She dreaded the moment wondering if he'd recoil in horror, or worse still, amusement before making excuses to leave. Maybe that'd be it. She'd never hear from him again, thinking her a deluded, screwy woman whose head was filled with crazy thoughts. Desperate not to ruin a promising relationship, CJ lay awake for nights worrying and rehearsing it in her head. It always ended badly with her blustering and his leaving without a backward glance. But she owed him the truth, this man with whom she was falling in love, and *he* had to know what he was getting.

*

They stood side by side, leaning on an old farm gate on the edge of a field of ripe corn. She told him everything, hardly pausing between sentences and nervously turning the gold bracelet on her arm as she spoke. She looked at the blue sky, with its summer cumulus clouds, and at the myriads of wild flowers that edged the field. She looked anywhere but his face, afraid to see traces of mockery or disappointment in those dark eyes.

She told him about Georgie, Jenny and the pretty lady in green. He neither laughed nor interrupted, watching her every movement. When at last she'd finished, he held out his hand.

146

She gave him hers and he pulled her towards him, taking her in his arms. His mouth found hers in a lingering kiss, his hands drawing her body closer.

"I love you, crazy lady," he whispered, his lips brushing her hair, breathing in her scent, his desire for her growing with every moment.

"You *believe* me?" She drew back, her face searching his for signs of mockery. There were none.

"Of course I believe you, CJ. I'd believe you if you told me the moon were made of paper. In my country things you call superstition are part of everyday life. Men disbelieve at their peril."

All the angst of the past few sleepless night floated away with his words.

Did she dare believe this was real? That this man understood? It was far from the reaction she'd expected. Her heart leapt. Yes, this *was* real. She wanted him to possess her and share her life with him.

He took her hands again. "Marry me, CJ, and let's grow old under that paper moon up there. Because if I'd only got one hour left, I'd want to spend it making sweet love to you." He tilted her chin and she looked into his eyes.

"Make love to me now, Sam."

He pulled her down on top of him and the promise was well and truly sealed amongst the rather flattened, but ripened, corn.

Sated, they lay in each other's arms.

"Do you ever see them?" asked Sam, carelessly chewing the end of a piece of straw. CJ sat up, her fingers tracing circles in the fine hair on his chest.

"Occasionally; mostly, I just hear them. I saw Georgie a couple of times some years ago. He's a wiry little man with a flat cap and a thin moustache, and smells of Brylcreem and pipe tobacco. He's from Yorkshire, and *very* straight-talking. I only hear him nowadays. I saw Jenny though, the night after she died. I'm sure Georgie brought her home to prove a point because I was so terribly angry at her passing. I woke and there she was sitting on my bed."

"I'd have been rigid with terror," said Sam.

"It wasn't like that. She wasn't ghostly or anything; not cold, grey or translucent. She was … well, she was Jenny. And we talked the way we always had. Then, I fell asleep and in the morning, I understood a lot more about gifts given in trust and why we can't influence the outcome of things. Only God can do that."

"Do you believe that it's God?" asked Sam.

"Yes, I think so, but it doesn't matter what name you give Him."

"Or Her?" Sam grinned broadly, picking a piece of straw from her hair.

"Or Her!" She grinned back. "I believe there's a higher power controlling all this." She gestured a circle. If left to our own devices, we humans would create chaos and anarchy within ten minutes. I learned something else, though."

"What's that?"

"That if a gift's given to a chosen person it can't simply be ignored or returned like a parcel. It has to be used, developed and passed on to our children."

"Oh," said Sam with a raised eyebrow, "we're having children, now, are we?" She found the gesture strangely sexy.

"Good grief, man! You've only just asked me to marry you."

"You didn't give me an answer."

"It's yes! A hundred times, yes!" She threw her arms around his neck.

Sam untangled himself and held her at arm's length. "There's just one proviso, though."

"Err … yes?"

"Georgie stays on the *outside* of our bedroom door!"

CJ threw back her head and laughed. "I'll tell him."

*

The memory of the cornfield brought CJ's soul-searching to an end and her mood lifted. She'd had her rant. There was a hand to heal without further need of boredom and self-pity.

The Land Rover pulled noisily into the drive and CJ met her husband at the door. "Sam, Sam, I've had enough of this lot." She waved her bandaged hand dismissively. "I've allowed boredom to creep in for far too long." She followed him as he walked into the kitchen to put away the shopping. "Sam, if I watch one more Jeremy Kyle Show I'll go insane! I have to *do* something."

He turned from the open fridge door and wagged a finger. "Oh, no! No going to work. The ban is still in place."

"Oh, I know. Not that. Cleaning, cooking – anything!"

"That bored, eh?"

"Sam, my teaching doll's disappeared. Will you help me look for it?"

"Why do you want it?" He stuffed plastic carrier bags into a drawer. "You're not going back for weeks yet." CJ paused and bit her lip, an odd look in her eyes.

Sam placed a hand on her shoulder, gently.

"What's the matter, babe?"

She looked uncomfortable, ran a hand through her hair and sat at the table, idly turning the bangle on her wrist.

"It *is* about work. I've never been away this long. I feel I'm losing my confidence a bit." Sam sat opposite.

"I'm sure people will tell you that it's normal after such an accident." He paused, thoughtfully, "CJ, is this about that wretched doll?"

"It's as if the thing's vaporised. I just don't understand it. I looked everywhere. It's even got my name written on its foot."

"Perhaps it left home," Sam quipped, to lighten the mood. "C'mon Gracie … say it. CJ's lost her dolly. CJ's lost her do …" He was silenced as a pair of slippers hit him.

"Don't you dare teach him anything else," yelled CJ as Sam deflected a flying cushion. It was bad enough the bird had somehow learned to shriek "Screw the Aussie bastards!" during the Ashes tour. Worse, he now considered it his party-piece whenever anyone came to visit. The only way to ensure the foul beak stayed shut was to cover the cage. The parrot probably thought that night was a three-times-a-day event.

"Seriously, though," said Sam, "by the time you've got the first day over, it'll be like you were never away." CJ nodded.

"Perhaps, I'm just being silly."

"Look," Sam continued, "I'm due loads of leave. Why don't we get away for a bit?" CJ brightened.

"Now, *that's* a great idea!"

"How about France?" said Sam, raising his eyebrows suddenly thinking of his family near Limoges. CJ frowned.

"I was thinking of somewhere a bit warmer," said CJ, leaning on one elbow. Sam thought for all of a second. A look of hope crossed his face.

"Australia? That's warm."

"What? After three months sick pay? Are you mad?" CJ huffed.

"Screw the Aussie bastards! Screw the Aussie bastards!" shrieked an excited voice. CJ glared at the occupant of the cage.

"It's France, then. I'll organise it. It'll give me something to do and a bit of purpose in life." The parrot squawked again. "Now get that damn bird's cover, for heaven's sake!"

Chapter 19

Shooting had become a regular feature in Mike's life. It seemed a long time since the seed of this hobby had been sown at a dinner party with friends. Now it'd become their habit to go a couple of times a week and sometimes more. It might have *started* as a joke, but now was a serious hobby.

Mike had only gone along to indulge his friend, saying he 'couldn't hit a barn door at ten paces'. To his utter astonishment, he discovered he was rather good at it. That was an understatement. He'd a natural aptitude for the sport.

At first, Mike had little idea how to even *hold* a rifle and certainly did not understand the mechanics of the thing, but he was a quick learner. With a little tuition, Mike was soon hitting the 25-metre target with ease. As the weeks went by, he was achieving scores to rival Joe's.

"Are you *sure* you haven't done this before?" Joe asked suspiciously.

Mike assured him he'd never held a rifle in his life, but was thoroughly enjoying the experience. Sensing a new member with a rare natural ability, there were always experienced chaps willing to pass on tips. Enthusiastic members were generous with both their time and teaching, and Mike was grateful for it. A friendly rivalry developed between the two friends that only served to ensure both improved; each constantly having to 'up their game'. Mike had a natural abhorrence of blood sports. He was a born-and-bred, card-carrying, devoted 'townie', to whom even a duck was considered a wild animal. But this sport was as far removed from hunting as it was possible to get. It was just as well as he'd never contemplate killing *any* creature. He couldn't even squash a spider, no matter how much Denise screamed; simply carrying it gently in his cupped hand to liberation outside. Mike was pleased that Joe hadn't exaggerated this point. The rabbits really *did* pause to feed beneath the targets, totally unconcerned by the loud cracks. In the history of the club, no one had ever hit one.

Dale Bank shooting range was housed in an old limestone quarry at least five miles from the nearest civilisation. Targets were set out in lines at 25 and 50 metres from the old, ex-army, wooden hut from which the members shot. Having the benefit of a long, raised veranda, it afforded shelter in inclement weather. This was a year-round sport, and inside was a well-stocked bar and social club.

As with golfers and cricketers, the members liked to get together after an afternoon's sport to chat about whatever men do. Solitude and target shooting are far removed from each other. Contrary to popular belief, in the wake of tragedies such as Hungerford and Columbine High School, competitive marksmen are rarely loners. Nor do members of approved and well-regulated gun clubs become homicidal maniacs with a small arsenal tucked inside their jackets. What people believe is often a different matter.

The members consisted mainly of young to late-middle-aged men and a couple of women, indulging in a hobby requiring exceptional skill and discipline. Not one harboured a desire to kill or maim anyone or anything. The police checks were rigorous to say the least, and the legal requirements and safeguards extensive. The penalties for any slight infringement were hefty and the club would have been disbanded, with members losing both gun licences and weapons.

There was the added element of self-policing. It was in everyone's interest to weed-out anyone showing an unhealthy fascination with either guns or the sport. The police would quickly have been made aware of anyone suspected of having a motive other than sport. Lying flat on your belly in often freezing temperatures, trying to hit a target 50 metres away, is surely where any madness lies.

And Joe and Mike loved every second of it, having both achieved competition standard within six months.

"Not bad for a chap whose only weapon in the past was a water pistol," said Mike on the way home one evening, "and I wasn't on target with that."

The end of the summer saw them shooting 2:2 rifles for the county with high hopes of being selected for Bisley the following summer. Joe was delighted, gloating without apology.

"We're going to make the national championships in less than a year, mate," he told Mike. "How cool is that? It must be something of a bloody record."

Back home, Eleanor shared Joe's pride at their success. She was glad he'd something to do apart from work. Although not choosing to participate herself, she often accompanied them to local competitions. When she'd had enough, she went shopping. Eleanor always did have a low boredom threshold.

It was a completely different matter where Denise was concerned. She'd a deep hatred of guns and all they represented. The first outburst of dissent at the dinner table was followed, in time, by a grim acceptance, of sorts. It was *Mike's* hobby and she'd no wish to share it, and was not even willing to discuss the subject further. Whenever it came up in conversation, she'd noticeably become fearful and anxious to the extent that it'd become a taboo subject. Guns were dangerous and no one would convince her otherwise. She preferred to think of it as 'the boys off playing' and dismiss it from her mind. The others had little choice but to accept it.

It was, however, this very subject that was to cause the worst row she and Mike ever had; one that was to mark the beginning of the end.

*

At their last quarterly meeting, the shooting committee decided it was time for a social event. On November 5th there was to be a bonfire extravaganza with fireworks for families and friends. It would be preceded by a display of target shooting by the members under floodlights and, later, a barbeque and disco for the children. There'd been no shortage of volunteers to help, with everyone eager to make the night a success.

For Mike, there'd been just one problem. Denise refused point-blank to go. He pleaded with her, spreading his hands in exasperation and, when that failed, he got angry. It degenerated into a row with them both yelling at each other.

"For God's sake, why, Denise?" he shouted, "Ellie's going. Why can't you join in? You don't even have to watch the bloody shooting if you don't want to. Stay in the hut with your fingers in your ears." She waved him away with a gesture of irritation. He wasn't finished, but lowered his voice. "Come later then, for the food and a dance, but please don't humiliate me by staying away."

Denise turned, angrily, her face contorted. "It's nothing whatever to do with humiliation, Mike, and you know it. I *can't* come. Why can't you see that?"

"What do you mean, you *can't* come? Ellie's coming. She's making the effort *and* she's just had twins, for Christ's sake!" He stared hard into her face with its uncompromising stare, her lips set in a thin, determined line. He was *really* angry. Denise's red face was inches from his.

"For fuck's sake! You won't even do it for me, will you? You're a selfish bitch, Denise." The words were spat out from between clenched teeth.

She froze. He'd never sworn at her like that before – never! He swore, of course, but never *at* her. She saw the venom in his eyes as he said it. Catching her breath, Denise slowly turned her back and folded her arms. Mike grabbed her shoulders and forcefully turned her to face him, her hands instinctively coming up to push him away. His strong hands held her firmly.

"Listen, woman, I've had to put up with your crazy behaviour for long enough." The low tone of his voice was threatening as he held her rigidly in a grip that hurt and she winced. Her eyes widened in shock.

"What do you mean?" she demanded, struggling in his grasp. He let her go and she staggered, falling to her knees, grabbing the sofa for support.

"Well, since you ask …" Mike was angrier than he could ever remember, but no longer cared. "Since you ask …" he said again, "like buying stuff and not knowing, like funny old ladies who didn't exist and that other bizarre crap that's was probably all in your mind."

"What do you mean, 'didn't exist'? Are you saying I made the whole thing up?"

"Denise, listen to me. I went to that shopping centre and I went to the café you said you were in. It was only a few days after, but no one remembered seeing *any* strange old lady. The waitress remembered you. She said it was *you* who was behaving oddly. She said you sat alone at a table in the corner and you spoke to no one. You were alone, Denise, talking to yourself. There *was* no woman with a pram and no old lady. So I decided to ask around, as she'd told you she was often there – or so you said. Several older shopkeepers remembered her, and her name was Alice, just as you'd described, and I was so relieved.

"There you see, I told the truth," Denise cried, jumping to her feet again. How can you say it was all in my mind after that?"

"Because, Denise," he said, his voice calm," there was no way you could have seen her on that day because Alice Arbourthorne died 20 years ago!" Denise stared, confused, and slowly to the floor.

Mike knelt beside her. She shrugged off his proffered hand. Suddenly, all he wanted was to put some distance between them for fear he'd shake her until her teeth rattled. He rose and walked to the window to stare out, leaning on the wall.

Denise lay on the carpet, sobbing with rage. "I'm not crazy, you … swine!" Mike turned and looked at her with pity, unable to find the words to end this. He moved to kneel beside her again in an act of pacification, his voice soft and pleading.

"You must see, Denise, during these last couple of years your behaviour has been … well, strange to say the least, love." He spread his hands, helplessly. "But when the twins were born, I thought you seemed so much better … happier." She fixed him with a glare of contempt.

"So, I wasn't good enough the way I was before?" Her face was contorted and red with barely controlled anger.

"No," said Mike, desperately. "I didn't say that. But it's as though you'd a new purpose in life. Those babies have been good for you … for *us*." He reached out again and tentatively touched his wife's arm, his eyes pleading. He paused. "Please come, Den. Ellie's got a babysitter. It'll be like old times; the four of us together again." Denise stared at the floor for a few moments, breathing hard.

"And *who's* going to look after the babies?" The tone was demanding. Mike's exasperation returned. Irritated he put a hand to his brow.

"I don't know! Her mother, I expect. Maybe Joe's cousin. I've really no idea."

"And, have these people looked after them before?" Denise continued to demand. "Or don't you know that either?"

"For God's sake, Denise, I'm sure Ellie knows what she's doing. It's not your problem. Look, are you coming or not?" Her eyes locked on to his like a deadly weapon on target as she answered slowly and quietly.

"No. I won't. It can *never* be like it used to. Why don't you understand that? You go, because I'm not coming. I'll care for the babies and protect them whilst you're off enjoying yourselves."

Mike sat back on his heels and looked at her curiously. "Why on earth should they need protecting?"

"Because they do! You could never understand." There was a faraway look in her sad eyes that disturbed him. She didn't look like his Denise any more. Mike told himself he was just a man and didn't understand any of it. He closed his eyes.

"I'm trying, Denise. God knows I'm trying!" He voice degenerated into a strangled sob.

"I'll keep them safe from harm." The words that came from her mouth were like a chant, not like her voice either. Mike swallowed hard.

Oh God! Am I imagining things now? "Look Denise, all that's required is you feed and change them, give them a bit of a cuddle and they'll sleep – end of story." He drew an imaginary line in the air to emphasise the last part.

"You can't possibly understand." She stared sadly into the distance.

"What the hell are you going on about? Look, you silly woman, they're not *your* babies!"

Denise gave a cry like a wounded animal, the colour draining from her face. Without warning, she drew back her hand and slapped his face hard. Shocked, beyond reason, Mike recoiled, his hand going to his cheek, fighting the instinct to strike her back.

"You're bloody insane." The words spat out as he rose and left the room, leaving the door quivering on its hinges; his pride hurt, more than anything else.

Chapter 20

Mike lay on the bed in the spare room for what seemed like hours, turning events over in his mind and trying to make sense of it all.

It's happening again. He sat up on the edge of the bed, head in hands, staring at the floor. *Whatever was wrong has returned to claim her sanity again.* At that moment, Mike was uncertain whether or not he could go through it again. He took off his shirt and lay down, pulling the quilt over his head, but sleep wouldn't come.

Through the wall he heard Denise sobbing quietly. He couldn't – he wouldn't – go to her. Not this time, even though it was the saddest, most heart-wrenching sound he'd ever heard.

Mike knew there were things he must do. He'd try a new way of handling it this time. God knows, all the love and tolerance in the world hadn't worked; maybe tough love was the only way forward. For if this was some odd form of seasonal affective disorder, it would all begin again soon. The weight loss and the black moods would start and, with the coming of shorter hours of daylight, melancholy and poor memory. And he knew that it would be a very long winter for them both.

*

An owl hooted in a nearby tree. The creature halted briefly and turned its head towards the sound. Although the night was still and moonless, it could see well enough; its eyes accustomed to the dark. Its sensitive ears were tuned to the merest movement unheard by the range of any human ear. It crouched, keeping vigil in the stillness, waiting for any miniscule movement of grass or earth. Tonight it was hunting in the practised way learned from its mother and generations of mothers before her.

Soon, when the opportunity arose, it would capture and eat its kill. On other nights, after the chase, it may taunt its prey, creating terror for pleasure alone, before killing and discarding the corpse, but tonight it would kill swiftly and eat. The shrew provided only a morsel, but sated the creature's blood-lust for the moment. Moving stealthily around the lake, it lay concealed in the long rye grass. A barn owl swooped low over the water, its ghostly, silent form hunting also. The creature looked out through the tussocks of stiff grass to the island where ducks and coots roosted safely. They were beyond the reach of the hungry vixen that broke cover to skirt the water's edge. She paused briefly some ten feet away to investigate a rubbish bin, her sleek, red body taut as she stretched, then, finding nothing, prepared to leave. She stopped suddenly, her nose raised, sniffing the still air as she caught scent of the creature and noted its presence before slinking away.

He watched her go. There'd be no meal here for him tonight. The vixen's musk-trail would alert all the small foraging creatures sending them scurrying back to their burrows. His efforts thwarted, he rose and headed away from the lake, and turned for home.

Then, he heard it: the sound like a sudden rippling breeze disturbing the otherwise still air. The fur on his back stood up; his senses were alert, ears pricked. He flattened his body to the ground and watched silently.

The low hum came from the direction of the lake, becoming louder, vibrating as it approached. The pitch rose to a whine hurting his sensitive ears, the darkness deepening as it came closer. It was nearly upon him; the sound settling to a low menacing growl.

Like a bullet, he broke cover and ran. It pursued his flight, matching his speed. Black shadows within shadows, with a groaning, throbbing core, threatened to overtake him as he fled through the night. Adrenaline fuelled, he reached the gate and leapt, clearing it easily before bolting up the path. He crossed the lawn in several bounds then cowered, dropping his body flat against the soft, damp grass. The black shadow stood between him and the door. It pulsated, emitting another low growl of warning. He'd reached home, but there was no way in. The shape moved towards him exuding pure evil.

He rose on his haunches and prepared to fight to the death, rocking his hips from side to side. He stared into the very depths of the black mass before him with wide staring eyes, lips peeled back in a ferocious snarl of white, pointed teeth.

The thing rose above his head, passing over him before turning to disappear as it seeped into the very fabric of the house. Bunbury's house; the house he now couldn't enter to watch and wait.

* *

The mechanics of life went on as before. Rows of long duration are hard to sustain, but, although mealtimes remained rather silent affairs, a kind of tolerance developed between Denise and Mike. However, in unguarded moments, the hurt showed in both their faces. Too many things had been said that couldn't be retracted.

Trust had been destroyed, and, as Mike would later remark to Joe, "Trust's like virginity – once it's gone, it's gone." It was probably pride that made him stick to his plan, as he ignored her weight loss, moods and supposed SAD. The nights were getting longer, the hours of daylight fewer each day. And in the long nights he'd lie awake wishing he felt like making love to her. Facing the wall, he lamented that it was going to be a very long winter until the sun, once again, made all the bad dreams go away.

For her part, Denise was still angry and the feeling *wouldn't* go away. Although they'd returned to sleeping in the same bed, she didn't crave contact with his body, sleeping or waking. She accepted with grim determination that it was to be endured – this horror – and the ray of hope was that, with the coming of spring's warmth, it would stop. Just like the last time, and the time before that.

161

Bonfire night saw Denise happily alone with the babies. Eleanor had taken some persuading that she wasn't just being a martyr, but still felt a bit selfish for allowing her to stay whilst they all went out. Mike put in a final word.

"Just let her do it, Ellie. It's just Auntie Den doing what she does best." Insults were no longer traded, hurt was less and a kind of apathy had set in.

As soon as the three of them left, Denise crept upstairs to the nursery. The babies were now in adjoining cots, but their heads still turned towards each other whenever they slept. Pictures of Pooh Bear and Tigger looked down from the pale, primrose walls. Denise knelt on an orange rug that lay between the cots, her face level with theirs.

How they're growing! She smiled gently, stroking Shaun's outstretched fingers, which seemed to reach out through the cot's rails for his sister. They were more active now and not lying still like new-borns. The hair on the backs of their little heads had begun to rub off and the colour was changing. From the hue of ripe corn at birth, his had darkened. Hers was lighter and fitted like a soft, downy cap. Marianne pursed her lips in sleep; a rather petulant pout, endearing somehow.

For ten, perhaps 15 minutes, Denise knelt gazing at them, thinking how addictive this new pastime was and revelling in its pleasure. The curtains began to waft as a breeze blew up. Rising, she closed the window as the first splashes of drizzle hit the pane. For a few minutes she stood looking out over the garden at Joe's newly installed solar lights along the path.

How annoying. I hope it doesn't spoil the fireworks.

The tall poplars at the foot of the long garden began to sway gently, their last remaining leaves dancing in the perpetual motion that comes with winter's approach. The moon shone intermittently as rain clouds crossed it in the ever-darkening sky. Briefly, the fish pond was illuminated by a shaft of light and, beyond it, the rose pergola.

That pond will have to be filled in before the two of them start walking, or ...

A sharp pain shot across her eyes, vision crazily zig-zagging. Denise gasped and pressed her fingertips to her temples.

"Oh, God!" she muttered under her breath. Stepping back, she closed her eyes for a moment and, rocking on her heels, the pain subsided. "Phew." The room began to spin and she grabbed the side of Marianne's cot for support, staring down and holding her breath.

Mist rose from the dark pool she now stared into. It was no longer the safe nursery with its pale walls and colourful posters, but quite a different place. In the cot that once held a child, lay water, menacing and dark, and emanating from it was the fetid stench of decay. Unable to believe what she was seeing and paralysed with fear, Denise could only stare, compelled to watch. A shape appeared from below the dank surface. It rose, limbs floating upwards in a delicate dance. There was a face with wide, sightless eyes and lips open as if in a final cry. She caught her breath at last – a huge gasp of air and shock as she stared into the face of a drowned child no more than a couple of years old.

"Marianne!" Denise found her voice and shrieked, grasping at the form in the water, its fair baby curls encrusted with mud and weed. Desperately, she struggled to free the cot side as the room started to spin again, colours engaged in a crazy dance.

Then, she fainted.

*

A thudding sound like the wheels of a train filled her head. It throbbed mercilessly, as did her whole body. She rolled over to grasp the sides of Marianne's cot, pulling herself up, consciousness returning and with it those last horrifying images. She blinked.

In their cots the infants were fast asleep, soft blankets tucked around their little bodies. Denise sank to the floor, her back resting against the cot side. Her heart pounded as though it'd burst as she tried to slow her breathing to regain some sort of control.

Oh my God! What's happening to me? Is this what it's come to when the mere sight of a pond gives me visions of drowning? She shivered, pulling her cardigan up around her neck and waiting for some semblance of normality to return. When it did, Denise went downstairs and searched her bag for the tablets she kept for emergencies. She took two and lay down on the sofa wishing she'd gone to the party with the others.

As the sedatives took over, calmness returned and, with it, rational thought.

This is ridiculous! It can't be anything more than a panic attack. I've always had an overactive imagination; my English teacher said it time and time again! I'm not allowing this damn thing to beat me or make the whole thing more important than it is. Firmly, she remonstrated with herself, asking why she hadn't put aside her fear of guns and gone – for Mike's sake. She'd been incredibly selfish and stubborn, too. If she'd gone, maybe all the rows would've been averted and prevented their marriage from slipping further towards oblivion.

I wonder what sort of time the three of them are having. I bet the fireworks are wonderful. She rested her head on a cushion and put her feet up on the deep upholstery of the brown leather sofa. *This is all crazy! I've got to start again with Mike. It can be like it was before. I'll make it like it was, because nothing's worth throwing away so many good years of marriage. After all, Mike's my future.*

Her eyelids fluttered and closed as the sedatives took effect, and she drifted into a deep, dreamless sleep.

*

Mike and Joe were pleased with themselves having shot near-perfect scores on the exhibition range. Ellie added to the congratulations with a bit of back-slapping amid the grins and handshaking. She shook her head at the speed of how the pair was learning to love the limelight. They'd qualified easily for the national championships at Bisley next summer – though Joe was aiming higher still. *He'd* set his sights on a gold medal at the next Olympics!

Beaming with pride, he handed Ellie a drink. She shivered. "I'm glad they lit the bonfire. I was getting cold out there and the wind seems to be getting up a bit. It looks as though it might rain. I hope not."

Mike unfastened the straps of his leather shooting jacket. "It won't matter after the first couple of drinks," he said raising his glass. "Cheers. This *was* a great idea, wasn't it?" The others nodded and drank.

"If you're both off to Bisley for a couple of weeks next summer," began Ellie, "then I don't expect you'd mind if us girls went somewhere warm." She looked from one to the other.

"You mean you're not coming to cheer us on?" asked Joe, scowling a little.

"I don't mind you boys going off and indulging your toy-soldier dream, at all," said Ellie, "but I can't imagine Denise enjoying anything less. So, I think we'll go off to a Greek island somewhere and take *your* children to play in the sand." She shot Joe an enquiring look.

"Fine. I don't have a problem with any of that. How about you, Mike?"

"Great idea. It'll do you good." He smirked at Joe, the words 'freedom' and 'beer' crossing both their minds simultaneously. Ellie smiled, thinking how predictable the male species was.

Indoors, the party was in full swing. The fireworks were wonderful and the rain held off until just after the last rocket exploded in a hail of blue and red shooting stars to the "oohhhs" and "aahhhs" of the crowd. Joe handed his wife her third hot dog with raised eyebrows.

"Well?" she said with a petulant look, "I'm breastfeeding and I need the calories." The men knew better than to argue with a hormone-fuelled new mother. Joe spread another forkful of fried onions on his hamburger and shoved it into his mouth, struggling to speak.

"I need the calories too; no particular reason!" Mike grinned. Two pints were helping him ignore the fact that his wife wasn't with him. Ellie finished her meal and, putting down her plate, rummaged in her tote bag.

"Boys, I think I'll just check if all's well at home." Joe scowled.

"I wondered how long it'd be. Oh, Ellie, Den can manage. She's in her element. If there'd been a problem, we'd have heard. She'd be on the phone by now. Stop worrying."

"Well, I'm going to ring anyway," said Ellie, finally retrieving her phone from the overstuffed bag. Joe caught Mike's expression, which told him not to argue further. He gestured toward the bar and the two sloped off to get another couple of pints. Ellie hit the pre-set button on her phone.

Chapter 21

Denise awoke with a start. She sat up quickly and wiped beads of perspiration from her brow – her hair damp with it. She knew it wasn't another nightmare; in fact, she hadn't dreamed at all. A quick glance at the mantle clock said she'd only been asleep a mere 15 minutes, but her head was thumping again, with a noise that seemed to come from within.

Grasping the arm of the couch, she struggled to her feet, eyes still heavy with sleep and the confusion that comes with waking suddenly. She shook her head to clear it, but still the noise was bouncing off the walls of the room. Then, as clarity of thought returned, she realised. It was the babies – the babies were screaming with an urgent intensity she hadn't heard before.

She leapt from the sofa, and ran into the hall and up the stairs, taking them two at a time in her anxiety to see what was wrong. At the top, she punched the landing light switch. The bulb flashed briefly and popped. Feeling her way in the dark, she found the knob of the nursery door. It wouldn't turn. She pushed harder, rattling it to no avail as the infants' screams filled her head. Panic-stricken, Denise put all her weight behind a shoulder-charge to the door to no avail, only succeeding in hurting her arm.

"Oh my God!" she said aloud, "what the hell …?" Frightened, she felt her way back along the landing and downstairs to the light switch at the bottom, realising a fuse must have blown. Stumbling over obstacles, she made her way to the kitchen. Joe kept a torch under the sink; she was sure of it. Fumbling, she knocked over the soap powder, granules spreading everywhere, before her hand found what she was looking for. With a sigh of relief she pressed the button. A dim shaft of light struggled into the gloomy room from an obviously low battery.

"Why can't men ever maintain things?" She muttered furiously, banging the thing on the work surface. The beam improved just enough to light her way back up the stairs to where the screaming had reached a deafening pitch.

"Right," she said forcefully, and grabbing the door knob put her entire body weight behind one last, concerted shove.

The door opened easily and the forced momentum propelled her across the room. She hit the far-window wall and fell down, banging her head hard on the corner of a small chest of drawers. Shocked, Denise lay on the floor between the cots, panting, tears running down her cheeks.

With a groan, she clutched at her temple; fingers becoming wet at once with warm stickiness from a deep cut. She must get up. Confused and disorientated, she felt around for the torch, which had fallen from her hand in her flight across the room. A sudden rush of warmth flowed down the side of her face and a wave of nausea overcame her. Denise frantically felt for something solid. She found the torch, which had rolled under the radiator by the window, its beam barely a glow now. Angrily, she threw it aside, finding the wooden bars of one of the cots.

Grasping them, she tried to stand, dizziness almost overwhelming her as a fresh wave of screaming came from the respective cots. Fighting the pain in her head, she struggled to lower the side; aware blood was dripping from her chin into the cot.

With a supreme effort she scooped one shrieking infant up into her arms and turned to retrieve the other. The room spun. Knowing she couldn't make it downstairs with both squirming in her arms whilst needing a free hand to steady herself, she placed Shaun gently on the carpet near the door.

"Good boy, now just lie there a second."

Holding Marianne close, Denise sat on the top stair and shuffled down on her bottom. No longer screaming, Shaun could be heard sucking his fingers noisily. On her knees, Denise made slow progress into the lounge. The glowing embers from the fire provided just enough light for her to reach the settee.

I must get to the phone and call for help. Ring the others. Ellie will certainly have her mobile. Blood still dripped from her head wound as she settled Marianne on the sofa between two cushions. After a brief respite from bobbing downstairs, the baby resumed her screaming; the noise unbearable to Denise's throbbing head. One hand reached out instinctively to caress the child, as another wave of vertigo caused her to sway.

"Oh, no! Please don't cry, Marianne." She begged, her voice failing. "I don't like it when you cry. I don't know what to do for you." A rocket burst over the house and lights flashed in front of her eyes.

The curtains! Open the curtains!

Holding onto the furniture for support, she threw them back. Intermittently, light from fireworks lit the room.

"Oh, Marianne, why didn't I think of that before?" She knelt and picked up the infant who nuzzled against her, mouth searching for food.

A deeper darkness filled the room. Denise looked slowly towards the ceiling, the child on her shoulder. The blackness above her head began to swirl, spreading outwards down the walls like a creeping fog. Her eyes widened in horror as she stared into the jet-black eye of its core. She clutched the infant tighter, a scream dying in her throat, and she cowered. Another rocket burst outside, filling the room with light. Seizing the moment, Denise got to her feet and ran with the infant clutched to her chest, making for the far corner of the room where she knew the phone was.

Her hand was almost on the receiver when she heard it: a menacing sound like the low growl of a hunting animal. Terrified, yet compelled to look, she slowly turned her head. A huge, black mass towered over her, pulsating evil. It was hunting her; its fetid breath so near her face she wanted to retch. Icy coldness pervaded the room and she clutched the child even closer, at last finding her voice, drawing herself up to face it, whatever it was, and she screamed.

"Don't come near this child! In the name of God you shall not harm this child. You won't have her! Take me instead." She stared into the eye that formed in the centre of the black, swirling mass above, challenging it with her diminutive frame as she prepared to face it. There was a terrifying roar as the wind blew through the room like a hurricane, so strong she feared the clothing would be torn from her body, but she held firm.

Barely able to breathe, her arms tightly encircling the infant, she prayed, as a crackling around her feet seemed to lick unseen flames upward from the floor to claim her. She must stay still no longer. It was too powerful. Courage deserted her and she ran, pain overtaken by sheer terror and the will to survive. Running for the door, she upended the occasional table with its flower arrangement. The crystal shattered as the vase hit the hearth, water and roses spilling onto the carpet. A half-drunk mug of cold coffee spread an ugly stain on the thick, beige pile.

Stumbling into the door frame, she almost dropped Marianne, her screams mingling with the infant's own. An angry bruise formed on Denise's arm where she'd hit the woodwork on her flight from the room. Blood dripped again where the door catch caught her flesh. Slamming the door behind her, she held onto the handle frantically, expecting at any moment it would be wrenched from her grasp. But the door remained closed.

Terrified now and unsure what to do, she realised the only phone was in the room she'd just left. In panic, she ran to the kitchen. She *had* to get the children away from the house and whatever was occupying it. Frantically, she headed for the back door.

The sudden realisation that Shaun was still upstairs stopped her dead in her tracks. He was alone and unprotected. At the mercy of whatever that thing was! Marianne gave a howl.

Oh, God. I have to stop her crying. Denise fled back through the kitchen and up the stairs in the darkness. Marianne continued to scream. The crying would surely allow that thing to find them. What was left of her reasoning was now focused on getting to Shaun. Opening the cupboard door on the landing, she placed Marianne inside, laying her on a pile of blankets and towels. She shut the door quietly, hoping it would muffle her screams.

Running to the bedroom, she grabbed Shaun, falling twice in the process, her shins now bruised and battered. The child protested with a sob and she slipped down the last few stairs to land in a heap at the bottom. Breathing hard and hauling herself clumsily to her feet, she ran for the door expecting to be cut down in her tracks at any moment.

She reached the car, threw open the driver's door and, with Shaun in the passenger foot-well, fumbled in her jeans' pocket for the key. The engine started on the third attempt and she drove away like the hounds of hell were after her. She must get away from that house – far away.

On his blanket beneath the dashboard, little Shaun lay still. In her dread and disorientation, it hadn't occurred to Denise that she'd left the other baby behind.

*

"There's no reply. Joe, …" Ellie called above the noise of the packed bar. "There's no reply from the house!" There was deep concern on her face now. The first couple of times, she'd thought Denise was probably in the toilet or making a cup of coffee, but now … "Joe, Mike! There's something wrong. I know there is!"

The boys had consumed a few beers by now and with that'd come overconfidence. Ellie knew that. Joe's speech was slurring slightly as he put his arm around his wife's shoulders. "She'll be feeding them, most probably. Now, *stop* worrying."

Mike put down his glass. "Den will be totally wrapped up in whatever she's doing," he added. "Looking after the two of them is what she likes to do best. She probably won't even have *heard* the phone," he nodded, with a note of irony. "You know Denise, nothing else exists."

Half an hour and several phone calls later, Ellie was practically dragging them to the car; saying if they didn't come, she'd leave on her own. The mood changed dramatically the moment they drew up outside the house. It was no longer 'the woman twittering on about nothing'.

Denise's car was gone and the house was in darkness. The men exchanged perturbed glances as they got out of the car, sobering up instantly as Ellie rushed up the path. Halfway, she stopped dead and gave a strangled cry, not taking her eyes from the open front door; her mother's instinct saying something was *very* wrong. The door swung on its hinges, back and forth in the wind. She shouted, blind panic evident in her voice.

"Joe! The door's open!" She gasped, fear etched on her features. Rushing inside, Ellie called insistently. "Denise … Denise, where are you?" In her wake came the two men. Joe flicked the light switch by the front door on and off.

"No lights." He went to the under-stairs cupboard where the fuse box was and pressed the reset on the trip switches. The lights came on immediately. Ellie, her recent surgery forgotten, was already at the top of the stairs breathing heavily. She threw open the door of the nursery.

A long, protracted scream brought the men to her side within seconds. Fighting her way past them she ran to the other bedrooms with renewed sobs of horror – finding nothing. Throwing open the wardrobe doors, she rummaged through shoes and other fallen detritus as if expecting her children to be hidden there, her voice fast becoming a series of strangled sobs.

"My babies, Joe. They're gone!" she screamed "Where are they? Where …?" She sank to the floor between the cribs clutching the bars, staring into the emptiness that'd once held her infants. Joe knelt, facing his wife, and took her gently by the shoulders.

"Ellie … Ellie, listen. There *has* to be some rational explanation for this. People just don't disappear." He looked into her red-rimmed, frightened eyes. "They're with Den, Ellie, wherever they are. So you know as well as I do they'll be safe." Ellie plucked at the cot blankets as though the babies were somehow hidden beneath them. It was the action of a desperate woman, almost deranged with worry.

Mike had done a quick search downstairs for Denise, as soon as the lights came on, before he'd heard Ellie scream. He'd taken in the devastation in the lounge with growing fear.

"Joe," he said softly and indicated with his finger that they should go downstairs. Ellie's head whipped around, her senses sharpened by terror.

"What? What is it? What have you found for God's sake, Mike?" Up on her feet again, she was already pushing past the men to get downstairs, defying all Joe's attempts to grab her flailing limbs. They reached the lounge. Ellie stared at the broken glass, overturned coffee table and the scattered roses.

"Marianne … Shaun …" she whimpered, "Mari …" then sank to the floor curling into the foetal position, rocking and sobbing, the blood vessels at her temples bulging.

Mike strode purposefully across the room. "Don't touch anything, Joe. I'm calling the police."

*

The police came quickly as they always do when children are involved and a doctor summoned. Joe carried Ellie upstairs to the bedroom where she lay on her side clutching Marianne's pink toy rabbit beneath her chin. No longer hysterical, she stared at the wall, silent tears falling onto its fur.

The family doctor drew yellow liquid into a syringe and, with a practised flick, expelled the air from the needle. There was a soft knock at the bedroom door and he paused.

"Come in."

A young WPC stepped quietly into the room holding a bundle. "Eleanor," she began her voice gentle. "I found this nice bit of medicine hidden in the cupboard. It looks as if she's just waking up." She held out the bundle of blankets. Ellie let out the primal scream of a mother protecting its young and froze.

"Is she …?"

"It's okay, Eleanor. Your baby girl's fine."

The doctor discarded the syringe safely, putting it in a sharps container, as Ellie proceeded to examine every inch of her child, then held her close as though she'd never let go again. Tears of relief ran freely down her cheeks, tempered with the knowledge her other child was still missing.

Downstairs, the questions went on forever; the investigative process was in full-swing. Although the police adopted a softly, softly approach, nothing could ever reassure the parents of a missing child. No amount of tea and sympathy, or the quoting of statistics could stop Ellie believing anything other than that her child was dead. As the hours went by, it became unbearable, with the house designated a crime scene and all that goes with it.

When the forensic team finally finished in the room, Mike sat in the chimney corner, a cold mug of tea at his elbow. Deep in thought and misery, his head rested in his hands. Everyone seemed to have forgotten *his* wife was missing too. Taking a deep, quivering breath, he let it out slowly. He shook his head, eyes burning, trying to dispel the nagging feeling deep in his soul that somehow Denise was at the centre of all this chaos.

Chapter 22

Sergeant Glyn Franks – 'Franksie' to just about everyone who knew him – was praying for a peaceful shift. His arthritis, troublesome of late, was giving him gip tonight.

"It's old age and poverty, lad!" Mary said before he left the house and Glyn laughed it off in the way he always did, not wishing to moan. But it was damp nights like this, far too many of them pounding the beat, that made it worse.

"It's the job, Mary, luv," he'd replied patiently for the umpteenth time.

And it *was* the job – his job: keeping his beady eyes on what the local villains were up to instead of doing what any sensible 55-year-old *should* have been doing – staying at home, tucked up in a warm, cosy bed with a good woman.

Glyn could have retired years ago; he knew that. He'd done his service and his pension was assured. After all, Mary was forever nagging him to finish. Soon, he'd give in.

For donkey's years, her sister in Australia had been inviting them to go and stay for a couple of months. Mary told him she'd book seats on a jumbo jet the very moment he – "You awkward, old bugger, Franksie!" – decided to call it a day. She'd done her service, too, over the years she reckoned, alongside her husband as a wife!

Glyn knew it was true and he couldn't have *had* a better one. She'd taken him on when she was just 17, and pregnant, but they didn't speak of that. Folk didn't in those days. They just got married quickly and said t' child was premature.

Glyn sat down on a park bench, chuckling to himself.

By God! You wouldn't get away wi' it now. Folk aren't so gullible and they have scans these days, even before t' kid's barely conceived!

But they'd managed to fool everyone just enough to avoid him getting a pasting from her father. Bending forward, he rubbed his bad knee and sighed.

"How did I get into this game? And why am I still doing nights at my age?"

At 16, Glyn followed his dad 'down t' pit', as did most Yorkshire lads in those days. As soon as he set foot in the cage on that first day, he hated it. He'd never been afraid of hard graft. Yorkshire folk were like that.

But it was donkey work. *Up to your waist in water for twelve hours a day. Lying on a conveyer on your belly just to get to the face and through a murky tunnel not much wider than you.* He patted his ample stomach and chuckled. *You'd be struggling to get through now, Glyn, lad! No human being should have to go through that for the purpose of keeping others warm and the wheels of sodding industry turning.*

Mercifully, and with hindsight it was a mercy, his career in the darkness and muck was halted by a snapped coal-cutting chain. It whipped across the rail track, killing two of his mates and left him lying in a pool of blood, barely alive. The metal chain inflicted a deep wound across his lower back taking out one of his kidneys. That would've been it had it not been for the skill of the doctors in Sheffield where he'd been taken.

Glyn recovered slowly but surely and, with the same Yorkshire, self-deprecating resilience, chose not to talk much about *that* either. Six months after the accident and fully recovered, he knew he was never going down that pit again and joined the police force as a 'bobby'.

Mary was so proud from the first time she saw him in uniform. That pride continued, never sending him out looking less than perfect. He stuck out a foot and looked at his boots, polished until you could see your face in them.

You're still fussing over the details, Mary, after all these years.

He loved her more than ever. She'd put on a bit of weight over the years, of course, but so had he. Glyn patted his stomach again at the memory of all her lovely hotpots and meat-and-potato pies. He licked his lips in anticipation, wondering what was in his lunchbox tonight. His father said if a woman could cook, a bloke couldn't go far wrong. He'd never doubted they'd grow old together, greying and slower of movement maybe, but still blissfully happy – he and his Mary.

A flash in the darkening sky brought him quickly out of his reverie. A rocket shot skyward, exploding in a hail of red stars. He watched until the last one fell to earth and disappeared, then, with a final rub at his knee, got up and continued on his beat.

It'll be quiet tonight. Bonfire night always is. Everyone will be out enjoying themselves and eating far too much to bother with making mischief. The park was quiet too and a stroll through it would give him plenty of time for reflection.

Glyn loved his beat. He was what he wanted to be: a jobbing copper who still believed there was a place for the old-fashioned way of policing. If you *talked* to people and showed respect, they'd respect you too. It worked most of the time! He'd had his share of 'collars' and dealing with all the local villains. Times were changing, though, and he missed not being able to dispense 'instant justice'. It wasn't allowed to give a cheeky kid a quick cuff round the ear any more. *More's the pity! In the old days if a chap gave his missus a good hiding, he could generally expect one back.* His kind of policing was now obsolete. Glyn shook his head. *Shame! It worked for some.* He sat down on the memorial seat by the park lake to give his troublesome knee another rub. *Maybe blokes like me are dying out – just like the dinosaurs! We're only good for sitting behind a desk and filing. Soon there'll be none of that either. Typewriters are okay, but that World Wide Web – oh my God! Whatever happened to talking to folk face to face? You can't tell when someone's lying by that email. You need to look them in the eye. No bloody computer can ever tell you that!*

"Ah, well," he said aloud, "best get on." Another starburst of fireworks exploded overhead, lighting up the night sky like fairyland. It was followed by another and another. Glyn sighed.

I bet that's the best part of a hundred quid gone up in smoke! What a bloody waste of money. He got up from the damp bench dusting the back of his trousers. *Oh, 'ell! I am getting old. What a miserable old bugger I've become.* He pursed his lips. *Maybe after Christmas I'll think about packing it all in.*

Any further internal wrangling was interrupted as his police radio crackled into life.

"Base to four-nine-one ... four-nine-one, come in please." Glyn pressed the button on the handset.

"Four-nine-one, receiving."

"What's your position, Glyn?"

"Four-nine-one ... Sandrine Road, on the edge of the park."

"Okay, proceed to the south side of the estuary bridge. There's a report of a young woman on the bridge ... repeat ... young woman on the bridge. It looks as though we may have a potential 'jumper'. Acknowledge, four-nine-one."

"Understood."

"Four-one-six and four-three-seven on their way. Base out."

Glyn re-clipped the radio securely to the top pocket of his jacket and quickened his stride. The young constables who'd been sent were the same two Glyn had 'puppy-walked' when they'd first joined the force. New lads were always placed with an experienced officer to learn the ropes and they didn't come more experienced than 'Franksie' Franks. He proceeded up Sandrine Road as fast as his bad knee would allow.

*

Glyn arrived at the bridge at the same time as the two younger men. The eager looks on their faces were dispelled as he held up his hand, signalling them to stay where they were and deal with any traffic.

The bridge had been built ten years ago; a single span over the river below. It was nothing like the size of the Humber Bridge, but still rose some 60 feet above the estuary. It carried two lanes of roadway and a pedestrian walkway. At intervals were a few raised observation platforms, well railed off, though not impossible to climb for anyone determined enough – provided they hadn't a bad knee.

Glyn stood at the south end of the roadway, now free of traffic thanks to the efforts of the young constables. Looking down the road, he could see the woman about a quarter of the way across. He took a deep breath, taking in the fact that the tide was out. If she fell, she'd not hit the water. Mist mixed with smoke from fireworks hung over the mud below.

He watched as the slight figure turned her back towards him. Slowly, deliberately, he began to walk forward, knowing the procedure like the back of his hand. He didn't need to think or plan, as calmly he continued to move forward. Specialist backup would come later, but, at this moment, this situation was his alone to deal with.

Glyn sighed. How unemotional he felt. This was clearly a supreme crisis in someone's life that'd led them to this. None of that would help him now. It wasn't his concern. There was a job to do. The rest would come later when the psychiatrist had done his job. That was assuming he could persuade her not to jump.

If he bungled it and she went over the edge, it'd be a matter for the police surgeon, frogmen and undertaker – *and* a hell of a lot of paper work. Glyn didn't allow the second option to invade his thoughts for long. That was to acknowledge failure before he'd begun. What was needed now was calm, quiet conversation with a troubled stranger in the most dangerous of situations.

Talk to her and gain her trust, gently, almost imperceptibly, and find a way to bring her back from the brink. Get to know her a little, be a friend, talk and listen. Make her believe there's a resolution, that it's not hopeless – that all things are possible if she'll just walk a few steps to safety. He ran through the procedure in his mind as he walked.

Talk, Glyn. You can do it, mate. And, when she finally trusted him enough to take his hand, he'd put his greatcoat around her and lead her to safety. Away from the perilous edge of darkness and into the arms of the professionals. And, like the last time, the smell of her perfume would linger on the collar of his coat until he next put it on as if to remind him just *why* he was doing the job; the reason he was out on this damp, unforgiving night.

That's where his role as a copper ended. Care, by all means, but not *too* much; that's where madness lay, taking the job home with you. You went home, set it aside and did normal mundane things for a while. It was impossible to take on the troubles of the entire population. The job – much as he loved it – was *not* about that.

*

"Hello luv. What's your name?" The voice was soft with its matter-of-fact tone, like a chance meeting and a chat in the park on a warm Sunday afternoon. The woman turned her head slightly, her eyes not moving from the rail she clutched with one hand, her knuckles white.

"Keep away from me. Please don't come any closer." Glyn noted her voice. It was steady, calm and deliberate. "Don't come nearer or we'll fall."

Not 'jump', thought Glyn. *She said 'fall'.* That was encouraging.

Slowly, he held up his palms in a placating gesture and stood still. "Okay. Steady then." He paused "They call me Glyn by the way. Perhaps you'd tell me what I can call you and, when we've been introduced, maybe we can have a little natter." The woman sniffed.

"Denise. It's Denise." She half-turned to glance at him nervously and at that moment, Glyn saw she was clutching a bundle of blankets close to her chest. His stomach lurched, a neck vein above his starched collar pulsating.

My God! She's got a baby. This was an entirely *different* matter. The sky lit up again as more fireworks burst overhead, long enough this time for him to see what a precarious position she was in. He swallowed with difficulty, his throat drying.

The woman was balanced on a narrow inspection platform beyond the safety rail. He forced another swallow. One false move – a mere stumble – and that'd be it.

Come on, Glyn, you can do this. Slowly, he took a step towards her as she rocked the bundle against her chest.

Fifteen feet.

The child seemed still and peaceful. Too still! For a brief moment Glyn wondered if something dreadful had already befallen it.

"What's baby's name, luv?" His voice was controlled and had a gentleness that belied his panic. She looked up, her gaze soft against the darkling sky and two pairs of eyes from different generations met for a second before hers returned to the child.

"Shaun. His name's Shaun." She clutched the bundle of blankets tighter, still rocking them against her.

"How old is he?"

"Four months."

"Oh ... don't you think that's a bit young to be out in this weather, luv, especially with all this smoke and ash floating about." He paused, gently stretching out an arm towards them; slow, measured. He took another two steps.

"Here ... let me help. Take old Glyn's hand and we'll do it together." He moved forward, a step further.

Ten feet.

She turned towards him, one hand on the guard rail.

"That's the way, gently does ..." The police radio burst into life. The woman cried out, clutching at the rail and almost losing her footing on the narrow ledge. For what seemed an eternity, though it was only seconds, Glyn held his breath until finally she steadied. He withdrew a few yards and grabbed the radio, sweating despite the cold November night. Swearing under his breath, he pressed the button, eyes still on the woman and her precious bundle.

"Four-nine-one, receiving."

"She's Denise Duval, aged 27, and reported missing an hour ago. Four-nine-one, she's a young baby with her ... repeat ..." Glyn cut her off. "Yes, I'm aware, and they nearly fell when you called. Suggest radio silence for the moment and put the

necessary in place. This is a *very* tense situation, so repeat …
radio silence."

"Understood, four-nine-one. Back-up on the way."

Glyn's heart, pounding in his chest despite his outward
coolness, slowed a little. He pressed the button on his radio.

Back to square one, then!

Slowly he began to inch forward again, this time talking as
he went.

"Sorry about that, Denise. Some folk are always bothering
you when you don't want them to. Don't *you* find that? There
are times when we just wish everyone would go away and leave
us alone. Don't we?"

Eight feet!

"But you see, Denise, there are times when it wouldn't be
right to leave, would it? Like now?" He waited for a response,
but none came. "Just tell me one thing, Denise. Is little Shaun
okay? Because he's awful quiet. Is he asleep perhaps?" The
woman glanced down at the bundle and nodded, slowly.

"He's okay." Glyn breathed a sigh of relief.

"That's good." His voice was soft, soothing. He took a few
more small steps.

Six feet!

"Who's baby is he, Denise?"

"Mine!" The voice was suddenly forceful.

"No, now … that's not *quite* true, is it? His voice was butter
soft. "But it doesn't matter. He's fine and that's the main thing."
He paused. "Shaun *is* fine, isn't he, Denise?" Slowly she turned
to look at him and he saw the panic etched on her features. Glyn
held up a placating palm. "It's okay, Denise, but I bet his mum's
fair out of her mind with worry. Why don't you let me take you
both home? Little Shaun needs to be fed, changed and tucked
up in his nice, warm cot." He paused. "Don't you think so?"
Another pause. "Of course you do, because you've taken really
good care of him, haven't you?" He took another step. "Yes, of
course you have. No one's going to hurt you or little Shaun."

Suddenly, Denise let go of the rail and with both arms started to rock the baby furiously. "Please, please," she pleaded, tears escaping from her lids, "don't cry! I don't like it when you cry!" Glyn stood stock still. There'd been no sound from the blankets; no struggling movements like you get from an angry baby. He remembered that from the grandkids – a mass of arms and legs.

Christ Almighty, she's killed him already! The paralysing thought raced through his brain like a train. *He has to be dead. No baby is ever that still!*

Slowly, as if reading his mind, Denise turned towards him again, her back precariously close to the gap in the protective metal railing. She stood one pace backwards from certain death.

Glyn didn't move, fixing his eyes upon hers. There'd be no heroic grab; it wouldn't be possible. She'd walk away from this willingly or … Her eyes pleaded with him and, at last, she spoke.

"I have to protect him. I must – don't you see?"

"What do you have to protect him *from*, Denise?" Glyn asked softly. There was another pause. Slowly, he offered his hand again. He could, at that moment, probably have leapt forward and grabbed them both if he'd been a bit younger and not had the curse of a bad knee. He wasn't ready to give in yet.

"Denise, what do you have to protect the little fella from?"

"Terrible things!" She was beginning to breathe harder, her chest heaving. "The shadows in the night that creep around me; evil black things that come to claim him. I have to get him away from the darkness. Can't you see that? There's only me left to do this now!" Glyn reached out his hand further towards the terrified woman.

"Come on, Denise. Take my hand and let's, you and me, walk out of the darkness together and we'll go where the light is."

Defeated, her chin dropped to her chest and, clutching the child, finally held out her hand to Glyn. He felt the soft, cold flesh brush his own.

At that moment a huge burst of fireworks cascaded above the bridge in an arc of fire. Denise started violently and stiffened, a look of surprise on her face. Her body arched as a powerful rocket hit her in the back. Sparks flew all around her, illuminating her face like a madonna. Glyn looked on in horror as she screamed and reeled backwards. Galvanised into action, he sprang forward in a desperate attempt to grab her. For a brief moment their fingers reached out for one another and their eyes locked as, with another massive burst of fireworks overhead, she fell from the parapet, her mouth wide open in a final scream. Glyn fell to the ground, perilously near the edge himself; face down, his head on the cold steel floor of the bridge.

"No!" he screamed. "Noooooo!" He'd been a second …a hairsbreadth from rescuing them both – and he'd failed. His chest tightened and he rolled away from the edge, not wanting to see. He couldn't breathe and tore at his collar certain he was having a heart attack. The world around slowed as he stared at the smoke-filled sky and waited for death to come. Stinging tears cascaded from his eyes unchecked.

"Four-nine-one. Four-nine-one, respond please." Glyn took a painful breath and realising he wasn't dead, wiped his nose on his sleeve and reached for the radio.

"They've gone over." His voice was flat. "God help her… … she's killed them both!"

"Glyn … Glyn! Are you okay?"

The only audible answer was the sob of a man in acute distress.

*

Help came quickly. Three squad cars with sirens blaring screeched to a halt just behind the two young coppers that Glyn left at the end of the bridge.

"Come on, Franksie, let's get you up." Between the two, they hauled Glyn into a sitting position. "You okay, mate?"

Glyn nodded, looking at the ground between his legs. "Yeah, sure."

"Let's get you back to the station. I expect you could do with a cuppa or summat a bit stronger." Glyn looked up at the young copper with the ash-blond hair and un-lined face.

God! He seems too young to even shave! "Not just yet, lad. I've summat to finish first. Well, *two* things actually." He pointed to the river below. "Now, drive me down there, will you?" The look of grim determination on his face forbade argument and the two of them helped him to his feet.

*

Glyn watched silently as police frogmen pulled the body from the mud and onto the river bank. They laid her, arms still around the child, on the soft grass and covered them with a blanket. A couple of CID officers ushered Glyn forward as the forensic team assembled, ready to begin their grim task. He took a sharp breath as a young, white-suited, female officer removed the blanket.

"God! She was a pretty lass." He said to no one in particular. "What drives a beautiful lass to this, eh?" The forensic officer looked at him.

"Ready?"

He nodded. She peeled back the sodden baby blanket, now caked in estuary filth. Glyn gasped as he found himself staring into the expressionless face and sightless eyes of a midwife's teaching doll.

*

Back in the warmth of the squad car, the young, blond copper, asked.

"What was the second thing, Glyn? You said there were *two* things you had to do."

"Ah, yes." Glyn smiled. "Give us your phone, mate." He phoned Mary.

"What's wrong, Glyn? What's happened?" Her concern was evident. Her husband *never* phoned her from work.

"Now don't go worrying, luv … I'm fine. I'm just ringing to let you know you can go out first thing tomorrow and book seats on that jumbo jet!"

*

An hour later, they found Denise's car in parkland on the south side of the bridge. It was a sight the young police constable who discovered it would never forget. Shining his torch in through the window he saw a baby, howling with indignation and hunger. He lay beneath the dashboard on a car rug; cold, but unharmed.

Chapter 23

CJ's ordeal was just beginning; the lengthy police interview compounding the shock of such a tragic and unexpected event.

Had CJ been at home, she'd have probably seen the report on the BBC local news. And, as with 9/11, she'd have watched as the horrific story unfolded. On *that* day she'd stood, coffee mug in hand and clicked the remote just as the plane hit the first tower. Then remained motionless, hardly daring to breathe, as the second hit the skyscraper. As both towers collapsed, the mug with its now cold contents fell from her clammy hand. Two hours later she'd still been standing there trying, like the rest of the civilised world, to make sense of the unimaginable.

*

The police were waiting outside as she drew into the drive after a visit to the local supermarket. They'd come to ask interminable questions about what she knew. They were kind, sympathetic and thorough in their questioning, but CJ was left in no doubt they were looking for reasons from anyone who'd been in a position to influence Denise's actions. In other words, had this witness played any significant part in the tragedy?

After an hour, the officers seemed satisfied CJ was merely doing her job and said so, *but* the insinuation that she might have had some influence was not lost on her. Ultimately, it would be for the coroner to make a pronouncement on Denise's state of mind and how this led to the events that unfolded.

The police also returned her doll: the ugly teaching dummy with CJ's name written in Biro on the underside of its foot, now almost obscured by stinking river mud.

The lovely young woman was dead and by her own hand it seemed. The same one who'd sat in her conservatory and poured out her heart amongst safer talk of coffee and cats. The person she'd watched walk down the path, get into her car and drive away. It was the woman who'd later brought her flowers.

And the same one who'd stolen the doll.

CJ watched as the officers left, through tears and the haze of rain that was pouring down the window. She picked up the filthy doll and stared at it, the sightless eyes fixed in a silent stare that pierced her soul. Then the guilt came, and, with it, gut-wrenching fear that was almost overwhelming. Hot bile rose into her throat. Her heart raced, her pulse thudding in her temples and, throwing the doll down, she sank to the floor, hugging her knees and weeping. The young woman was dead! Where was Sam when she needed him? The two-day funding conference in Harrogate had been very ill-timed and he'd booked into a hotel. With cold, shaking hands, she dialled his mobile, but got the usual answerphone message. In frustration, she clicked it off.

Probably still in an evening session. With grim resignation, she abandoned the attempt at contact. After all, what could he do? How could this have happened? Denise seemed so full of life and was coming to terms with her problems. CJ wept silently at the pointless loss of a young life.

After a few minutes she wiped her eyes and blew her nose loudly then, knowing she must ask herself the questions, prepared for her own recriminations.

Did I do anything wrong? What did I miss? There must have been something. Oh, God! Was I out of my depth here? Did I in some way contribute to her death?

And with each unanswered question, the bile rose again, burning her throat.

With her chest tightening, she tried Sam's phone again. There was still no answer.

"Damn! Where are you?" The room spun in a giddy merry-go-round and she felt sick. Stumbling to the window, she pushed it open and gasped as a blast of cold air rushed in. Clutching the sill with both hands she fought for control.

Help! I need help! Quickly, she scribbled a note for Sam.

She knew what she had to do, where she must go, and, grabbing the keys, ran for the car through torrential rain.

*

Pieter Van Reger was completely taken by surprise at the hammering on his front door. He almost dropped his late-night whisky, juggling the lead crystal glass clumsily, the amber contents ending up in his lap.

"Blast! What the hell ...? Putting the glass down, he went to answer the door, unprepared for the sight that met him.

CJ was drenched, her hair plastered to her head. Rivulets of mascara coursed down her cheeks, with eyes red from weeping. She was shaking with cold and distress, her teeth chattering.

"Cordelia ... for God's sake ... *what* has happened?" He stepped forward to take her firmly by the shoulders and ushered her inside. She stood still and silent, dripping in the hallway. Quickly, he fetched a plaid rug from the cupboard, wrapping it around her shoulders.

"Pieter ... I ... I ..."

"Don't talk, child." He commanded. "Whatever it is will wait until you're dry and warm. You'll catch your death like that." Gently, he led her along the passageway to the downstairs bathroom and, sitting her in the rattan chair, proceeded to run a deep bath, throwing in sweet-smelling geranium oil for good measure. "Come on, child, get those wet clothes off and have a soak. You'll find a spare robe in the cupboard." He turned, his eyes softening. *"Then* we'll talk."

He left, closing the door behind him.

*

Pieter stood with his back to the fireplace, hands clasped in front of him. In his own practised way, he appeared deep in thought, but was watching CJ carefully as she sipped whisky laced with honey – the perfect relaxant, in his opinion.

He thought she looked even smaller swaddled in the soft, white, oversized robe, her hair tousled and curly from shampooing. She'd scrubbed her face of make-up, her skin pale and child-like. He'd never seen her like this. It was a far cry from the bright self-assured woman who lit up a room just by walking into it and who lit up his life just by being there. This was a vulnerable, frightened child and he was staggered at how protective he felt.

Pieter poured himself another whisky and topped up her glass, despite her protestations. He sat in the armchair opposite and rested his head on the back whilst CJ told of what happened to Denise. He made no comment nor interrupted her. When finished, she sat cradling her empty glass, the whisky bottle sitting on the rosewood table nearby, its contents depleted by several more inches. After some minutes of thoughtful silence, CJ lifted her head and looked directly at Pieter. She'd been unable to meet his gaze since she'd stumbled through the door.

"It was *my* fault, wasn't it, Pieter?"

"What makes you think that?" Pieter's pale-blue eyes pierced hers, his face showing no emotion.

"It *must* have been something I said – something I did. I keep going over and over it in my head trying to remember every detail."

"Re-examining facts is fine. Introspection is an exceedingly bad thing! That's elementary psychology. I don't need to tell you that!" Pieter knew his words were cold and business-like. It was quite deliberate. "Do you suppose *you* could have really made a difference to what that disturbed young woman did in the end?" His gaze hardened further. "I think you're in danger of overestimating your importance, child."

"Pieter, don't call me that … please" It was a whispered plea.

"Then don't act like it!" he snapped. "You don't tell people what to think. You let them talk and by doing so reach their own conclusions. You're *just* the catalyst, the facilitator who allows someone to make a change in their behaviour, or to *accept* their situation and live with it." CJ sighed deeply.

"And what if *I* can't live with it? What if *I* can't live with what's happened?"

"Then you'll die with it!" Pieter's voice was raised, his eyes flashing. "If you don't resolve this, it'll never leave you! You'll be haunted by something that will progressively get out of your control. It'll eat at you like a cancer and *never* let you go." He paused to finish what was left in his glass and looked at her with eyebrows raised. "Well? Am I right?" CJ lowered her eyes, too choked to speak. "Don't you *dare* cry," he commanded, "the time for crying's over." He pointed a finger, "By all means, grieve." He paused. "We know so little about the people who come to us, and have only what they choose to tell us and we take *that* at face value." He raised his free hand in a gesture of impatience. "There are tried-and-tested treatments for schizophrenia, paranoia, personality disorder and all manner of things. So, tell me if you can, how do you treat distress? Sympathy? Empathy? Dismiss the whole damn thing and tell them not to be so silly? There *is* no magic formula, no quick fix for distress, but one thing's certain, it *will* get easier. In the meantime, or until whatever ails them has run its course, we provide the stop gap. We give them permission to speak the unspoken, to think the unthinkable. Just long enough for them to work through their pain; a diversion if you like, to consider another angle, a different point of view." Pieter sat forward in the armchair, hands on his knees, his voice more forceful, the words clipped.

"That's why we *never* give advice or try to provide answers." Clients *have* to do that for themselves. This woman, Denise, what she did was *her* choice, her solution, and there'd have been nothing you could have done to change that. I think you know that, Cordelia."

CJ nodded.

"Now," said Pieter, "we're going to re-live that interview with Denise one last time and *then* you're going to lay it to rest, along with her, and move on."

*

The old grandfather clock in the hallway struck 3.00am.

"We're done" said Pieter, standing up. "You may take my bed."

CJ tried to protest and, struggling to her feet, began to sway. Quickly, he caught her arm to steady her.

"Whoa! I think I drank a little too much, Pieter". She took another unsteady step, threatening to fall this time. Deftly, he caught her, sweeping her up into his arms, her own circling his neck. He sank to the sofa, CJ upon his lap, her head resting on his shoulder.

"Pieter?"

"Yes?"

"Can I cry now?"

"If you must." He smiled and closed his eyes.

"S'okay. I'm not going to."

He stroked her hair gently as she slept. The closeness of her body seemed the most natural thing in the world and he never wanted it to end. CJ shifted in her sleep, stretching. Her eyes remained closed.

"You should be in bed, child," whispered Pieter close to her ear. She nodded sleepily. Peter shuffled sideways and stood, then, lifting her gently, carried her to his bedroom. Lowering her carefully, she turned onto her side disturbing the robe. It fell from one shoulder revealing a breast with its perfect, pink nipple.

Peter gasped, then, bending, he kissed her tenderly on the forehead; a trembling hand so close to her pale, skin he could feel its warmth. It matched the growing heat in his groin. He closed his eyes, allowing his hand to remain poised for a few seconds more before replacing the stray robe and settling the soft, downy quilt around her. Then, turning, he left, closing the door with a gentle click.

Chapter 24

The distinctive smell of old-fashioned hair cream filtered through the air.

The parrot, which up until then had been chattering away between crunching fell silent, his steady gaze fixed on the armchair. CJ looked up and closed the regency novel she'd been engrossed in.

"Hello, Georgie. I haven't heard from *you* for a while. Just where the devil were you when I needed you?" The voile curtains wafted gently, swishing to and fro, and then were still. Back came the familiar voice.

"It weren't me tha needed, lass."

"I always need you, Georgie. I was beginning to think you'd gone forever." She laughed. "No such luck!"

"Cheeky little bugger." There was a pause. "Tha couldn't help 'er, tha knows – that woman."

"I know that, now."

"Should 'ave listened to me. I said she were trouble! Dint I say that?"

"Yes, Georgie. You did, but we can't always choose who we see." CJ laughed out loud at the irony of the parallel.

"She wants peace."

"Hasn't she found that?" There was silence, but CJ knew he was still there. She could feel it and the parrot was still glaring at the armchair.

"Georgie?"

"No. There are too many bad things in the way – and some bad, bad people. There's power 'ere you've no idea about. Find the truth, and then she'll be able to rest and move on."

"Sorry, Georgie, you're not making any sense. How do I even start to do that? What power? What bad people?"

"It's no good! You'll not listen to me." There was a pause. "Just look at the tube, then you'll understand better."

"What tube, Georgie? You'll have to give me something better than that."

"That tube over there. Look at the tube!"

And with that he was gone.

The parrot squawked loudly and spat out a piece of shell.

*

CJ looked around the room with exasperation.

What the hell is he talking about? "The tube?" she repeated aloud, walking round the room. "Pipes? Cables? The Underground? No, he distinctly said 'over there'. Over where, Georgie?" She raised her arms in a gesture of frustration. CJ looked at the ceiling then at the floor and all the space in between. Impatiently she grabbed the TV remote. "Oh God! I don't know, Georgie, for heaven's sake. How do you expect me to work …?" She looked down at the remote in her hand. "Wait a minute!"

The TV had been on standby. CJ clicked it into life. *The television! When it was invented it used to be called 'the tube'.* She remembered her grandmother referring to it like that. Someone from Georgie's era would certainly say that. She stared at the screen. "But what am I looking for?"

Sitting down, she began to scroll through the channels with no clue what she sought. *News, children's programmes, antiques, more children's TV, Time Team …* It went on and on. She was just about to throw the remote at the wall in frustration, when something caught her attention: the History channel.

Framed on the screen in close-up was a man in Nazi uniform. Although in black and white, there was something about this man's eyes that mesmerised her. He took off his officer's cap and turned to look directly into the camera lens, smiling and relaxed, putting on a show for the camera.

CJ started violently, hands going to her mouth. Those huge eyes, those hypnotic eyes, seemed to be staring directly at her, holding her gaze. Grabbing the control for the DVD recorder, she hit the record button.

CJ's mind was racing. There was something about those eyes all right and she felt sure she'd seen them before.

"Georgie," she pleaded aloud, "why the devil can't you just tell me things instead of all this … this … subterfuge. You're driving me crazy. Just *what* is it you want me to do?"

*

Sam leaned forward, one arm resting on the table, and looked at his wife over the rim of his wine glass. He gazed steadily for a few moments, then emptied it in one gulp and set it down.

"Okay, woman … so what have I done now?"

CJ looked up from pushing salad thoughtfully around her plate.

"Sorry, darling …?"

"What've I done? You've hardly uttered a word during dinner. You're here, but your mind isn't." He gestured, an open hand moving across his face. "The lights are on, but no one's at home."

"Oh, I'm sorry, honey …"

"Is this still about that woman?" He reached to refill the glasses. CJ screwed up her nose and said nothing.

"Because if it is," he went on, "I think you should reflect on what Pieter said, and if you're going to continue to counsel, then you have to draw a line under it and carry on. You know, it may not be the last time something like this happens, due to the very nature of the kind of people you're dealing with. To quote Freud, 'shit happens, baby'."

CJ laughed for the first time in days. She shook her head. "I don't think Freud said that."

"He must have done, we've all said it! Now drink up and talk to me. Or are you still angry that I was away when you needed me most?"

"No, I was never angry with you. Anyway, how do *you* know what Pieter said?"

"He phoned me."

"*Did* he now?" CJ's eyes widened.

"Don't look so affronted. He was worried about you."

CJ wrinkled her brow. "Are we talking about the same Pieter here? Tall bloke … South African accent … bloody abrasive at the best of times …"

"The very same." Sam sat back in his chair.

"What else did he tell you?"

"Aaahh." Sam tapped the side of his nose, and then held up his hands in submission. "He told me not to let you go off investigating and looking for reasons why." CJ cocked her head on one side and looked at him intently.

"And *you* wouldn't *dream* of doing that, of course."

"I know you've got to get answers … right?"

CJ nodded.

"Thought so. So did Pieter."

"God! That man!"

Sam leaned forward again, hands cupping his face, both elbows resting on the table.

"So, then, where do we start?"

CJ smiled enigmatically. "With a documentary."

Chapter 25

It was raining; a persistent, misty drizzle that's relentless and shrouds everything with damp. It was a thoroughly unpleasant day, as if the world were protesting at a young life cut short.

CJ hadn't worn black, choosing instead a pale-olive dress and dark-grey jacket. A black, animal print scarf was tied loosely around her throat against the chill of early morning. This wasn't a fashion show. She'd no wish to stand out from the crowd as the woman who'd done the counselling – perhaps the holder of secrets. She wore soft, flat shoes so as not to clip-clop on the flagstones of the old church, further drawing attention to herself.

*

Mike Duvall had come to her house personally to deliver an invitation to the funeral. But for that, she most likely wouldn't have gone. Though initially declining her offer of coming inside, he'd thanked her warmly for the way she'd cared for his late wife. Unexpectedly, there'd been no hint of blame, saying she'd made a real difference to Denise and helped her look at her problems in a totally new light.

CJ said how very sorry she was for his loss, her hand reaching to touch him on the forearm gently – a gesture of comfort. It proved to be some sort of catalyst. He looked at her intently for a moment as though wrestling with some inner question and not knowing how to begin. Mike took a deep breath and blew the air out gently.

"Do you think perhaps I might come in for a moment after all? That is, if you're not busy?"

"Of course. Come into the warm, and I'll make us a cup of tea or something." CJ led him into the conservatory.

"She'd obviously very deep-seated problems, my Denise," began Mike. "And I didn't have the first clue how to deal with them. In my ham-fisted way, I thought if I ignored it, then it'd all be okay – whatever *it* was."

"There's no reason to blame yourself, Mike, but no matter what I say – or anyone else says for that matter – you'll do *just* that. It's human nature. When someone we love dies, it's normal to wish we could go back and do things differently and have a second chance to say all those things we wish we'd said."

Mike nodded, his eyes closed, chin on his chest.

"I held a secret, you see." He raised his head and looked at CJ, searching her face for whether he could trust her. He knew he could. "We had a party some time ago to celebrate our ten years together and it was Denise's birthday. The organising was a highly clandestine affair. I invited friends from way back. Denise *had* no family you see. She'd been brought up in an orphanage after her parents were killed in a skiing accident in the Austrian Alps." He accepted the proffered cup of tea. "Thank you. I expect she told you all this so I'll not go into it."

Denise nodded and sipped her tea. "Yes, she did. She said how happy she'd been there."

"The highlight of her night was that I'd managed to find two very special people: the two 'aunties' who'd cared for her at Belmont. They lived a very short distance away in Wensley – *still*, after all these years. I could hardly believe my luck. You see, they'd been *far* more than just carers. Lucy and Hennie treated Denise like their own child. She'd talked about them for years and always with such great love; I knew I had to find them." The cup rattled on its saucer. Mike steadied it with his free hand and looked at CJ. "I wish I hadn't. Oh, God, maybe if I hadn't things would've been different."

CJ stared back, an arched brow questioning. Her mind raced, wondering how two gentle old ladies could have made such a difference to someone's life.

"What is it, Mike," CJ prompted softly. "What happened?"

"I overheard a conversation I wasn't supposed to." He paused for a few moments collecting his thoughts. "The pair had gone into the front room, probably to have a rest from the music and enjoy a quiet cuppa. I was serving birthday cake and, when I got to the door, I could hear they were in the middle of a conversation. Not wanting to interrupt, I stood outside the door and waited for them to finish. It was *what* I heard." Mike paused.

"Go on," said CJ.

Mike swallowed hard and sat back in the chair.

"The pair knew some sort of secret about Denise's background, and had for a long time. It was obviously too terrible to tell and, when I asked what it was they were referring to as 'that she must never know', Lucy said it'd do no good. They'd obviously made a pact and *I* was never going to be party to it. What was most disturbing was the two gentle old ladies immediately became steely-eyed. It was a conversation never meant to be overheard. So I left it. The party wasn't the place to pursue it, anyway. I decided that, after a few weeks, I'd arrange to see Henny and Lucy, perhaps on neutral territory." He paused whilst his cup was refilled. "You see, CJ, I was intrigued. Looking at it from the lighter side … if my wife, let's say, had 'disposed' of several other partners, then I'd have quite liked to have known to expect a knife in my back!" He laughed before remembering his situation. "You see, I tried to look for the ridiculous and figured, after ten years, well, if she hadn't done me in by now then I was fairly safe." He sighed sadly. "Isn't that what any reasonable person would have done?"

CJ nodded.

"Then, Denise began to act strangely, distracted, forgetting things and there was that shopping trip. She'd been seeing things that didn't exist: an old woman that apparently died 20-odd years before."

"Mike," began CJ, "a disturbed mind is more than capable of playing funny tricks. It can make us *believe* we're going crazy."

"Do *you* think she was crazy?" His eyes locked on hers. This was a man she couldn't lie to even if she'd wanted to.

"No, I don't," said CJ emphatically. "She seemed anxious when we first met, but that soon dissipated as we chatted and by the time she came back two weeks later she seemed so much better. She looked better. She sounded better and she confirmed that." CJ sighed deeply, spreading her hands in a helpless gesture. "Perhaps I was wrong, Mike. Did you ever go and see the old ladies?"

"I intended to. Then, when Denise began to act strangely, it got pushed onto the back burner again. It was only last week, after she died, I took the bull by the horns, so to speak, and the three of us met at Lucy's cottage. I'd this idea I might discover something that could be of use at the inquest. I guess I was so desperate by this time I was looking for answers – any answers to explain what happened – to make it all seem less terrible than it was. Maybe I was clutching at straws and …" His expression became dark and brooding. "And then, *what* I found out … there's no way I was going to repeat any of it at a public enquiry. I wasn't about to allow my wife's memory to be sullied or ridiculed. And, then, there was the press. *They* were going to hang on every word and pounce on it like the vultures they are. Get a bit of sensationalism and they'd have never left it alone. I wasn't going to let that happen."

He sat for a few moments, eyes focused on the patch of carpet between his feet. Denise sat quietly watching his inner turmoil until he felt able to continue.

"Whenever she spoke of her father – and bear in mind she was only small when they were both killed – it was with love, though I wonder how much she *really* remembered and how much was *what* she'd been told." He massaged his temples in a somewhat desperate gesture. "So, how *could* I ever have told her that the father she loved …" Mike raised his head and looked into CJ's eyes, "that *her* father was a mass murderer?"

*

CJ sat alone in the conservatory, a large furry throw across her knees against the late-night chill. Sam had gone to bed several hours before, unable to keep his eyes open any longer after repeated showings of the documentary. She watched it once again, then ejected the disc and filed it carefully away.

So, it *was* him. She was never more certain of anything. The eyes were a dead giveaway. It would have been far too much of a coincidence, especially after the horror story Mike told her. And, all that aside, she trusted Georgie implicitly.

Knowing there'd be no hope of sleep, CJ went to the fridge and took out a bottle of Chablis before returning to the warmth and comfort beneath the throw. She sipped the icy drink, Mike's words bouncing around her head. He'd told her about a massacre during the war, perpetrated by Denise's father and the SS – and, finally, about the curse.

God, thought CJ, *no wonder he'd kept it from the coroner!* She could only have imagined the response if the press got hold of *that*. The family would've never been left in peace again. But was it all really true? Or just one of those things that get passed down the generations and altered with repeated telling? CJ had asked Mike if he believed the story and, if so, whether he also believed his wife was cursed. He sighed and said he didn't know. "I like to think I'm a rational, level-headed person ..." He shook his head sadly. "So why am I even entertaining the possibility, except I'm hard-pressed to come up with anything else."

After he'd left, CJ sat asking if *she* believed in curses. Didn't the victim have to believe it themselves? Surely, it was all based on fear – a bit like voodoo. But Denise had no knowledge of her father's past, so that didn't even enter the equation. The only people who *did* know were the two old ladies and, but for Denise's untimely death, *they'd* probably have taken the secret to their graves.

"So what is this, Georgie?" she whispered to the empty air, "The sins of the fathers visited on the children?" She shook her head, suddenly impatient, cross with herself for believing in far-fetched fairy tales. "Oh, *now* we're entering the realms of fantasy!" She poured another glass of wine and sipped it thoughtfully, trying to find reasons that weren't obvious. Before he'd left, Mike asked her to come to the funeral and he'd implored her to help him.

"Help me, CJ, the way you helped Denise. When no one else could, you took the time and trouble to get to know her. Help *me* find the answer to all this because if anyone can, it's you. I'm not expecting miracles. Nothing can ever bring her back. I just want to find the truth; a reason to hang on. I want you to tell me that it's not been for nothing and that she's at rest."

CJ stiffened. His words struck a chord. Georgie said she wasn't at peace. She promised to attend the funeral. There were so many questions left unanswered. Once more, CJ took out the disc and fed it into the DVD slot of the recorder and pressed the 'play' button. She sat back and watched as the handsome man in Nazi uniform turned to look into the camera lens, his piercing wide eyes flirting with the camera. CJ paused the recording. Once again, the eyes seemed to look directly at her, an unwelcome penetration, and she shivered. Then taking a deep breath, she stared back defiantly.

"So, I've found you at last," she said aloud. "You thought you could hide, but this is where it has to end. I *will* put you to rest for the sake of generations to come. There'll *be* no more hiding places for you, my friend." Beneath the direct gaze of the mesmeric eyes she shivered again, pulling the throw around her shoulders as a chill descended on the room. She didn't break her gaze, as reaching for the control, she blanked the screen.

As CJ drained her glass she was sure of one thing. She knew what she must do and where she must go; one thing was certain – this was far from over!

Chapter 26

Quite without shame, the two most important men in CJ's life had taken part in a huge conspiracy. There'd been late-night phone calls and clandestine meetings involving the consumption of copious amounts of whisky. As far as either knew, CJ hadn't suspected a thing about the elaborate plans being drawn up for her protection.

Sam knew she'd pursue it, like a dog with a bone. She was incapable of leaving anything alone once the mood took her and she'd made a promise to Mike. If she was anything, his wife was honourable – sometimes annoyingly so. Sam was sure she was putting herself in danger. He also knew that without a blazing row, which he probably wouldn't win anyway, he was powerless to stop her.

"It's your penalty for marrying a strong-minded woman," he told himself. On this occasion, she wasn't merely strong-willed, she was driven. She'd started something and it had to be taken to its conclusion, whatever that was.

Pieter needed little persuasion when invited to accompany them. He also feared CJ had got herself in a little deep. Though every fibre of his scientific, academic soul told him to fear the living and not the dead, there was a nagging feeling that kept him awake until the small hours. Ever since the night at his house after the woman fell from the bridge, he'd felt uneasy with his protégé's reaction to the events.

And France in August would be extremely pleasant.

Lecture tours from his past life in academia left him well-practised in the art of rapid preparation and frugal packing. That's not to say his little luxury items would be left behind. Pieter never 'did without'. His idea of what he thought essential for a trip was different from other people's. He took what he considered absolutely necessary and that included fine cologne, the odd Cuban cigar and well-tailored trousers with at least one expensive dinner jacket. Oh yes, and a few silk ties. There'd be a gift for his host, a little 'something' in gold.

Sam had often spoken of Aunt Caron in the past – now well into her eighties. He already felt he knew her as a cherished family member of good friends *and* Sam's aunt on his father's side. She always referred to CJ as "Ma petite fille".

Pieter *needed* a holiday. He assured himself he deserved it. His eighth book was with his editor and he could take time off from the hospital whenever he chose. So he'd chosen.

It was also a great opportunity to spend time with CJ ... and, of course, Sam. Secretly, it pleased him to be needed, though he'd have rather died than admit it. A trip to France and the chance to meet the enigmatic Caron were not to be missed. He *would* repay the kindness by treating the pair of them to a lavish trip to his beloved South Africa later in the year, or, at the very latest, the following year. CJ's well-known love of animals could be well and truly sated beyond her wildest dreams with a safari in the bush of the Western Cape or perhaps to the open grasslands of the Veldt. They'd stay in luxury bungalows, surrounded by all the wildlife his country had to offer. It'd be *her* treat and he'd spoil her. And Sam could come along, too!

He joked with his subconscious constantly, but, in fact, Pieter was extremely fond of Sam and could have wished for no better a man for his surrogate daughter. It made up for the misfortune of not being young enough to marry her himself. But Sam would do very nicely. He was a good husband and deeply in love with her. What more could a woman need?

Pieter could provide any scintillating company she may be lacking, and he would see to it she and Sam wanted for nothing whilst he was alive.

She was rarely far from his thoughts and the fantasies he allowed himself from time to time gave him pleasure; so, where was the harm? He loved her. He'd done so from the first moment and *that* would never change. It'd be his obsession until he took his final breath. He'd accepted long ago she belonged to someone else. He'd *never* tell her; he'd never actually speak the words. How could he? Deep down, he suspected she knew, pretending to put aside any embarrassment she felt for the greater good. In her soul she'd know he'd never compromise her or make her so uncomfortable she ran away from him.

So how does she see me? He allowed his sharp, analytical mind to wander for a few moments. *A benevolent, older uncle? God forbid! No ... not that! A trusted and careful friend? That's better.* He was sure of one thing: he cherished the relationship enough never to put it at risk. For to give in to vanity and confess his real feelings would be to lose her forever – and he couldn't bear the pain of that. For, never to see her again or hear her voice, experience the smell of her skin or to feel the aura of her presence ... A lack of any of those things would be intolerable. What would be the point in living? Never before in his life had Pieter experienced anything like the effect she had on him.

"No!" he said aloud.

He'd *never* tell her. Not until either of them were dying and probably not even then. He sighed deeply, looking at his dapper reflection in the cheval mirror. *Pieter van Reger, you are a fool and will remain so. Now go on holiday with the woman you love more than life itself and, above all, keep her safe.*

He turned abruptly, then picked up the valise from the bed and headed for the door. Stopping suddenly in mid stride, he turned, put down the case and went back to the dresser to open the top left-hand drawer. Prising two fingers under the rim he deftly released a tiny gold catch. A shallow drawer slid out; a hidden compartment. With his fingernail, he pressed another ridged catch, almost invisible to the naked eye, and another thin drawer, spring-loaded, was released. The quarter-inch-deep space seemed too small to conceal anything. Carefully, Pieter took hold of a thin, black cord between his finger and thumb, pulling out the faded black-velvet pouch, before closing the hinged lid and replacing the secret drawer. It closed with a faint click. He took the bag and, after fingering the velvet briefly, placed it in his inside jacket pocket.

"Insurance," he told the man in the mirror. "Just a little insurance."

Then, picking up his valise once again, he strode quickly from the room, closing the door behind him and, after locking the house, left for France.

Chapter 27

Sam spoke in perfect French, his accent superb with no trace of his Barbadian heritage. "Tante Caron, permet-moi de te présenter Monsieur Pieter Van Reger, professeur et mon ami." Aunt Caron stepped forward, extending an elegant hand with long, manicured nails. Pieter took it, raising it to his lips.

"Enchanté, Madame."

If she was impressed, Caron showed no flicker of it, merely lifting a finely-shaped eyebrow. She continued in perfect English.

"Welcome. It is good to see you, Pieter. I've heard so much about you – you clever, clever man." She turned to CJ and held out her hands, "Ma petite fille." They air-kissed on both cheeks. The hugs and deeper shows of affection would come later, away from public gaze. It looked, at first glance, comical as this woman dwarfed CJ by a good 18 inches.

Caron stood over six feet tall in her heels. She appeared ultra-slim in her black, haute couture dress, far too elegant for the heat of midday. Her hair was coiffured, her makeup flawless. Though 80, she carried her back ram-rod straight; no doubt a testament to the prolonged ballet lessons of her youth. Despite the strong French sun her complexion bore few lines.

"Now, my friends …" With a flourish she clapped her hands, turning towards the house calling loudly. "Patron! Where are you? Our guests, they are here." Two more claps. "Vite, vite."

Whatever Pieter had expected, whether an immaculate wine waiter or a liveried butler, it certainly wasn't the man who hurried through the farmhouse door clutching two bottles of champagne in one large fist and crystal flutes in the other with surprising delicacy. *This* man was nearer his own age and, judging by the state of his muddy boots, clearly the local farmer.

His stained trousers were precariously held up by worn red braces stretched over his belly.

Caron beamed and went from her clap-clapping to vigorous applause. She didn't stop until the man reached the group, puffing somewhat. Sam looked on with amusement having witnessed the spectacle many times.

"Bonjour, Papa Philippe!" He relieved the older man of his burden before greeting him in the French traditional fashion. Beaming broadly, he held him by the shoulders at arms' length.

"Comment ça va, you old rascal?"

Philippe pursed his lips, rocking his hand from side to side, palm downwards, chubby fingers splayed. "Comme ci, comme ça." He chuckled deeply and held out his arms to CJ whilst attempting to shake Pieter's hand at the same time.

"La famille," he enthused, "together once more!" CJ was hugged with vigour and for a few moments was quite unable to breathe.

"Here, Uncle," said Sam, "allow me to pour for you."

Sam did so as Philippe explained to a rather bemused Pieter that he *wasn't* the local handyman but 'Patron' was how Caron always referred to her husband. "And in my case," he went on with a resigned expression, "it means 'The Boss'. Oui!" He patted his wife's bottom before looping his thumbs through the braces. "I am ... how you say? The love of your life, am I not, ma cherie?"

"Yes, you are!" retorted Caron, "and I know very well you speak perfect English so stop showing off." Caron leaned forward to whisper to Pieter. "He was in the Resistance, you see." This was clearly meant to explain everything. Pieter shook his head, amused at such a seemingly mismatched couple. CJ had been watching him and moved close to his ear.

"Whatever you're thinking, you'd be wrong. They're a perfect match, believe me." Pieter turned and shot her an incredulous look. Good God, the woman seemed to know what he was thinking now! "I know," she whispered. "I'm a witch."

"Do you see me arguing, child?" he asked out of the corner of his mouth.

*

The old farmhouse shimmered in the midday sun. CJ never tired of coming to gaze at it with the same excitement she felt the first time, soon after she'd met Sam. The stone building was at least 300 years old, now pale and mellow where bougainvillea and honeysuckle competed for space across the old façade, threatening to invade the red-tiled roof. The long racemes of wisteria were still at their best, draping the building with purple as if dressed by an exclusive designer, colourful against the well-bleached stone. No one remembered how old the wisteria was, but, judging by the thickness of its gnarled stems, its age was clearly in excess of a hundred years; it was a perennial haven for butterflies and bees.

On either side of the low entrance stood cones of bay, meticulously trimmed by Philippe; sentinels sharing their perfume with anyone who brushed past. Lavenders thrived in the stony, gritty soil close to the foundations and reached up to meet geraniums tumbling haphazardly from large boxes beneath each window. Once three farm-workers cottages, Philippe had converted the place into its present eight bedrooms, with the original three staircases snaking around the building.

Later, CJ sat at the kitchen table, a meticulously scrubbed, old, pine affair. Papa Philippe stood beside her, truly at peace in his domain with his second love – cooking.

She'd sat here many times with a glass of chilled white wine as he chopped, pared, braised and baked, producing whatever he decided the day's fare should be. Whether delicate brioche for breakfast or fine cuisine for later in the day, he was always the same, sleeves rolled up and wearing his blue-and-white striped apron.

As she looked at this benign, white-haired old man at peace with the world, it would've been easy to forget this was 'Jules'. He'd lead an entire battalion of resistance fighters and doubtlessly been the bravest of the lot. After they'd captured and tortured him, the Germans took him to the notorious Paris headquarters of the Gestapo. He escaped, but was darn near shot to pieces.

Now, Philippe had found peace in his Limousin kitchen, surrounded by pots and pans, with his bed of herbs growing just outside.

Aunt Caron always had an air of mystery. She seldom spoke of the war. If the subject was raised, she would give an enigmatic smile and wave a hand with its manicured fingernails in a dismissive gesture guaranteed to silence the most persistent enquirer.

Philippe paused from peeling vegetables to refresh CJ's glass, an expression on his face she'd come to recognise. He wished her to talk to him privately, here in his sanctuary. Words were not necessary. He could ask with the mere raise of an eyebrow.

"Yes, Philippe?" she responded. She'd always thought he possessed incredible perception that often set her wondering if he, too, was like herself.

"So, ma cherie," began Philippe, moving on to the preparation of the filet mignon and fixing her with an outwardly soft gaze that said much more. "I think perhaps you are about to put yourself in mortal danger." She looked away.

"May I help you with that?"

"Non!" Philippe allowed no one to assist and, anyway, Sam had made sure tales of her hopeless culinary attempts spread across international borders. Philippe was settling for no such diversion. "Well?"

"There's something I must do. Oui."

"Then tell me." Carefully, he put down the large kitchen knife, and, wiping his chubby fingers on the apron, sat and poured two more glasses of wine. He frowned and CJ sensed disapproval in the way he tilted his head to one side, like a parent talking to a misbehaving child. Linking his fingers across his belly, he leaned back and prepared to listen.

Chapter 28

The intensity of Papa Philippe's gaze, sharp enough to cut, threatened to lay bare her soul. CJ had never been able to hide even a snippet of information from this man. He was far too perceptive, sometimes scarily so. She shuffled under his scrutiny.

Philippe leaned forward in his chair and, although she sensed his imminent disapproval, CJ knew there was no escaping an explanation. She felt like a small child again, about to be chastised for some indiscretion, as Philippe linked his fingers, thumbs beneath his chin, and rested his elbows on the table.

"Ma cherie," he began, "I've known you a long time and I love you beyond words, so you'd better relent and tell me what foolhardy mission you're about to embark on under the pretence of coming to see this elderly uncle."

CJ began to protest, but he was having none of it, holding up a firm hand and stoically waiting. She took a deep breath and began, telling him the whole story. Philippe sat passively, his expression as unchanging as the face of the moon.

*

Two hours later, exhausted, CJ sat back and drank the contents of her glass in one thirsty gulp.

"More?" asked Philippe, refilling it with a hint of surprise at how she'd sloshed his precious cru down her throat. There was silence for a few minutes as she drank and Philippe considered. When he spoke it was measured.

"I've two pieces of advice. The first you may choose to ignore. The second, I'm afraid I *must* insist on. These are my conditions. Oradour's a sad place that has seen much pain. The tragedy of what was done there still lurks in the old, crumbling walls." CJ looked up, surprised. "Yes, I *believe* that." He paused to look deeply into her eyes. "But you *know* that, don't you, CJ? *You,* above all people know such murderous acts don't just disappear and you *will* be in danger. Believe the words of an old man who's witnessed the evil men do. That evil remains – I've seen it." Before she could ask, he added, "You see, the kind of peril you're facing is unseen; the result of the vile actions of men." He lowered his voice and whispered. "It's your very soul that's in danger."

"I'm well protected, Papa."

"You may *think* you are, but this is beyond your understanding." He paused to drink. "However, I also know you *have* to do this. That is why I impose my conditions."

CJ searched his face.

How he could possibly know this? There was no clue – just the gaze of a benevolent, elderly uncle whose goose-grey eyes seemed to hold the wisdom of ages. She reached across the void of the table top to take his hand.

"Darling Philippe, I'll do anything you say. What *are* your conditions?"

"You must take utmost care – and this I'm sure you will *not* do!"

"And the second?"

"Take Pieter. He *must* go with you."

"Pieter? Not Sam?"

"No … I will amuse Sam."

"Okay, Papa Philippe. I'll do this. I don't understand, but I *will* do it." Rising from the table, she kissed his cheek. He clapped his hands.

"But tonight," Philippe's face brightened, jollity returning, "we feast and drink!" He raised his glass and drank deeply, cautious in case CJ should see the fear in his eyes.

Chapter 29

It was morning. CJ lay on the soft, feather mattress, reluctant to move. The carved bed enveloped her and she felt lost in its generous proportions.

This room at the top of the house was where she and Sam always stayed. It was one of the guest bedrooms, with traditionally large French furniture. CJ shuffled and breathed in the aroma of old wood. This was the room where, as a new bride, she'd spent her honeymoon and the evocative smell of cedar still excited her as it had then. It held a special magic of love, sex and fulfilled dreams.

Sam had allowed her to sleep in today, bringing coffee and croissants, which he'd left on the night-stand by the bed before kissing her gently on the forehead and leaving.

CJ yawned, stretched deliciously and sat up to pour coffee, which was, thankfully, still warm. Nibbling a croissant, she rose and threw open the shutters. Warm air and sunlight flooded into the room, the breeze ruffling her still unruly hair.

"Georgie, are you there?" She looked out across the manicured lawn to the rolling French countryside beyond, the land already shimmering with heat-haze.

"Georgie, where are you? I think I'm going to need you today." She listened intently, head cocked to one side. There was no reply – no smell of Brylcreem or Old Shag. "Obstinate old beggar," said CJ aloud, reaching for another croissant and shoving half of it indelicately into her mouth where it melted. A warm, pulsating blast of air suddenly rushed around her. She turned.

"Georgie?"

"I've told thee before … I'm not a bloody Alsatian tha knows!" CJ joined in the last three words, mimicking him. She felt his irritation with a poke in the ribs and could imagine the pursed lips and furrowed brows.

"I was beginning to believe what they said in *Blythe Spirit*, Georgie."

"And what were that?" asked a bad-tempered voice.

"I think it was Madame Arcarti, the eccentric old medium, who doubted spirits could travel over water."

"Huh?"

"Clearly she was wrong!"

There was a grunt. "Water – air – fire – stone-cold porridge. Don't really matter over 'ere, does it? Seems a bloke *still* can't get any peace – even when he's dead! Bloody 'ell! Nagged by women all me life; thought when I went I'd get a bit o' rest. Hah! Not on yer flamin' life. Must have done summat *really* terrible to get saddled wi' a silly bint like thee."

"You know you love me, Georgie."

"What makes thee think such a notion?"

"Because … well, because … I enrich your life." She laughed. "Sorry … death … err … soul. Anyway, you'd soon get bored with only your halo to polish."

He gave a throaty chuckle. CJ was forgiven. She'd known Georgie a long time and was absolutely certain that he'd never have qualified for a halo – dead or alive!

There was a pause and CJ finished her coffee.

"Tha's not *really* intending to go to that place?" he said presently. "Leave it alone, woman, can't tha? Past can't be altered."

"I've got to, Georgie. If I don't settle it, then it'll just go on and on and Denise's death will have been for nothing. It needs a line drawing under it once and for all."

"And tha thinks that thee's t' one to do it?"

"I can't see any other way *and* I made a promise."

"Aw God!" He interjected. "Is there nowt I can say to change thy mind? Listen, woman! There's evil inside them walls like yer can't imagine. Take my advice and leave it alone!"

"I can't, Georgie."

"Things happened in there that are beyond your worst nightmares; men, women and bairns ..." He stopped. CJ stood still gazing out over the tranquil fields for a few moments.

"Georgie, are you still here?"

"I'm 'ere," he said quietly. "I want you to listen to me – I mean *really* listen."

"Go on."

"Understand this, CJ. Evil doesn't allus *want* to be stopped. In those ruins are things that'd trample owt that gets in t' way. It'll shake you off like you're nothing. Think hard. I'm begging yer now."

CJ had never been begged before. It was not Georgie's way, but the tone of his voice told her not only was he deadly serious but also he was afraid.

*

CJ knew all about Oradour and what happened there from the television programme. Framed on the screen stood its protagonist, smiling and posing for the camera. Under different circumstances he'd have been considered handsome; straight and proud in his Nazi SS uniform, its swastikas clearly visible on the collar and sleeves.

As for the rest of the story, it'd been easy to research for anyone skilled at using the Internet. All the facts quickly fell into place as CJ sat at the computer. Forty years ago this wouldn't have been possible; now all the information was at her fingertips. She'd found what she was looking for.

Now she must seek justice for an innocent woman who'd been cursed by an accident of birth.

Chapter 30

"**D**enise Duvall." CJ said her name and remembered their cosy chats in the conservatory at home – safe talk of cats and coffee and never-to-be-born children. A ghost of a smile played on her lips before her expressive face hardened with the memory of a promise. Her mouth set into a tight line. She turned her back to the window, warm sunlight shimmering around her like a security blanket.

There'd been little comfort in what she'd found out about *that* family. It'd all fallen into place with surprising ease. German military records matched the dates and led her to the family's background in Bavaria after the war. There were detailed family trees, birth, marriage and death certificates, which beckoned her seductively through time.

With each revelation she witnessed the descent into hell of an aristocratic German family – one of its sons destined to wreak mayhem on the innocent. By his murderous actions, he'd been cursed by an old woman; a powerful incantation dragged from the depths of darkness, born of hatred and horror. And such was its power that it would go on … until it was stopped.

"Thou shalt not make unto thee any graven image, or any likeness of any thing … Thou shalt not bow down thyself to them, nor serve them: for I, the Lord your God, am a jealous God, visiting the iniquity of the fathers on the children unto the third and fourth generation of them that hate me …." (Exodus 20:4–5).

CJ stared into the cheval mirror opposite the window and suddenly understood. The graven image had come in the form of an unremarkable grocer and his obedient servant; then a young, blond Lieutenant charged with making sure the residents of a sleepy French town paid for their alleged treachery – and he'd be cursed for all time.

The avalanche that came unprovoked out of a clear blue sky killed him and his wife swiftly, silently, leaving an innocent child too young to have been taken to the high slopes to ski. She was the sole survivor to inherit a fortune – and a curse.

A child sent away to be kept safe by strangers in a foreign land with no memory save for a haunting lullaby and the angel singing it. But, even *she* couldn't hide. Innocence wouldn't stop the inevitability of the curse.

Visited upon the fathers and the children …

So that was destined to be her fate. Denise, who inherited her father's cornflower-blue eyes that she didn't remember and her mother's soft voice that she did. CJ stared unblinkingly at her reflection and bit her lip. Denied children, maybe the curse would end, but the evil *would* go on.

She must stop it, forever. She'd no idea how, but was never more certain that when the time came, she'd be shown – somehow.

*

The café, with its four tables outside, was deserted save for Pieter and CJ.

They sat facing each other across one of them in the patch of no-man's land between the old and new town that the small café straddled. It was hot for mid-morning. The old walls provided a little shade, though in parts were beginning to crumble. General de Gaulle had commissioned the new town soon after the end of the war and had decreed the old would be a designated war grave to lie forever alongside the new. It was a shrine to the lost and a lesson for future generations of the evil that men do in *anything* but God's name.

The new Oradour seemed a quiet little town much like any other in western France, but by the old walls there were few people – not even tourists. Living in the shadow of a shrine was obviously unpopular, but several residents sat outside their rather drably-painted houses. They were black-clad, wrinkled crones and a couple of elderly French men wearing the traditional beret and blue, serge smock. Pieter patted the pocket of his cream, linen jacket.

"Damn! Left my cigars behind."

"There's a tabac in the centre of town," said CJ sipping her coffee. "I remember passing it. It's, maybe, five minutes' walk, if that."

"Do you mind if I pop back and get a couple?"

"Of course not, Professor, but don't be too disappointed if they haven't got your 20-quid-a-throw Cubans. Avoid throwing a 'Benny' in the shop, won't you?"

"What in heaven's name is a 'Benny'?" Pieter's voice took on an exasperated tone. "I can't understand you sometimes."

"Oh, he was a character in *Crossroads*."

"And where exactly *are* these crossroads?"

"No, no … it was a television programme. Oh, sorry, darling! I forgot you only listen to Radio Four. Now pin your ears back and let me teach *you* something for once."

"Why do I need to know this? I'm never going to become a devotee of a soap opera, or any other television programme for that matter."

"Oh, so you *know* it's a soap opera. Then you *have* seen it! I'll bet you were secretly in love with Miss Diane."

"Who?"

"Miss … Oh, stop it, Pieter. I never know whether you're pulling my chain or not. So listen carefully. I'll be brief."

"Must you? Oh, I *do* hope so!" He drained his espresso in one gulp.

"Yes, my darling boy. You don't know half enough."

"Now you're mocking me!"

"Of course. Now sit still." CJ sat back 'Pieter-style' and steepled her fingers. "Benny was a half-wit; no, that's not very politically correct, is it?" She cleared her throat. "He'd special needs; you know, a bit simple, I suppose."

"You surprise me!"

"He was devoted to Miss Diane and ..."

"Shut up, Cordelia! I'm going to buy cigars. Then I can *really* ignore you."

"I'll wait here, then." She sat back in the white plastic chair and smirked. "Do you have your cream on? It's going to be *very* hot."

"You sound like my mother!" Pieter shook his head, reached for his Panama and set off down the street. CJ watched him go. At the corner, he raised his hat to two elderly women who were sweeping the road in front of their houses.

"What a gentleman you are, Pieter," she said aloud.

CJ leaned back in the white café chair, her eyes wandering to the entrance of the old town. The gates were long gone, but their sturdy, stone supports remained; sentinels left on guard. She shivered despite the heat, goose bumps rising on her arms. Instinctively, she ran her palms over her flesh and shuddered again.

Why do they call it someone walking over your grave? It's rubbish! She closed her eyes, lifted her chin to catch the sun and yawned. *What am I doing here, Georgie?*

"You know very well." His voice was a mere whisper, but had an air of resignation that accepted that mere words wouldn't change her mind. CJ yawned again, her head slowly sinking forward to rest, chin on her chest.

✳

"But why, Papa?"

The child looked up into the man's adoring face with the screwed up frown only a nine-year-old is capable of. She persisted. "Why can't we paint our house in bright colours like Aunt Amelie does?" She pouted, sending auburn curls corkscrewing in perpetual motion.

"Aunt Amelie lives in Limoges, ma petite." The man stroked the child's head gently, stilling her curls, but she was not about to give up easily.

"But why can't we do that *here*, Papa?" Her father gave an indulgent smile and scooped her onto his lap.

"We can't, ma cherie. When you're a little older, perhaps you'll understand."

"But, Papa, I'm nine … and a *big* girl." Her brown eyes were as wide as saucers. "I want to plant geraniums in a blue box outside my bedroom window just like Aunt Amelie." Her father sighed and folded his newspaper, all hope of reading abandoned.

"One day when you're a little older, I'll tell you all about it, Sophie."

"Papa, I want to know *now*, so tell me, *please.*" She tugged at his sleeve. "You *must* tell me why no one is allowed to grow pretty flowers in our town and why the houses are all grey? I want to live in a blue-and-yellow house like Aunt Amelie in Limoges, with geraniums and lavender on the window sills. Why can't we live in a blue-and-yellow house, Papa?" She climbed down from her father's lap to stamp her foot on the ground. He knelt, his hands gentle on her shoulders, his eyes on hers.

"Sophie," he began, "it is General De Gaulle's wish that we don't do that. It's to show respect. You see, a terrible thing happened here a long time ago before you were born. It's the way we must remember all the people who used to live here in Oradour." The child put her head on one side and thought for a moment, the look of petulance returning.

"When I'm all grown up, I'll *go* away from here and live with Aunt Amelie in Limoges. Then I'll paint *my* house whatever colour I choose, whether General de Gaulle likes it or not!" Her father shook his head sadly.

"Yes, I fear you might, my little one – you and all the others. He looked towards the new Oradour, which wore its memorial shroud so proudly. He sighed deeply keeping his thoughts to himself.

*

"Cordelia! I can't believe you're sleeping. For heaven's sake, child, I've only been gone for 20 minutes!" CJ was awakened by his voice, the sharp tap on her shoulder *and* the pungent aroma of an unfamiliar cigar smoke that assaulted her nostrils.

"Oh, Pieter ... I'm sorry! I must have dropped off for a moment." She stretched painfully, bare flesh below her shorts welded to the cheap, plastic surface.

"Didn't you sleep well?" Pieter adopted his authoritative tone, which he was well aware irritated her immensely.

"I suppose I was thinking about this place and what it represents," she said.

"Then you *are* worried about coming here."

"No, not really. Errm ... no."

"That means you are. I've known you long enough to recognise bluster."

"Okay, Pieter. Perhaps a little. I was lying awake thinking of Denise."

"Ahh, I see."

"No. I was thinking how none of what happened was her fault. She was an innocent. We can choose our friends but not our relatives. What do you suppose is more important, *who* we are born or *what* we choose to become?"

"I take it you mean nature or nurture?"

"Yes, that's it."

"Well, say so, child!" CJ chose to ignore his supercilious tone.

"But, surely," she began, "if you're completely unaware of who your relatives are, it's impossible for even notoriety to affect your values? Whether your father was a saint or a mass murderer, how can that affect you if you don't know?"

Pieter said nothing, a thin smile fixed on his lips, silently questioning; interrogating her.

"I hate it when you do that, Pieter."

"Do what?"

"You know very well! That bloody 'I'm going to make you work it out for yourself' face. I'm surprised students didn't chuck things at you." CJ took a deep breath of irritation and sniffed.

"It's called genetics, Cordelia."

222

"Are you seriously suggesting that it's inbred in you to abduct or murder or suffer like your parents did just because you share the same blood? You'll be telling me next that *you* believe in curses and prophesies."

Pieter said nothing, amused at the incredulity that flashed in those beautiful, hazel eyes, now firmly fixed on his. He considered the question, elbows resting on the table, fingers intertwined. After a few moments, he took another cigar from his jacket pocket, lit it and puffed contentedly.

"Do I believe in curses?" he mused, finally addressing the subject.

"Well?" said CJ, "How can you? You're supposed to be a scientist! *Do* you believe in all that?" Pieter exhaled.

"Not directly, but I'm sure both can be self-fulfilling to those who fear and believe them. Take voodoo ..."

"This has nothing to do with voodoo. This is civilised Europe, not Haiti."

"My child, the principle is the same. Our brain patterns and the associated physiology can be inherited. I'll give you a simple example: depression. It's the *tendency* that's inherited, like an addictive personality. Whether you exhibit that tendency depends on what else is going on in your life, your particular circumstances and how you react to them." He paused to draw on his cigar. "And, then, there's the XY chromosome." CJ watched him intently.

"The sex chromosome? What's that got to do with anything apart from whether or not you end up with a willy?"

"Oh, so *elegantly* put, CJ. Actually there've been many reputable studies by some *rather* eminent psychologists."

"Like you?" ventured CJ with some amusement.

"I'd a little input on one occasion," he said, not revealing he was responsible for the entire study. "It was carried out some years ago in high security prisons with the more violent offenders. All were male and many were found to have an extra chromosome of the type we call Y, so they had an XYY sequence.

There *were* exceptions. Some ex-prisoners had it and went on to become useful members of society. However, the majority of the really violent offenders had XYY. There were other factors, of course." He placed his spent cigar in the ashtray.

"Such as? We seem to be back to genetics."

"Cordelia, it was a *very* long study, and, yes, the XYY *was* passed on genetically. Those who went on to rape, torture and murder repeatedly usually followed a pattern. They'd been abused as children, had a history of animal cruelty, dropping out of education, petty larceny, brawling and so on." He waved his hand in the air in illustration.

"And those who *didn't* have XYY?"

"Stability at home, reasonable education, employed ..."

"So how can we predict who'll go on to offend and who won't? Unless we're going to take DNA samples from everyone at birth, then have three 6s with a question mark tattooed under the hairline of the ones who happen to be positive."

"We can't take DNA from everyone. Not that there aren't do-gooders out there who'd love to demand it! Is it ethical to label a person over a possibility?"

"Tell that to the families of murdered children. What about those who are XYY and supress it? God, it's open to all sorts of interpretations."

"And *not* admissible in a court of law, thank God! It begs the question 'Did they decide to kill or was it pre-determined?'" CJ drew in a sharp breath at the implications.

"Can you see a time when it could be used as a defence?" Pieter laughed. "Who knows? Another coffee?"

"No, thanks." She pointed to the old gates. "Shall we go?"

"Only if you're sure."

"I'm sure." CJ reached to touch his fingers across the table. "Oh, I'm well aware you're humouring me, Pieter."

"How so?"

"I know you don't believe in all this stuff because it can't be explained scientifically, but I'm glad you're here anyway."

"Someone needs to take care of you whilst Sam's playing golf." Quickly, he withdrew his hand on the pretence of replacing his hat to divert his mind from how her very touch was like an electric shock. He took an ill-disguised deep breath and patted his Panama.

"Do you like taking care of me, Pieter?" The question took him completely by surprise. He stared at her, momentarily wondering if she could be flirting with him.

"Whatever *do* you mean, child?"

"It's just that you're always so good to me, Pieter; so generous to Sam and me. I'm not your intellectual equal – far from it and I never could be. Why do you care so much for me, Pieter?"

Briefly, he looked away then fixed her with a reproachful stare.

"Because, child," he said, "you are my muse and it pleases me." He wagged his finger. "And never underestimate your intellect!" He stood and turning his back walked slowly towards the old gates of Oradour.

At that moment, he wanted to gaze deeply into her eyes, to draw her close into his arms, to caress and kiss her tenderly. Then to sweep her up and carry her to his bed and remove her clothing slowly, kissing every inch of her fragrant skin. He ached to run a finger along the cleft of her velvet softness and when she arched at his touch, he'd make love to her. He called over his shoulder knowing she was following.

"Why? Because you interest me. I want to discover how you know the things you seem to and what goes on in that rather-fascinating mind of yours. I want to see what you see, to hear what you hear and understand what makes you the person you are. It's all in the interest of science, of course!" CJ caught up and walked slowly at his side.

"So, I'm just one of your studies to feed that all-absorbing, hungry mind of yours, Professor?"

"What else, child?" She was silent.

Because I love you and want you with every part of my being.

"Pieter?"

"Yes?"

"You *will* continue to be there for me, won't you – as my friend?"

"You know I will." *Until my dying breath.*

She smiled. "Why?"

"I told you, you're my muse."

"And your study subject."

"Yes."

As they walked slowly past the gate posts, Pieter was grateful that he'd worn his loose, linen trousers.

Chapter 31

They stood on what had been the main street of the little town. What remained was no more than a dirt track, although the house frontages on either side remained. There was no glass, of course, but the sturdy walls still stood. The old tram-track ran down the middle of the street, though no longer led anywhere.

"According to Philippe's guide book, trams used to run all the way to Limoges." said Pieter. I suppose that's where people worked if they didn't farm the land. I wonder ……"

"Listen," interrupted CJ, her eyes raised to the blue sky overhead.

"I don't hear anything," said Pieter.

"That's just it. Silence. It's eerie. Even the birds aren't singing." She looked down the street at the rows of houses interspersed every so often with what had been shops. Some still bore the names of their proprietors which could still be made out despite the peeling paint.

"La Boulangerie: Mon. Yves Fouquet," read CJ aloud. It wasn't hard to imagine a bustling street with fresh-baked bread in the window awaiting customers. As in towns and villages across France, Monsieur Fouquet would've been up at 3.00am to bake the first batch. And, like his father and grandfather before him, he'd have repeated the process later in the day for the teatime rush.

They meandered a little further past the boucher and the one-time premises of a seamstress. The skeletons of several ancient sewing machines stood in the bare bones of the ruined shop belonging to Mme Argent. In fact, many of the houses seemed to possess sewing machines, or what was left of them.

After the Germans set fire to the town only the metal frames remained.

"I suppose *everyone* learned to sew," said CJ softly, unaware she was whispering, but the atmosphere commanded it. "Luxuries such as new clothes would've been frowned upon in wartime, don't you think, Pieter?"

"Make do and mend!" he quoted. "It would've been a rite of passage that young girls learned the skills needed to become wives one day. It was important, the ability to sew and cook."

"Look, Pieter, what are they?" CJ was pointing to where the telegraph wires once were secured. Green, conical glass orbs hung like huge marbles strung from each pole.

"They're conductors," said Pieter, "still intact after all this time. Amazing! Not one mischievous small boy has thrown a stone."

CJ didn't think it that amazing. Perhaps children were afraid to enter the gates, warned by their mothers against entering the abandoned town where the ghosts of so many massacred souls must still reside. Restless spirits searching for loved ones amongst the horror and never to be re-united.

When the Germans came, the men were separated from the women and children, and then murdered; all burned alive after being shot to incapacitate them. The men and older boys were driven into Laudy's barn; the women and children led into the church. God's sanctuary would become *their* fate in the roaring flames. There'd been four survivors out of the 450 inhabitants who'd the misfortune to have been in the town on that fateful day in June 1945.

Both Pieter and CJ were familiar with the story, but being here was creepy. No wonder the birds didn't sing inside the walls of Oradour-sur-Glane, with its pretty river running nearby. CJ stopped at a house and placed her hand flat on the stone upright by the entrance, her eyes tightly closed. On the other side of the street, Pieter read the guidebook. He'd heard of this place, of course, along with Khatyn in Belarus and

Łomazy in Poland. These were only a couple of the villages that suffered the same fate. The History channel on his infrequently watched TV seemed to specialise in war and its atrocities. Could there ever be forgiveness for so many? Perhaps for some, but not the French! There would be neither forgiving nor forgetting.

Even with her eyes closed, CJ could sense Pieter standing beside her.

"Oh, Pieter, this is terrible." Sadness was etched on her face. "There's the remains of a pram in here. Couldn't they at least have spared the children?"

"They couldn't risk leaving any witnesses who might have been able to give evidence against them," said Pieter.

"But babies were no threat." Pieter placed his hand gently on her bare shoulder.

"Can you feel them, CJ?"

"Oh, God, yes. I feel them!" She leaned her forehead against the cool stone and murmured softly. "I feel their bewilderment, panic and their fear."

The documentary she'd watched in the safety of the conservatory a few weeks before began to replay in her head like a bad dream. The Germans had come early in the morning, parking their trucks on the road just outside the town. The officer had been a good-looking young man, despite what his uniform represented. In another life, he might have been the lad next door, the one who punched your ticket at the tram stop or the butcher's boy on his bicycle, the one whose smile both captivated and put you at ease. Those eyes were capable of kindness and could well have been those of a lover as they gazed from the screen. All CJ had seen was an officer in Nazi uniform with ice-cold, cruel eyes as he posed, flirting with the camera lens. His mouth was set with the mere ghost of a smile that said, "I'm in charge here. Cross *me* at your peril." In his hand he held a thin horse-whip and there was no mistaking his authority.

As CJ watched, she shuddered despite the warmth of the room. She stood, suspecting *no one* dare sit in the presence of such an imposing figure.

The soldiers entered the town obeying their orders, quietly and in a non-threatening manner so as not to cause alarm to the inhabitants. After all, the war was nearly over. The Allies had landed on the Normandy beaches and, with that event, all patriotic Frenchmen breathed a huge sigh of relief. The Germans were all but defeated, so what could a small company of retreating soldiers do? France stood on the brink of freedom.

But these men had a very different agenda. They'd come in response to an informant who'd reported Resistance activity in the area. An officer had been killed and retaliation was to be swift and decisive. It was the final act of a defeated army, led by a monster who at that moment sat in his Berlin bunker planning his own demise.

*

CJ's hand began to tremble as her fingertips read the story imprinted on the stone.

An old lady stood cooking at her stove, content as she stirred the pot. At the table sat a young woman rocking her new-born infant. The tranquil domestic scene hurriedly changed to one of confusion as she saw them walk down the dusty street towards the town square. The younger woman held the baby in one arm as she helped the older woman. CJ felt them pass with a blast of cold air that made her gasp and she turned. Taking her hand from the wall she knew she must follow.

"Cordelia," Pieter spoke from close by. "Are you okay?"

"We must go to the town square – all of us. Don't worry. We'll come to no harm." She began to walk slowly, a dream-like look in her eyes. Pieter followed a few steps behind, matching stride and watching her closely, a curious expression on his face.

She stood silently in the heat of midday, her hair damp at the neck. A trickle of perspiration ran down between her shoulder blades, wetting her clothing. Surrounded by people, her eyes were fixed on the young officer who stood before her. With an air of defiance, she held the gaze of his cornflower-blue eyes, the infant in her arms crying.

"The child is ill, Madame?" His grasp of her language was impeccable.

"Non, Monsieur. It's very warm and he's but two weeks old." She instinctively tightened her grip on the bundle as he reached to stroke the infant's face then, seeing her reaction, slowly withdrew his hand. A thin smile played around his mouth.

"We won't keep you out in this heat for very long, Madame," he said, his eyes softening. In different circumstances, it might have been easier to trust this man, to start a conversation or even to have let him stroke the child's head. But that uniform and what it represented formed an impenetrable barrier. The officer made a courteous bow, clicked his heels and turned away.

In the heat-haze, the young woman looked at the surrounding crowd and all the people she'd grown up with: Madame Moreau, the school mistress; the charcutier, still wearing his straw hat and apron; and the Berton twins, indistinguishable from one another, hiding behind their mother's skirts. Behind them was Padre Matthias, hurriedly summoned from his devotions by the ringing of the church bell and wondering why it stopped so suddenly. Practically all the town's families were represented, though many of the men were away at work. Monsieur Fouquet, the boulanger, was agitated and grumbling. He'd just put a fresh batch of bread in the oven when they were summoned to the square. On the edge of the crowd stood the mayor, his face expressionless.

The air around CJ seemed to swim and swirl, and she feared she may faint. Suddenly, there was shouting from the guards and the men began to move off slowly in the direction of Laudy's barn. CJ turned.

"You must go to the barn, Pieter."

"Where?"

"The barn, Pieter. It's down the road where the fairground sets up in August, the big, thatched building on the left."

"Why?"

"Pieter, please trust me. You must go."

Looking down, he placed a firm hand on each of her shoulders, holding her gaze.

"Cordelia, are you all right, child?"

"Yes."

"Are you absolutely sure?"

"Yes, darling, I'm fine. Now go with the others."

"What others, CJ?"

"No matter, darling, just go. *I* must go to the church." She pointed. "Don't worry, it's just over there."

Pieter put on his hat and, turning, walked slowly across the square with a couple of glances over his shoulder to where CJ stood motionless and completely alone.

Chapter 32

The huge, carved, oak doors loomed before the snake of humanity that wound its way towards the church. There was a perceptible air of relief at the prospect of finally being out of the hot sun. Though the soldiers' machine guns were menacing, they were not levelled at anyone.

CJ was grateful to enter the church's cool interior with its high arched ceiling and stone pillars. The ancient flagstones kept the building at an equal temperature throughout the year. The mothers with their prams and pushchairs gravitated towards the nave where there was room to sit. Most of the pews had been removed from the main area of worship and stacked in the centre of the aisle, hymnals and order of service sheets carelessly thrown in amongst them.

For a while, people were relatively quiet, chatting softly to their neighbours and friends, relieved to be out of the oppressive heat and in the promised safety afforded by the house of God.

All that changed suddenly with the shutting and barring of the doors. What followed were excitable raised voices and shouts of alarm. Children began to cry as they sensed the unease and panic of their mothers. CJ fought to breathe in the close proximity of so many bodies pressed together. There was a single gunshot and with renewed cries of anguish, the multitude cowered on the floor trying to hush their distressed children lest they attract the attention of the blond-haired man with the pistol.

Like a wave they backed off to the barrier of the sacristy's carved, wooden screen and crouched against it. An eerie silence hung in the air; a poisonous fog of expectation and fear, as though at any second something bad was going to happen. Women were praying on their knees, begging for salvation that the ordeal would be over. Suddenly from outside, came the unmistakable rat-a-tat of machine-gun fire. Mothers clutched at their children in horror, fear etched on their faces.

"My God! They are shooting the men," shouted an anguished voice. CJ clasped the infant to her breast rocking him gently, not recognising her own voice amid the cacophony.

"Don't cry, my sweet; not now, please. I don't like it when you cry." She cowered with the others by the sacristy wall, placing the child beneath her arched body to protect him from the pressure of people around her. From her position, she saw two soldiers carrying an oblong box. There were tapes trailing from it across the floor. They set it down at the foot of the great stack of pews.

A tinder box!

In stunned silence, she watched as the soldiers stretched the tapes down the aisle. Then, when they were a safe distance away, they pulled and the strips of fabric grew taut.

Pandora's Box from which all the evils of the world were set free. And, when all evil had escaped, there was one thing left inside: hope.

CJ tore her eyes away and looked around at the terrified women and whimpering children.

There's no hope here!

At some unheard signal, the tapes were pulled forcibly and there was a tremendous explosion setting alight the hymnals and paper. Smoke coursed upwards and flames began to engulf the wooden pews. The soldiers had vanished. Only the tall, blue-eyed officer remained, readying himself to take aim at those closest. Six shots rang out in rapid succession and women started to fall.

Mass panic ensued. People backed away towards the sacristy wall where CJ crouched holding the baby, now in immediate danger of being crushed under the fleeing tide of humanity. Hunkering down lower in an attempt to protect them both, she gasped for air as the fire took hold and the church started to fill with smoke. Frantic people scrambled roughly over her as she crouched helplessly and prayed. Another volley of shots rang out, a pause, then more … and more. People fell, their combined dead weight pinning her to the ground as the sacristy wall collapsed with a huge crash. Had it fallen the other way, she'd certainly have been dead … and the child under her, if it wasn't already so.

A hand suddenly grasped her wrist and somehow she supressed the urge to scream. The fingers tightened; bony gnarled fingers, the third wearing a wedding ring. There were more shots, but fewer now. All was becoming quiet and still. The next shot would surely be for her. CJ closed her eyes and prepared to die. The gunfire stopped. When she opened her eyes it was to look into those of an old woman.

"Go, child," she whispered, "crawl to the window behind the altar. Use the smoke as cover." CJ shook her head frantically,

"How can I do this, Grand-mére?" The old lady tightened her grip.

"Go," she whispered, urgently, "for the child."

"Grand-mére, I … I …" Tears ran freely down her cheeks, her voice breaking.

Grandmother held up her hand.

"Do one last thing. Help me up … then go!"

In the gloom, CJ began to crawl over the limp bodies in the sacristy, the infant held securely in the shawl across her chest. Her tears fell and mingled with the tangled limbs under her feet, urging her forward in a desperate attempt to live.

Slowly, painfully, the old lady dragged herself to her feet and began to pick her way through the dead and dying towards the crackling fire.

The officer turned slowly, surprised by the presence of this defiant old crone who stood amongst the carnage of the charnel house, soaked in the blood of neighbours and friends. Slowly, he raised his pistol.

Marie Chourade didn't stop or flinch. Her dark eyes fixed him with a hard, uncompromising stare that bore into his soul. A wave of terror engulfed him. His hand, which held the pistol, began to tremble and he could neither move nor speak, paralysed by her malignant gaze.

Raising her arms, the old lady cursed him and his issue for all time. Consumed by fear he could only watch as, with arms still raised, she walked into the flames, her gown catching alight at once. She screamed and a great plume of black smoke spewed from her mouth and shot towards him with a deafening roar knocking him to the ground. When he dared look, she was gone. All was silent save for the crackling fire and, from the sacristy, the plaintive cry of an infant.

Slowly, deliberately, Kessler reached for his pistol.

*

CJ reached the altar and stepped into the space behind it, grateful for the barrier from the terrible scenes on the other side. Horror-struck at what she'd witnessed, she slid down the wall. Cool, fresh air rushed in from the shot-out windows and she took long gasps. Then, in renewed blind panic and aided by an altar stool used for lighting the candles, she began to climb. Terror spurring her on, she grasped the sill with her fingertips and with a huge effort, found a foothold and hauled herself up. The baby began to cry.

"No, not now, please." She rocked him, clinging with one hand to the stone frame. The unmistakable sound of footsteps approached and not daring to look backwards, she knew she must jump from the window.

"Halt!" She froze, clutching the child to her, her lip bitten and bleeding. "Turn around!" Slowly, she turned, forcing herself to look away from the gun barrel and into the Lieutenant's cornflower eyes now locked on her own.

"Sir, I beg you, spare my child. For pity's sake." He raised the gun, levelling it at her head. She wet herself.

"No ..." she screamed and turned to jump. A tremendous thud between her shoulders sent them both pitching forward and they fell from the sill through fresh, clean air.

Chapter 33

Pieter reached the barn and stood quietly looking around. He could imagine the scene of sudden gunfire with men desperately trying to protect their sons and sons trying to shield their fathers.

When the firing ceased and all were lying dead, the soldiers set the straw alight to burn the evidence of their atrocity.

Pieter looked up to the now roofless space, leaving the building to the mercy of the elements, the stones blackened in places, but still standing in defiance. Staring at the blue sky, he could almost hear the screams of the wounded and dying as they suffocated and burned to death. It was an oppressive place.

There are ghosts here! He shivered despite the heat as a strange feeling of foreboding overcame him. "Cordelia! Oh God … Cordelia." He must get to the church and find her. Turning on his heels, he ran from what remained of Laudy's barn, picturing the cracking of timbers and the acrid, cloying smell of smoke in his nostrils. He began to call her name with increasing urgency.

Breathing hard, he reached the church and stumbled through the gap where the heavy doors had once been. He fell and dragged himself back to his feet, aided by the wall. As he rose, he saw something.

In the middle of the church was a black-clad figure. It was swirling and full of menace. Pieter gasped, hardly able to believe what he was seeing. He felt his knees weaken in its presence. The apparition began to move forward, drifting above the ground leaving a trail of blackness and a stench in its wake. He couldn't tear his eyes from it and he grew faint. With a supreme effort, he reached into his jacket pocket, fumbling and cursing himself for his ham-fisted efforts.

Suddenly, out of the blackness, the plaintive wail of an infant cut the air. The figure seemed to swell before him forming a dense, black mass with a cowl-covered head.

It turned at the sound and he saw it head for what had once been an altar. As he watched, mesmerised and disbelieving, he saw her.

She was high up on the stone window-ledge, long-since devoid of its stained glass, clinging precariously to the pitted stonework. Pieter gave an ill-suppressed cry as he saw it was CJ and she was in the direct line of the advancing figure.

"Stop!" he screamed. "No!"

The figure paused and turned to fix its attention on Pieter. At that moment, he'd never felt such terror or malevolence. His knees gave way, as under its red-eyed gaze he sank to the ground, his mind whirling like a dervish. With his last vestige of strength, he found what he was looking for and his fingers touched the velvet bag in his pocket. Feeling inside, he took out the diamond-encrusted gold crucifix. With it in his hand, he felt some strength returning and struggled to his knees. He held the cross aloft and, with a scream, addressed the demon in the name of the God he didn't really believe in.

"Get back to where you came from!" he shrieked. For an instant the figure swelled, then began to recoil as he crawled forward on his knees, the crucifix held before him. With a great crash, a huge stream of light seemed to come from nowhere. A woman screamed. Scrambling to his feet, Pieter began to run towards the altar as a shaft of blinding light hit the figure, lifting it up into the air. It disappeared, leaving the dreadful smell of burned, rotting flesh.

Pieter dragged his eyes away to the window where CJ had been clinging, helplessly.

She was gone!

CJ hit the ground hard, instinctively rolling in an attempt to lessen the impact, landing against the cool stonework of the church's outer wall. Her head spun and a wave of nausea overcame her. She retched; there was excruciating pain in her left leg. Desperately, she tried to turn onto her back, horrified to see her foot at a seemingly impossible angle. Gasping with pain, she looked up at an azure-blue sky; the salty taste of blood in her mouth. She shifted, with a cry of agony, to embrace the wall, the stone cool against her face, and she lay still.

After a few minutes her eyes began to focus and her concentration fixed on one block of stone that had a cross crudely scratched into its surface. With a renewed wave of agony, CJ knew she was slipping away and she wasn't afraid. There was a voice in her head, the persistent, soft voice of a trusted friend.

"I've brought him to thee, lass. Now do it!"

Do what, Georgie? CJ's semi-conscious mind asked. The voice in her fuddled head changed. It was now a woman's, frail and with the softest French accent.

"Cherchez l'enfant, ma soeur. Amenez-le en toute sécurité."

"I don't understand ... Je ne comprend pas. Je ne comp..."

"Find the child, my sister, for he is near. Bring him safely to where he belongs."

With a groan, CJ lost consciousness.

Pieter ran from the church and round the back to where he found CJ lying by the wall. He was sure she was dead, doubtful that *anyone* could survive such a fall. His despair on seeing her still body was unbearable. As he lifted her gently, her head lolled against his shoulder and she gave a cry of pain. She was alive! He thanked the God he was now considering the existence of. Bowing his head, he kissed her tenderly on the cheek before carrying her gently in his arms to safety.

Although concussed and with a badly-broken ankle that needed surgery, CJ was otherwise unharmed. A couple of weeks later they returned to Oradour; this time with the authorities to witness the removal of a well-preserved infant skeleton from its resting place. Gently they took it from behind the loose stone marked with a cross at the base of the church wall.

DNA testing proved, without a shadow of doubt, that the child belonged to Anouk Ferrier. They'd both been shot in a final, murderous act of revenge by a young Nazi officer in the dying days of the war. The same man who'd a young daughter back in Germany, a beautiful toddler with her father's eyes and her mother's smile. Who, when retribution came, had been sent to England and a new life. Sent to safety, far away from wagging tongues and curses. She'd been given a new name and identity, and she'd grown in a loving family; the real truth only known to two women who wouldn't live forever. She'd never know who or what her father was. And without that knowledge, how could any old woman's curse possibly affect her?

She was Denise Duvall, nee Ashford and she was loved.

CJ stood watching the sad exhumation. She'd been determined to, supported by her crutches, and the fussing of both Pieter and Sam. How the bones had come to be there one could only speculate. Anouk's husband found her broken body on his return from work in Limoges, along with all the other men who'd the good fortune to be away that day. Together they discovered the victims of the massacre. His child however, was missing and despite his search, never found – until now.

Perhaps one of the soldiers actually had a conscience amid the slaughter and, on finding the child, decided to give it a half-decent burial. CJ wondered if, in that sweet innocent face, he'd seen the features of his own little ones back at home. Maybe it was he who'd found the loose stone and placed the child behind it. Hidden from view out of some element of remorse? That was the sentimental version offered by CJ.

Pieter's reading of possible events was a little different and perhaps more plausible. The war was almost at an end. Defeat was imminent and the Germans knew it. Hitler had committed suicide after shooting Eva Braun and his dog in the Berlin bunker. He'd opted for the coward's way out, leaving everyone else to take the consequences for the crazed actions of a deluded madman.

Someone would have to pay for the mass-murder of Jews, gypsies and the mentally vulnerable. They'd have to be held accountable for the cold-blooded murder of men, women and innocent children in a sleepy French town – people who presented no threat and never had. Casualties of war were one thing. Indiscriminate slaying of babies and children was quite another. So, as Pieter pointed out, maybe hiding the murdered body of a tiny child was by way of a little self-protection. No one would ever know!

Weeks later, people gathered in their hundreds for the sad ceremony. Years ago, Anouk Ferrier's husband buried his young wife's body in a small clearing a short walk from the town square. Her grave was now disturbed one last time to allow a tiny snow-white coffin to be interred alongside her. They were reunited at last. No longer alone in the silent cradle where he'd been hidden. He was now with the mother who'd given her own life in an attempt to save his.

Gradually, the crowds dispersed until only CJ, Pieter, Sam, Aunt Caron and Philippe stood looking down at the stone-bordered grave covered in flowers. There was a new inscription.

'Anouk Ferrier, née Chourade, daughter, wife, mother and her son, Jean-Claude. Together for all eternity.'

With her ankle on the way to recovery, though still leaving her with the hint of a limp, CJ bent to place a bunch of forget-me-nots amongst the other flowers. Then, putting her hand flat on the rich, red earth between, she said "Goodbye."

The curse was spent, debts were repaid and the promise to Mike fulfilled. The storybook could be closed, for now it was at an end. She stood and took Sam's proffered arm on one side and Pieter's on the other, and they walked away from the grave, back through the past of the old town and into the future of the new one.

By the old gates she stopped suddenly and turned, stumbling a little. Sam caught her arm.

"Darling, I need a moment alone."

"It's far too early to be cavorting around on your own."

"Just give me a moment." Pieter placed a hand on Sam's shoulder and they withdrew a few yards.

CJ gazed over the old town. A light breeze ruffled the early spring foliage of the old orchard alongside the town square. A pretty young woman was looking towards the gates, holding her child against her breast with the breeze disturbing her fair hair. She raised her hand and waved.

CJ nodded and raised her own hand and then, with a smile, left them in peace.